The Duke's Despair
a Regency Romance

Colleen Ladd

Published by Marian Kelly
United States of America
Print Edition: June 2015

ISBN: 978-1-941881-03-3

Cover design by Laura J Miller
www.anauthorsart.com

This book was formatted by StevieDeInk.

Many thanks to Linda White (aka Regina Duke) for all her advice and encouragement over the years, not to mention the expert proofreading assistance, and to my family for believing in me even when it might have been smarter not to.

Chapter One

HER face streaked with tears, Lady Clarissa Seabrooke flew up the steps of Ransley House and through the front door before the butler got it fully open. Victor Mallinson, the Duke of Ransley, stepped down from his carriage and watched the coachman drive around to the mews. From inside the house came the thunder of feet on the stairs, followed by a door crashing closed. Ransley glanced up at the rattling windows. It wasn't too late to call the coachman back and go out to his club…. He mounted the steps with a sigh.

"Evening, Your Grace," Hailston said, as calmly as if tearful young ladies dashed through the house every day. Which wasn't far wrong, come to that. He deftly relieved Ransley of his hat and caped greatcoat. "A pleasant evening, sir?"

Ransley gave his butler a withering look and went into the library, where he poured himself a large brandy and drank it off standing up. He refilled the glass and seated himself in an armchair by the hearth, where a dying fire flickered lazily over the remains of the coals. Ransley propped his chin on his fist and stared into the listless orange flames. He didn't so much as blink when one of the downstairs maids rushed in to make up the fire, working awkwardly from the far side of the hearth to keep out of his way. She finished as quickly as possible, dropped Ransley a curtsy, and left.

Five minutes later, Hailston came in with a tea tray.

"I didn't order tea," Ransley said without looking up.

"Yes, sir." Hailston set the tray on the table at Ransley's elbow.

"I don't want tea." He swallowed the last of his brandy.

"No, sir." The butler took his empty glass and handed Ransley a dish of tea.

"You're a meddling old woman."

"Yes, sir." Hailston had been with Ransley far too long to find his master daunting, no matter what mood he was in. Though he sometimes found the man's imperturbability irritating, Ransley was grateful; some butlers would have given their notice rather than suffer through the constant upheaval of the household. But then, Hailston positively doted on Clary. Had ever since the poor girl was dropped on Ransley's doorstep after the death of her mother, his sister. In the decade since, Ransley ought to have learned something about the rearing of young ladies, but a man less suited to the task than himself, he couldn't imagine.

He obediently drank his tea and ate a handful of the ginger biscuits that shared the tray with the quietly steaming teapot. "Has my niece's maid gone up to her?"

"Lady Clarissa's locked her door, sir."

Ransley stood, swaying slightly. Two bumpers of brandy weren't enough to see him off, but it had been a long night, and they came atop the champagne he'd drunk at the ball. Just as well Hailston had brought tea and biscuits, or Ransley would have been in no shape to talk sense into his ward. Which was, of course, precisely why his butler had seen fit to impose tea on him in the first place.

Two flights up, Ransley hesitated outside Clary's door, nerving himself to confront the tempest within. One would think some sort of ease with such scenes would arise out of their constant repetition. One would be wrong. When he did knock, the only response was an increase in the pitiful sobbing.

"Come now," Ransley said. "I haven't the key, and I don't fancy going to Hailston for it. You don't want me breaking the door down, do you?"

"You wouldn't!" After a brief silence, Clary added in a small voice, "Would you?"

Ransley considered. "Yes, I rather think I would."

The door inched open, and Clary's tear-ravaged face appeared in the crack. "Really?" she asked hopefully.

"Really."

She disappeared, leaving the door ajar. When Ransley pushed it open, he found Clary huddled on her bed with her arms lashed around her legs and her expensive ballgown tucked inelegantly about her bare toes. Ransley seated himself on the edge of the bed.

"I don't mean to do these things," Clary said to her knees. "Really I don't."

"My dear girl, how can you possibly not have meant to tell Lady Carruthers about helping birth the lambs last spring?" He'd only left her for a moment to get her a glass of orgeat and himself some much-needed champagne. He'd returned to find her recounting the experience. In detail.

"Oh, I'm hopeless!" Clary wailed, listing sideways to fetch up against him. He wrapped her in his arms. "I'm always doing the wrong thing, or saying the wrong thing, and I'm too tall, and I haven't got any curves to speak of, and I have *freckles*, and I haven't any bosom—"

Ransley cleared his throat, cutting her off. "Your, ah, your freckles would fade, you know, if you'd remember your bonnet when you go out. And even if they don't, they're very fetching."

"They're hopelessly unfashionable," Clary said, her voice muffled in his chest.

"Not every young man can make himself find attractive only what Society deems fashionable." He listened to her snuffle against his collarbone, unconvinced, and finally added, "And you do have... curves. Ask your maid."

"Nothing like Alicia Stanhope."

Ransley cleared his throat again. He prayed he wasn't coloring, but if she kept her face buried in his chest, he supposed it was of little moment if he was. "Miss Stanhope is... overly gifted, Clarissa. In any case, there's more to a woman than her curves. There's certainly a great deal more to you." He stroked her shining blond hair, so like his sister's. "You really must try to *think* before you speak."

"I try. I do. But I never know I've gone wrong until it's too late." She sniffed, and Ransley fished his handkerchief out of his tailcoat pocket and handed it to her. "I wish Lady Ashburne were here."

"Lady Ashburne is on her wedding trip and we shall just have to muddle through without her." How he wished he'd taken the blasted woman's advice and held off bringing Clary out for another year. But he'd seen little point in waiting and several very good reasons not to delay. Not least of which was that the chit was eighteen and it was high time he fired her off before her racketing around the countryside did permanent harm to her reputation or she developed any more of a *tendre* for Lady Ashburne's blasted brother than she had already. He might no longer have reason to wish Lady Ashburne and all her kin to the devil, but that did not mean he wanted his ward married to a purse-pinched young man still at university and too bold by half. Had he waited, however, he might have had Lady Ashburne's assistance in reassuring Clary. Not to mention keeping her out of the briars.

There was no use crying over it now. It would not add to Clary's countenance to be seen fleeing back to the country with her tail tucked firmly between her legs. If only the girl could refrain from blackening her reputation every time she set foot outside the house.

* * *

Half an hour later, Ransley was finally able to turn Clary over to her clucking maid. He retreated to his bedchamber and managed to exchange his dancing finery for biscuit inexpressibles and a bottle-green coat of superfine without the assistance of his valet. Munslow would be most annoyed to learn that his master had attended to his own toilette, but Munslow was not there. Ransley had given him the evening off, not expecting to return before the small hours of the morning.

He traded his dancing slippers for polished Hessians, allowed Hailston to help him into his greatcoat, and left for his club, enjoining Hailston to keep an eye on Lady Clarissa while he was out. The butler cast his eyes skyward at the imposition of a duty he'd have undertaken regardless and wished Ransley a pleasant evening.

It was brisk out, low clouds threatening rain, but Ransley chose to walk to St. James's. He desperately needed a few minutes to himself, without someone hanging on his arm or his next word. He'd never much liked doing the pretty — dancing attendance on self-indulgent women preening themselves over their beauty, pawed at by a legion of matchmaking mamas and their marriage-mad daughters, elbowed by so-called gentlemen overly impressed with their own consequence, and generally finding himself at the service of everyone's pleasure but his own. Ransley had spent the greater part of the fifteen years since he came into the title rusticating primarily to avoid the social round. There were those who saw in the Season everything that was finest in the *ton*, mistaking the glittering show of jewel-bedecked women and elegantly clad men for something more worthwhile than it was. In Ransley's experience, the Season showed the *ton* at its worst — greedy, grasping, unprincipled, shallow, and unconscionably arrogant.

The business that brought him to Town to testify before the House of Lords had concluded satisfactorily weeks ago. Were it not for Clary, Ransley would have long since returned to Tynesfield Manse, favorite of his country estates. Fool that he was, however, he'd decided, since he had to be in Town anyway, to fire Clary off while they were there. He'd spent the last several years willfully blind to the fact that his niece was turning into a young woman. And a perfect hoyden. Were it not for Lady Ashburne's pointedly expressed opinions on the subject, he'd be blind still. However, it had been brought glaringly home to him that if he didn't find Clary a suitable husband in Town, she'd find *herself* a most unsuitable one closer to home. Even so, were it not for the matter of Lady Ashburne's brother, he'd likely have held off bringing Clary to London until next Season, or the one after. But Clary had been well on her way to developing a *tendre* for the boy, and while she could certainly afford to marry a man without a feather to fly with, Ransley would not sit by and watch her slide into such a marriage for lack of a more suitable match. Clary could do better. Unfortunately, she appeared to be doing as much worse as she possibly could.

Ransley had hoped she'd make some appropriate connection quickly and save him having to spend the entire Season in Town. Lady Clarissa was bright, pretty, well bred, well-dowered, and the niece of a duke — some young buck should have snapped her up right off the mark. But poor Clary seemed utterly unable to make it through two days together without some catastrophe befalling her.

The rain began just as he arrived at White's. Ransley hesitated, rain pattering down upon him, then went on. Too many people. Though it was early, and many gentlemen still squired brilliantly bedecked ladies through the social round, the doors of White's were busy with comings and goings. Ransley continued down St. James's and went in at a smaller, less-fashionable club. He surrendered his hat and greatcoat at the door and went into the card room. It was warm and welcoming, the subdued murmur of bets made and accepted paradoxically adding to the impression of quiet. The tenuous peace Ransley had found while walking held. He did not feel so hemmed in here as in a ballroom, and if there was no less grasping greed, at least it was admitted to openly.

"Your Grace," the majordomo intoned, his manner more arrogant than his position justified, with a thin veneer of subservience overlaid for Ransley's benefit. As it was, to the best of his recollection, the first time Ransley had ever entered this club, there must have been something of a scramble among the servants to identify him. "How pleasant to see you. Will you be dining?"

"No. Thank you." He'd supped before the ball, and had he any desire to eat again, he'd have gone to Watier's, which had by far the finest cook. "Brandy, if you please. "

"Of course, Your Grace. Would you care for a private chamber?"

"I would not." If he'd meant to sit alone and brood over a brandy, he'd have stayed home.

"Of course, Your Grace." The majordomo bowed and retreated. Ransley was glad to see him go. A simple "sir" would have sufficed, but the man persisted in repeating "Your Grace," as if to alert all in hearing to the presence of a duke in the club. Perhaps he'd made a mistake in not going to White's.

Ransley had plenty of blunt and enough skill at cards to acquit himself well, but now that he was here, he found he had no desire to play. He'd thought to lose himself in the banality of wagers won and lost, but all he wanted now was to drink in peace. Nothing, it appeared, would satisfy him tonight — he did not want to be alone, precisely, but neither did he want to be accosted or drawn into conversation.

He flipped idly through the heavy pages of the betting book, noting that not all the bets were as circumspect as those in White's, which were usually worded along the lines of "Lords A & B wager £500 that a certain gentleman will offer for a certain lady before the end of the Season," leaving Lords A and B to remember precisely which gentleman and which lady. Heaven help them if their memories didn't agree when it came time to settle up. A few of these bets were as judiciously worded, but others named names. Reputations could be ruined. Not that those placing the bets cared a fig for that.

That George S. will fall off his new horse within a fortnight, wagered by Lord Gore. Accepted by Lord Ormsby. There was no notation as to who had won, though the fortnight had long since passed. The sum of money was significant and Ransley wondered idly which of the lords had walked off with it.

That Lady Vi— will land a husband before Lady Th—, by M, accepted by K. Ransley's lip curled. The names of the ladies in question could no doubt be determined by anyone *au courant* with the day's gossip. The bet was distasteful, made all the more offensive by the cowardice of the bettors in concealing their names more thoroughly than those of their victims.

Lord T wagers that Lord C—d will not die a natural death. Several gentlemen had put their names down, wagering varying amounts against Lord T. Ransley snorted. Whoever Lord T was, he'd won himself a pretty penny.

Lord W accepts M's wager that VR will never get an heir.

"Ransley! What a surprise."

Ransley turned to find a man of overripe good looks bearing down on him. Josias Mallinson's rich brown hair was styled exactingly, his shirt points high enough to proclaim him a dandy without quite interfering with the movement of his head, and his waistcoat a bilious shade of yellow. He came at Ransley with his hand outstretched. Ransley wondered, as Mallinson's overwarm fingers closed on his, just how his cousin's branch of the family tree had come to so little resemble his own. "Mallinson."

"I knew you were in Town, Ransley — anyone who reads the papers knows that! — but I had no idea you were a member of Cocker's."

"I'm not." Ransley retrieved his hand.

Mallinson laughed. "I ought to have known. The Duke of Ransley is a member of any club he chooses to enter. Come, join us." He gestured to a table occupied by three men, none of whom glanced up from his cards.

"No, thank you. I must be going."

A waiter chose that moment to arrive with Ransley's brandy.

"Cocker's has a cellar to rival White's," Mallinson said. "You must at least sit down and enjoy your brandy."

"Very well." There was nothing served by being rude. Though a distant cousin, Mallinson was next in the succession and, as such, Ransley's heir. He allowed himself to be guided to the table.

"Ormsby, Ivison, Leynthall," Mallinson said, indicating each man in turn. "You know the Duke of Ransley."

Ormsby grunted without looking up from his cards. Ivison looked Ransley over briefly with watery blue eyes and nodded, and Leynthall laid his cards down long enough to extend his hand with a friendly smile. "A pleasure. What brings you to Town?"

"Stupid question," Ormsby said. "What brings any man to Town? Women. Gamblin'. Horses."

"Launching a chit," Ivison put in, a long-suffering expression lengthening his already long face.

Leynthall's smile turned self-deprecating. "Looking for a wife."

Mallinson's laughter was inappropriately loud, and Ormsby said, "Speak for yourself. One is more than enough for me."

"And me." Ivison tossed his cards on the table and drained his glass, signaling the waiter to refill it. "If you bothered to pay any attention to *on dits*, Leynthall—"

"Or, for that matter, the newspapers," Mallinson interjected.

"—you'd know that His Grace has been before the House of Lords half a dozen times in the last two months. Everything settled to your satisfaction, Your Grace?"

"Indeed." Ransley tasted his brandy and found it as excellent as Mallinson had promised. It was unfortunate that he no longer wanted it.

"Not certain I could have done what you did," Ormsby said with the unpleasantly friendly manner of the inveterate gossip. "Revisitin' the murder of your niece, ten years gone?" He shook his head. "Hard thing."

"One minute," Ivison said, his watery eyes blinking in such palpable confusion that the display was unlikely to be genuine. "Thought I heard His Grace was bringing his niece out this Season."

"Lady Clarissa Seabrooke," Mallinson said. "Sister to the girl who died."

"The Seabrooke chit's your ward?" Ormsby smiled unctuously. "Heard a bit about *her* lately."

"Oh?" Ransley looked at the man until he withered. "I can't think anything you heard bears repeating. Gentlemen." He stood, leaving his nearly untouched brandy on the table, and walked out.

Mallinson caught up with him when he was retrieving his greatcoat and hat from a footman and followed him outside. The streets were mired in mud and a wet, rank smell thickened the air. Ransley strode down St. James's, not acknowledging his cousin's presence until they reached a busy crossing, where they were forced to wait for a break in the passing carriages.

"It did not escape my attention," Ransley said, his eyes on the fancy equipages that trundled past, "that it was you who brought Lady Clarissa's name into the conversation. I will not have her name bandied about a gentleman's club, especially not in connection with her half-sister's death."

Mallinson's jaw twitched. "It doesn't need my help to come up, Your Grace."

Spying a break in the endless stream of carriages, Ransley strode across the street, a sweep clearing the crossing ahead of him.

"Your own actions in the House of Lords saw to that," Mallinson called from behind him.

Ransley tossed the little sweep a coin and continued home, wishing he hadn't come out, or had stopped at White's as he'd originally intended. Chances were it would have made little difference. No doubt Clary's name was on lips there as well — tonight's unfortunate blunder would already be making the rounds. And if it was not her name bandied about, voices falling away to nothing when he approached, it would be his.

It began to rain again. Ransley pulled up the collar of his greatcoat, though he was far from chilled, his blood still running high from the contretemps with Mallinson. When last he saw Mallinson, the man had been fresh from school, looking for a place in the world, and Ransley's habit of spending most of his time at Tynesfield Manse made it eminently practical to offer Mallinson the use of Ransley Manor. Smaller than Tynesfield and closer to London, the Manor was a suitable estate for a young man to cut his teeth on, especially as Ransley knew he could trust his steward to put the brakes on any too-ambitious scheme and inform him of any problems. How better to ensure his heir could be relied upon to take good care of the estates once they passed to him than to see to it that he learned the running of one now?

Ransley was in no rush to marry. He'd had his fill of scheming females when he first came into the title, and felt no desire to marry a woman whose so-called affections had less to do with his person than his money and the opportunity to turn herself into a duchess. There was no rush to get an heir. Mallinson's existence meant that the title and lands would not revert to the crown if Ransley died. Mallinson meant Ransley could do as he wished.

But Ransley found himself disturbed by this most recent meeting with his heir and could not put his finger on quite why. Had Mallinson's eyes been the littlest bit too small for his face all those years ago? His tone quite so unctuous? Certainly, he hadn't dared to set himself so obviously against Ransley. But then, he'd been barely a man then.

Rain spattered Ransley's face and he pulled the brim of his hat farther down. He crossed a narrow lane, this one without a broom-wielding urchin, miring the toes of his boots in mud. Munslow would be most displeased.

He ought to have stayed home, and not just from the club. The entire evening had been an unmitigated disaster.

Chapter Two

"Thea, dear, I don't mean to nag, but at this rate, we'll be late for Lady Ayleford's ball."

Althea Ravenshaw turned a quick smile on her companion. "It's fashionable to be late, Aunt Florence." She stepped into the dress her maid held for her and stood patiently while Chloe did up the legion of tiny clasps marching up the back of the dark blue ballgown.

"Just because it's fashionable doesn't mean it's not rude," Mrs. Florence Wellins scolded gently, settling herself in a chair to watch as Chloe completed Thea's toilette. Her hair was already beautifully styled, the inky tresses caught up in a complicated knot from which a few gently curling locks artfully strayed, and Chloe fussed about her, making the final touches to her dress and simple jewelry.

Thea regarded her fondly. "My dear aunt, surely you've learned by now that, in London, rudeness *is* fashionable. You're not buried in the wilds of Essex anymore, you know."

Neither of them had been for nearly four years now. Thea still felt it at odd moments: a light, sharp tingle rushing along her arms and across her scalp. Freedom. Freedom from the sickroom, from seven years of tending her grandmother through her final illness. Freedom from worry, her inheritance enough to keep Thea and her companion comfortably for the rest of their lives. Freedom from constraint, so far on the shelf that no one much cared what she did. And if her reputation was not pristine, it did not need to be, for she was not the least interested in finding a husband. She'd only just gotten free of one prison; she had no intention of locking herself up in another.

"None the less," Mrs. Wellins maintained with gentle severity.

"Very well, Aunt. If I meet your approval?" Thea made a slow turn in front of Mrs. Wellins, who nodded. "Then we shall be off directly."

Chloe had draped a wrap over Thea's shoulders and was assisting Mrs. Wellins into hers when one of the footmen scratched at the door. "Begging your pardon, Miss, but the Earl of Wilford is in the drawing room."

"Oh heavens! Thank you, Ned, I'll be down directly." The footman — she hadn't the least clue whether it was Edward or Edwin — bowed and left. It was the fashion to hire footmen as much like each other as possible, and there couldn't be two men more like each other than the twins, but Thea thought their mother had gone too far in the naming of them. The household was in the habit of calling them both Ned, since no one could tell them apart. "I wonder what Lord Wilford wants."

Mrs. Wellins hurried from under Chloe's ministering hands and followed Thea down the stairs. "My dear, you didn't—"

"Of course I didn't. I haven't the foggiest idea why he's here." Thea put on a pleasant expression and swept into the parlor, Mrs. Wellins following like a banty hen with one chick. Lord Wilford was bent over a small figurine, studying it so closely his nose was all but pressed against it. At their entrance, he jumped up and dropped his quizzing glass, which swung wildly on its cord.

"Miss Ravenshaw," he stammered, smoothing down his wild shock of pale brown hair, which instantly sprang up again. "How pleasant to, to see you."

"It is rather to be expected," Thea murmured, "when you present yourself at my house." Mrs. Wellins gave her a discrete poke in the ribs, and she quickly banished any sign of amusement and dropped Lord Wilford a curtsy. "How very kind of you to call, my lord."

"The honor is all mine," Lord Wilford said, sweeping her entirely too low a bow. He looked mildly confused when he straightened up, and Thea wondered if he'd forgotten why he came. No such luck. "Miss Ravenshaw, I wonder if I, if I might have a moment alone with you?"

"I would like nothing better, my lord," Thea said quickly, "but if we do not get on to the ball, we shall be very late indeed."

"What? I, yes! Yes, of course." He bowed again and gave her his arm, but stopped abruptly before they reached the door. "Which, ah... Refresh my memory, i-if you would be so kind, Miss Ravenshaw. Which ball?"

"Why Lady Ayleford's, of course."

"Oh. Quite. Quite." Lord Wilford blinked several times quickly, then started again for the door. His carriage sat before the house, Thea's own more modest equipage pulled up behind it, the horses stamping impatiently. Wilford led her to his carriage and handed her and Mrs. Wellins up, then climbed in himself. They sat motionless for a moment before he realized they weren't moving and stuck his head out the window to call, "What ho, coachman. Lady Ayleford's."

And with that, they were off, leaving Thea's hired carriage standing before the house. It would not remain there long; one of the Neds would soon send it back to the stables, and what a blessing it was to have servants who could think for themselves. The rain had stopped late that afternoon, and the sky was clear, a deep black chill descending on the city. Thea looked up from arranging her wrap more snugly about herself to find Lord Wilford watching her, his vague brown eyes beaming out of a round face. He was a washed out, rabbity kind of man, the butt of far too many "friendly" jokes, and Thea rather liked him, for all that his certainty she'd give him her hand in marriage if only he asked often enough was growing tiresome.

She would have felt guilty for the trick she'd played him, making him think he'd agreed to escort her to Lady Ayleford's ball, if it weren't the only way she could escape having to tell him no again. She'd had to do so twice already, and though her surprising lack of interest seemed utterly unable to prick his *amour-propre*, it was awkward and embarrassing to keep turning him down. She really didn't like hurting his feelings, even if they didn't stay hurt long enough to keep him from trying again.

When they entered the Ayleford's ball, Thea on Wilford's arm, Mrs. Wellins following after, hearing her name announced with his made Wilford swell up like a rooster. Thea winced inwardly, knowing she'd not be rid of him for the duration of the ball. He nearly always tracked her down sometime during the evening, but it usually took him a while to find her. This night, there would be no escaping him.

"Shall we sit here, Miss Ravenshaw?"

Thea took the gilt chair with a nod of thanks, Mrs. Wellins perched next to her, and Wilford took up a position at Thea's shoulder from which he clearly did not mean to budge. He stood stolidly watching the assembly swirl around the floor in a riot of color without the least attempt to make conversation.

Thea generally didn't mind Lord Wilford's company, but it wasn't long before she was wishing him heartily to the devil. His hovering put off any other gentleman who might take it into his head to ask her to dance, and before an hour had passed, she'd have welcomed anyone, from the greenest youth to the veriest rake. She never cared much who she danced with, so long as he was capable of a rudimentary attendance to the music and did not tread too often upon her feet, but tonight she'd have happily accepted even Lord Buncombe, who was hard of hearing and tended to forget which dance he was engaged in and switch without warning from a minuet to a country dance, setting everyone to sixes and sevens. It did not matter with whom she danced. Thea was not there to make a match; she was there to enjoy herself. Which was nearly as impossible as making a match with Lord Wilford in constant attendance upon her.

Thea fanned herself idly and stared across the sea of brilliant ballgowns that dipped and swirled with the music. Whites and pastels — colors suitable for a girl's come-out, though not always suited to the girls coming out — eddied erratically around gowns in every brilliant hue ladies married, widowed or on the shelf could imagine, and a few they ought not have. The men seemed almost afterthoughts, whether moments of black and white simplicity in the riot of color or splashes of extravagance as outlandish as the ladies.

The musicians struck up a waltz and a pain throbbed behind Thea's right eye. She dearly loved to waltz. But it seemed no man would ask her to dance while Wilford stood at her shoulder, and she knew better than to ask him, even were that appropriate. Wilford danced like an elephant with three feet roped together and the fourth on ice.

She sighed and rubbed her forehead. Sitting there was more exhausting than dancing. There was nothing to distract her from the stifling heat, nor the overwhelming scents of rose, lavender, costmary, starch, and bay rum, curdled by the ripe odor of those who'd foregone bathing for longer than they ought.

"Miss Ravenshaw?" Wilford touched the back of Thea's gloved hand. "A-are you well?"

"Fine." Thea forced a smile. "Though I believe I require some air, and perhaps a glass of champagne."

"Allow me to—"

"You might get me the latter, your lordship, but only I can procure the former." Thea stood and dropped Wilford a curtsy. "Please, my lord, do me the favor of keeping my aunt company until I return."

She shot the loyal Mrs. Wellins an apologetic look and slipped away before Wilford could object that she oughtn't be on her own — a patent absurdity at her age. She was no naïve chit in her first Season to need such close watching. As she made her way to the refreshment room, Thea half-hoped she'd be accosted by a man demanding a dance — preferably a gentleman who'd squire her around the floor for their mutual pleasure without a thought to how much she was worth. Though at this point, she'd even welcome the advances of a gazetted fortune hunter if it meant she could spend a few minutes lost in the music and a man's arms. If only *something* would happen.

Thea had cause to regret that thought later. When the chit in the peach-colored gown collided with her in the door of the refreshment room, however, the only thought she could spare was for her ballgown, splashed with whatever the girl had been carrying. Thea wrinkled her nose at the odor of almond and orange.

"Oh!" the girl exclaimed, blue eyes gone wide and round as her free hand flew to her mouth. She dropped the empty glass, which shattered, freezing nearby conversation, and fled.

Thea shook the orgeat off her skirt. At least the stain wouldn't show overmuch on the dark blue silk. When she showed no sign of falling into hysterics, the attention of those who'd witnessed the accident shifted to the progress of the chit across the ballroom.

The girl was tall and her honey-colored hair shone in the candlelight, making her easy to follow, as did her unrefined pace, which left a trail of disgruntled dancers and bystanders. Peach was a good color for her, though the dress was a little too fussy to suit her height. It was entirely too bad she'd be remembered for her dash across the ballroom rather than her excellent looks or whatever skill she might possess in the turn of the dance.

Thea watched the girl escape through a door onto the terrace and breathed a sigh of relief that the young lady was, at least, no longer under the censuring eye of the *ton*. A moment later, a tall man with pale hair slipped out the terrace doors after her. Thea didn't have to consider her reaction. She grimaced and headed across the ballroom herself. The girl didn't deserve to be ruined just for spilling orgeat down Thea's favorite ballgown.

Thea's progress across the ballroom seemed agonizingly slow, but in truth, it only took her a few minutes to reach the nearest door. She glanced about to make certain no one was paying her any mind, then slipped out onto the terrace. It was, after more than an hour in the overheated ballroom, rather like plunging into a cold lake. She sucked in a short breath and walked to the stone balustrade that edged the terrace. The moon had risen, throwing the evening into silvery relief, but as far as Thea could see, she was alone on the terrace. Nor could she make out any figures in the garden but the obligatory marble statuary.

Thea hesitated with her hands on the cold balustrade. It was possible the girl had become chilled and slipped back inside by a different door while Thea was making her way across the ballroom. It was equally possible that the man had only stepped out for a breath of fresh air himself, in which case he might return at any minute. To be found alone on the terrace with a man would ruin her nearly as thoroughly as it would the chit she'd come out here to rescue. Though Thea had less cause to concern herself with her reputation than most — having no pressing need to make a marriage match — she would find the Season deadly dull if she was considered too scandalous to be invited anywhere.

She sighed and turned reluctantly back to the door, only to spin around again when a faint noise reached her ears. Her heart pounding, she ran down the short flight of stairs, consciously identifying the noise only after she plunged into the garden. Someone was crying.

Pathways of crushed stone shone like silver in the moonlight. Thea drew in a steadying breath redolent of mud and grass and started down the path that led most directly toward the source of the noise. The garden rose around her, dark and silent but for the sound of sobbing. Making her task harder, the moon chose that moment to disappear behind the clouds for an extended period, dropping the garden into gloom. Somewhere along the way, she lost the path in the dark, knowing she'd done so only by the rich smell of crushed grass. Her dancing slippers would be ruined.

The sobbing grew louder, and Thea quickened her step. Her thin dancing slippers weren't meant for rushing about in a dark garden, and she was limping from a stone bruise by the time she spotted the girl. The moon chose that moment to return, and she could clearly see the chit seated on a stone bench, bent nearly double and sobbing into her skirts with the man looming over her. What Thea could see of his expression was forbidding.

"Is something amiss?" Thea called before she could think better of it. She quailed when the man turned, his eyes so pale in the moonlight that they looked nearly white except for the black of the pupils. He was taller than Thea'd thought, and his scowl was terrible.

The girl's head flew up, and she gaped at Thea in something like horror before dissolving into fresh hysterics. "I'm sorry, I'm so sorry, I didn't mean to—"

"Of course you didn't," Thea said at the same moment the man snapped, "That will suffice, Lady Clarissa." The girl subsided into sniffles, and the man said, "May I assist you, madam?" in a voice colder than the night air.

"I came to see if Lady Clarissa needed assistance. She left rather abruptly." Thea nerved herself to step closer and held her hand out to the girl. "Come, my dear. Shall we go in?"

The girl stared, her eyes flicking uncertainly between Thea and the man. What could he have said or done before Thea arrived to make the girl hesitate to escape the threat he posed her reputation, or worse, her virtue?

"Come, dear," Thea coaxed, her skin prickling at the man's closeness. Thwarted rage and something else that Thea couldn't identify spilled off him in waves that seemed to beat against her until she could barely breathe. She wanted nothing more than to grab the girl's hand and flee back inside. "Let's go in."

Lady Clarissa looked startled and on the verge of tears again. "Oh, but—"

"Don't take on so," Thea said quickly. She took the girl's hand, prying it lose from her wrinkled skirts. "We'll slip into a retiring room and do something about your face before we return to the ballroom. All will be well, I promise."

Lady Clarissa's free hand rose to her flushed cheek and she hauled in a shuddering breath. "Can we really—?"

"No, you cannot," the man said, and Thea was surprised to realize he was not nearly as close as she'd thought. "This has gone quite far enough. Clarissa—" He held out his hand, clearly expecting her to take it. "Come, girl."

"But Uncle Ransley!"

Thea took a breath, grateful for the coolness of the air, for she felt as if she might burst into mortified flames. She ought to have known by their coloring that there was some relationship, though his hair and eyes were a deal paler than Clarissa's. Hoping the moonlight hid her blushes, she steadied her voice and said, "I trust you will turn her over to one of the attendants in the retiring room, my lord. Her reputation will not be enhanced by reappearing in the ballroom with a tear-blotched face."

"We shall not be returning to the ballroom." There was no give in his voice. "Not that it is any business of yours."

Thea bristled. "Neither," she added, "will lingering in the garden help her reputation."

He gave Thea a wintery smile and she struggled not to shiver — she felt stripped to the skin by his pale glare. "There's no harm in a girl sitting alone with her guardian. But you, madam, might wish to have a care for your own reputation. It's generally frowned upon for an unattached woman to go unchaperoned into the garden with a man she does not know."

Thea sucked in a breath. "I came out here on my own."

"That does your reputation no better credit. And you are not alone now."

"Lady Clarissa needs to make a reappearance in the ballroom, my lord," Thea said doggedly, holding onto her temper with a white-knuckled grip. If, as she was increasingly inclined to do, she washed her hands of the whole mess, it was the girl who'd pay the price. "If she does not, her reputation will surely suffer."

"Whether or not it does is no business of yours. Good evening, madam."

Thea gritted her teeth. "Really, my lord, you must—"

"I must nothing."

"Don't be so pig-headed! Your niece—"

"M-miss Ravenshaw?"

Thea closed her eyes. Lord Wilford. Just what she needed.

* * *

Wilford hurried Thea back toward the house, the moist heat of his fingers penetrating the thin sleeve of her dress. He was quite as determined as she'd ever seen him, so much so that one might have thought some wild animal snapped at their heels.

When she recalled the nearly colorless eyes of Lady Clarissa's uncle and the reflexive snarl that bared his teeth when she presumed to contradict him, Thea wasn't entirely certain Wilford didn't have the right of it. She was still so angry she could barely see and had no idea if Wilford had extracted her deftly from the argument or merely mumbled something unintelligible and dragged her away.

It was only after she managed to gulp in enough of the chill night air to cool her fuming over that *gentleman's* high-handed mismanagement of the poor girl's reputation that she realized Wilford was talking.

"...taking it very well. And such a pretty dress, if, ah, if I may say so. Should have been watching where she was going, the foolish chit. I don't, I don't see how she could be so clumsy, and she the ward of a duke. Should have better manners—"

"He's a duke?" Thea blurted.

"Course," Wilford said. "Duke of Ransley. You didn't know?"

"There was no one to make the introductions." Except the girl, who'd been in too much of a taking to think of it. A duke, puffed up with his own importance and disposed to listen to no one's council but his own. And Thea'd pricked his arrogance by arguing with him, questioning his motives, and worst of all, failing to call him "Your Grace"! She thought again of those blazing pale eyes and shivered.

"You must be near frozen!" Wilford began struggling with his coat, an elegant affair of claret superfine so closely cut he surely couldn't get out of it without his valet's assistance.

"I'm fine," Thea said hurriedly. "Please, my lord, let's just go back inside."

Wilford looked down at the hand she'd laid on his arm to prevent him from trying to remove his coat and back into her eyes with a daft grin, and Thea quickly removed her hand.

"Ransley," she said before Wilford could think to propose again. She hadn't meant to say it so suddenly, and Wilford spun on his heel as if he thought the duke might be sneaking up on them. Thea smiled feebly. "Now why does that name sound familiar?"

"Familiar?"

"What do you know of him?" She tucked her hand into the crook of Wilford's arm, and he stammered a moment before managing to get both his mouth and his feet moving.

"Got more blunt than Golden Ball. Four country estates, or is it five? Plus the house in Grosvenor Square. Doesn't spend much time there, I, I hear. Doesn't go about much in Society either."

That explained why his face wasn't known to her, but it wasn't helping her place the niggling familiarity of his name. It hit her like a sudden downpour that she'd called one of the highest peers in the realm pig-headed. "What do you know of him personally?"

"P-personally?" Wilford stopped.

"Yes," Thea said, encouraging him on with a gentle tug to his arm. If they were spotted together in the garden, Thea might have no choice but to succumb to his marriage campaign. "What's his character? Is he generous, courteous, prone to take offense easily?" A man of his wealth and power would not find it difficult to make Thea's life untenable, were he inclined to take revenge for petty offenses. "My lord?" she prompted when Wilford did no more than eye her, an odd expression twisting his vague features.

"Ransley's a good enough fellow, I, I suppose." He started again for the house, but at so slow a pace, Thea had to grit her teeth to prevent herself from dragging him along. "Don't know if he takes offense easily; don't know anyone fool enough to offend him. Fact is," Wilford went on cheerfully, "Ransley can hold a grudge positively ages."

Oh lovely. Just the thing to reassure Thea. She didn't have any time to refine upon it, as Wilford was still speaking.

"Don't know i-if you've heard…." He hesitated unbearably, then shook himself and said, "Course you haven't, Miss Ravenshaw, stupid of me to forget that you won't, you won't have read the newspapers—"

Contrary to Wilford's assumptions and Society's dictates, Thea did, in fact, read newspapers. It was one of the rewards of her self-sufficient life that she had no guardian or husband to forbid her to look at anything but poetry, Minerva press books, and the latest fashionplates. The newspapers, of course, were where she'd seen Ransley's name, and not in the society pages, either. Thea ransacked her brain for the connection, vaguely aware of Wilford wittering away beside her.

"…dastardly behavior, but then, what can you expect…"

It was something to do with the House of Lords. And Thea was quite certain it had been sensational, though precisely how had been buried in the flood of overblown news items bruited across the papers since.

"…ten years he kept after his niece's murderer, though the, the fellow was already dead and gone. Or so—"

"Lady Amelia Holgate," Thea murmured. Ransley's niece, murdered when she slipped away from a house party held by her husband-to-be. It was the recent unmasking of the murderer that had brought Ransley, a decade after the fact, to testify before the House of Lords. "Lady Clarissa's sister? Oh, the poor girl, to lose her sister that way."

"Half-sister," Wilford said dismissively. "Different fathers. Rumor has it they scarcely knew each other." He cocked his head, looking like a particularly dense sparrow. "But how did you hear of the case?"

"I…." Thea swallowed her pride, not up to arguing with Wilford, who could be counted upon to stick to any belief without wavering, no matter what arguments were presented to the contrary. "I must have overheard someone speaking of it."

"Terrible," Wilford said, and Thea thought he was referring to the murder until he added, "Shouldn't speak of such things in front of a lady. Young jackstraw, no doubt, with, with no sense of propriety. Miss Ravenshaw, you need someone to protect you from—"

"Thank you for your escort through the garden, my lord," Thea murmured quickly. The terrace had finally come into view, and it appeared to be empty, thank heavens. "But we cannot return together."

"Oh, but I don't see what—"

"It would give the wrong impression," Thea said gently, removing her hand from his arm. This close to the house, it was imperative that she separate herself from him as quickly as possible. "Do you go in first, and I shall follow."

To her surprise, Wilford dug in his heels, a stubborn light in his eyes. "I, I couldn't possibly leave you out here alone, Miss Ravenshaw."

"I shall be perfectly all right. I will only pass a bit farther along the terrace and go in by another door."

"I couldn't possibly leave you alone," he insisted doggedly.

"Lord Wilford—"

"I wish you would call me Dart. E-everyone does."

"Dear Lord Wilford," Thea said, wincing when he flushed with pleasure. "You're too kind. Please, do go in. I'll be along directly."

Wilford looked back into the moonlit garden, then shook his head stubbornly. Perhaps he would relent if Thea went in first. She frowned, not entirely certain she could rely on him to wait an appropriate length of time before re-entering the ballroom himself. It would be as bad as going in together to have him return mere minutes after she did. He might easily run out of patience, forget why he was supposed to wait, or even enter prematurely with the aim of advancing his suit. Were he a more ruthless or a more intelligent man, he already had enough ammunition to force her to marry him. Pray Wilford never thought of that. He was a fine enough fellow, but she simply couldn't imagine spending the rest of her life with him. Harmless and dimwitted were not the words she wanted to use in describing her husband, assuming she ever wanted one at all.

"You are quite right, my lord," she said, and he looked startled. "It would never do for me to return to the ballroom on my own. Please do me the inestimable service of finding my companion and sending her out to join me." She stopped, afraid she was laying it on too thick, for he had a terrifically suspicious scowl furrowing his brow. He was directing it out into the garden, rather than at her, however, and when she stopped speaking, he looked back at her, blinked twice and suddenly beamed.

"My pleasure, Miss Ravenshaw." He bent far too low over her hand, then hurried onto the terrace and inside, the door creaking alarmingly. Thea hoped the music was sufficiently loud to cover the noise. Otherwise, some busybody was sure to notice first Wilford coming in, then Mrs. Wellins going out, then Thea and Mrs. Wellins coming in. For a moment, she considered simply going in on her own, but regretfully discarded the idea. Not only might it be noticed that she came in immediately following Wilford, but that gentleman might become difficult to handle if he felt she'd sent him after wild geese. She sighed and rubbed her temples. Dancing around the dictates of propriety was infinitely more exhausting than even the most vigorous country dance. A chill breeze sent leaves skating across the terrace, and Thea shivered, wrapping her arms about herself. She glanced back into the dark garden, hoping that Wilford would hurry. The only thing that could make this worse would be if the duke and his niece came up before she could get safely inside.

"Why Miss Ravenshaw," a baritone voice said pleasantly from behind her, "whatever have you been saying to Lord Wilford to puff him up so?"

Chapter Three

THEA spun, her hand flying to her throat. She had just enough presence of mind not to scream, which was extremely fortunate, as the last thing she needed now was to bring anyone else out onto the terrace. She knew the man who lounged indolently against the terrace railing, smoking a cheroot and studying her with cool gray eyes, having shared the occasional dance with him. Very occasional. Though he was handsome and extremely amusing, and she rather liked him for his irreverence and his devil-may-care smile, her reputation could not withstand any closer acquaintance with him than that occasioned by the odd minuet. And she'd been worried about Wilford. This was *not* an improvement.

"Lord Trenwick. How pleasant to see you. Please leave."

He blew out a cloud of fragrant smoke and smiled. "I've always admired your forthrightness, Miss Ravenshaw. Little did I know you could become even more charmingly blunt outside the ballroom."

"It is because we are outside the ballroom that I am blunt," Thea said reprovingly. "You have me at an unfair disadvantage, my lord, as I'm sure you're well aware. Please go back inside so I might do likewise." She kept her eyes on him and steadfastly forbade herself to look either at the terrace doors or the dark garden behind her. If someone stepped outside to take the air, or Ransley returned from the garden, and found her speaking alone with one of the *ton's* most celebrated rakes….

"It is inconvenient to speak to you from such a distance," Trenwick said. He had not put out his cheroot, even though it was not the done thing for a gentleman to smoke in the presence of a lady. "You might as well cease staining your slippers in the grass and come up onto the terrace."

"I have no wish to speak further with you, thank you. Please go inside."

He gave her a slow, lazy smile, his eyes dancing.

Realizing that she stood in full view of anyone opening the nearest terrace door, Thea moved a few feet to her left, keeping the railing between Trenwick and herself. The move took her out of sight of the door and nicely into the shadow of a nearby tree. That it also brought her closer to where Trenwick leaned on the balustrade was a coincidence, though he smiled as if it were not. "Now, my lord," Thea said, and had to admit that it was an improvement to be close enough to speak quietly, "if you would return to the ball…"

"I'm rather enjoying myself out here. I found myself curious to see what was about when I saw you and not one but two gentlemen dart out after the Seabrooke chit. I'm glad I came. I haven't seen Wilford so self-satisfied since he thought he'd won a substantial bet on a horse race. He seems to think he's stolen a march on all the other gentlemen vying for your hand."

"He's wrong," Thea snapped, "and so are you if you think there's anyone who's set their cap at me." She thought better of her sharp tone the moment the words were out of her mouth — Trenwick might be an unprincipled rake, but he was the son of an earl and welcome everywhere but Almack's and the homes of the highest sticklers of the *ton*. It wouldn't do to make an enemy of him, regardless of the circumstances.

Far from becoming annoyed, he laughed. "So he was about the race as well; his horse came in last. And so are you, if you think there aren't a dozen men within earshot who wouldn't leg-shackle themselves to you given half a chance."

"Surely you do not count yourself among their number," she said with some asperity.

He looked at her seriously, but devilry danced in his eyes. "If I but thought you would accept my suit…."

"Given your reputation, my lord, I would be foolish to take you at your word."

"Given *your* reputation, Miss Ravenshaw, I would be foolish not to mean it." He had the audacity to wink at her. "For certain, you would not accept anything *but* a serious offer. Even the wagging tongues will admit that your reputation is as far above reproach as mine is beneath it. Despite your unaccountable unwillingness to step into parson's mousetrap."

She smiled sweetly at him. "As unaccountable as yours?"

He laughed again. "*Touché*, Miss Ravenshaw. You've pinked me there."

"So, my lord, as we are unanimous in our preference for independence, will you not go inside before someone catches us out here and forces our hands?"

She thought he was bamming her when he murmured, "Perhaps I shouldn't mind matrimony so much, were my wife as quick-witted as you," but uncertainty made her heart beat faster.

If he took it into his head, Trenwick would be much more dangerous to her than Wilford ever could. And not just because he was far more clever. If she wasn't careful, he might just manage to turn her head with his looks and his charm. She reminded herself that marriage to such a man, while certainly less dreary than with Wilford, would not suit her, or any woman with an ounce of self-respect, for no man with such a rakish reputation could possibly be expected to stay true once wed. Before she could dredge up a suitable response, however, he straightened from his slouch against the railing and looked out into the dark garden. Thea forced herself not to turn, praying he had not suddenly espied Ransley and his niece making their way toward the terrace.

"Perhaps not so quick-witted as all that, now I think on it," he said in a more normal tone, gesturing with the cheroot he still held. "Running out into the garden after a foolish chit? Perhaps your attic is to let after all."

"Perhaps I did not wish to see the girl ruined for a simple mistake."

"It's hardly her first. Nor, like as not, her last."

"I thought better of you, my lord, than to listen to common chin-wagging," Thea said, and there was an edge to her voice she had not intended. What was Lady Clarissa to her, that she felt the need to defend her?

"The chit's well on her way to blotting her copybook for good." He drew on the cheroot and his next words emerged in a cloud of smoke. "Mind you don't get dragged down with her."

"Then perhaps we ought to both go inside, my lord."

He grinned. "Together?"

"You know that was not my meaning. Nor," she said, taking a chance, "your intent. Cut line, if you please, sir. I'm no ball of yarn to be batted about for your entertainment."

"Nor I a kitten, to take so *innocent* a pleasure." When she did not respond to his innuendo, his smile widened. He put the cheroot between his teeth and waved grandly at the dark garden behind her. "You do not wish to wait for the girl whose reputation so concerned you?"

"Her reputation is protected," Thea said dismissively. "Now, sir, about mine…"

Trenwick blew gently on the end of his cheroot to rekindle the embers. "You think so well of her chances?" he asked off-handedly. "Would you care to place a wager on it? Say… a waltz with me against her making it through the Season without having to retire to the country?"

A waltz with Trenwick would do Thea's reputation no favors, and wagering over Lady Clarissa could do that lady's reputation irreparable harm. "Unlike you, sir, I do not gamble."

"Nonsense. All of life is a gamble. You merely chose only to wager where you're certain to win."

"I don't know what you mean. You will not find me at the tables, Lord Trenwick."

"Yet you gamble nonetheless. Choosing which ball to attend is a gamble — will it be pleasurable or deadly dull? Shall you risk having your modiste fashion a gown out of a striking shade of blue — which looks lovely on you, by the way — or stick to a safer, less vibrant color?" He blew out a trail of smoke and watched it drift into the night sky. "For that matter, are you not gambling the highest of stakes each time you decide which man to dance with? You're wagering your reputation on his, when for all you know, he'll go out and ruin himself, and possibly you, before sunrise. I fail to see how my proposal is any worse for being made plain."

She'd never heard any man acknowledge the kind of balancing act a woman of the *ton* had to perform. Nor admit, even implicitly, that the poor choices of a man like himself might unfairly doom a woman for no reason other than that she was seen with him. His self-awareness made him doubly attractive, while making his proposed wager all the more objectionable. "You're greatly mistaken in me if you think that I would be so careless of Lady Clarissa's reputation, or my own, as to agree to such a wager."

"On the contrary, I have perfect faith in your care for her reputation. Though perhaps slightly less in your concern for your own." He grinned. "You are, after all, still talking with me."

"I would not be if I thought I could safely go inside before you, my lord," Thea said with some asperity, feeling that she might as well be hung for a sheep as a lamb. Besides, she was beginning to think that nothing she could say would do aught but amuse Trenwick. If she were certain she could trust him not to enter so soon after her that their presence in the garden would be connected and raise rumors, she would simply go inside. But given the way he was acting, she couldn't risk it.

"Ah! I am wounded," he said theatrically, and even went so far as to put his hand over his heart as if he'd taken a blow. "My reputation may not be pristine, Miss Ravenshaw, but I've never given anyone cause to doubt my honor."

"I do not doubt your honor, my lord. It's your sense of humor I'm finding chancy."

He frowned at his cheroot and stubbed it out against the railing. "Very well then, Miss Ravenshaw." He leaned toward her over the railing — she nearly took a step back despite herself — and murmured, "Take my wager, and I'll go inside."

"An infamous suggestion, my lord." The orchestra, which she'd been vaguely aware of playing a lively country dance, wrapped up the song, and in the lull, Thea suddenly heard voices from inside the ballroom. They were far too clear, she thought, to be coming from more than a few feet the other side of the terrace door. "Please."

"Take my wager, and I'll turn aside whoever that is before they can discover you. It's an excellent deal — your reputation is protected and so is Lady Clarissa's. I give you my word that the wager will be known only to you and I, and I have no doubt you'll win in any case. For I know well that you will take her in hand, if only to win your bet."

"I should have done so in any case," Thea said, though she wondered how far she would have pushed her way in there. Or could, with Ransley set against her.

"I know."

"Why wager where you expect to lose?"

"It's something to do. I find the Season deadly dull, don't you?"

Thea looked at him, her mind working frantically as the voices came closer to the door. If the wager ever became known, Thea's and Lady Clarissa's reputations would both suffer. But Trenwick had given his word that no one but the two of them would ever know, and whatever else was said about him, he was reputed to be true to his word. It couldn't hurt Lady Clarissa, therefore, whereas if someone came through that door and found Thea and Lord Trenwick together in the gardens, her reputation would be ruined for certain. Far more than if she simply forfeited the bet later and danced with him. A man's laugh, as loud as if he were already on the terrace with Trenwick, coupled with the rattle of the doorhandle stopped her heart. "Yes."

"Yes, you find the Season dull?"

"Yes, I'll take your wager," Thea hissed as the door squealed open.

"Done," she heard Trenwick say through the pounding in her ears. Then he was turning to the gentlemen coming through the doorway while Thea retreated as quickly and quietly as she could to the other end of the terrace. The moon reached that area less vibrantly and she kept back from the railing, but she knew she could not hope to remain unseen if the men came fully out onto the terrace.

After what felt like an eternity, during which her heart refused to beat and she could scarcely breathe, she heard the door creak closed again, and a man's footsteps came across the terrace.

"You can come out, my dear," Trenwick said in a normal tone of voice that sounded shockingly loud to Thea. "I've vanquished the dragons."

She stepped cautiously closer to the railing, but could see no one but Trenwick on the terrace. "I'm not your dear, and you cannot vanquish dragons, my lord, when you are one of them," she said severely, finding it irritatingly difficult to get her breath back.

"On the contrary, Miss Ravenshaw, how better to fight fire than with fire? Speaking of…" He began patting himself as if he expected to find something. "What the devil happened to my cheroot?"

"You stubbed it out, my lord," Thea said, though he could not possibly be so skimblebrained, or intoxicated, as to have forgotten. She wondered if he thought to put her off her guard by acting the fool or if it was just his idea of entertainment.

He grinned, his teeth flashing in the moonlight. "How foolish of me." He walked to the opening in the railing where they'd originally met and held out his hand. "Now, Miss Ravenshaw, clasp hands to seal the bet and then let us both go inside."

When she hesitated, he tipped his head at her, managing to look ridiculously avuncular. "You're like to freeze solid if you stay out here much longer."

Thea took a breath and came along the railing to meet him. He'd been smoking bare-handed, his gloves stuffed haphazardly into his tailcoat pocket, and the heat of his skin sank shockingly through her glove when she put her hand in his.

The terrace door opened with a creak that sent ice plunging straight through Thea's heart. She pulled her hand from Trenwick's and whirled. "Mrs. Wellins!" All the breath left her in relief, and she stepped up onto the terrace. "How lovely to see you here."

"You were gone so long, my dear," Mrs. Wellins said, without flicking so much as a glance at Trenwick, bless her heart. "I thought I'd best check to see you were well."

"I'm much refreshed." Thea turned to Lord Trenwick, who smiled sardonically. "Thank you for your escort, my lord. Mrs. Wellins and I will be along in a moment."

Trenwick bent briefly over her hand, his eyes positively twinkling, then headed off down the terrace. Thea sagged against the stone balustrade as soon as he'd taken himself back inside through the far door, which thankfully did *not* screech like a banshee. "Thank heavens for that. And thank heavens for you, dear aunt. But what took so long? Did not Lord Wilford send you out to me?"

"He did," Mrs. Wellins said comfortably. "But I thought it best not to say so before Lord Trenwick. As for the delay, you know as well as I how difficult it is to argue Lord Wilford out of anything he's set his mind to. I had all I could do to prevent him from following me back out."

"That would never have done. Thank you, Aunt Florence. Whatever would I do without you?"

"Heaven knows," Mrs. Wellins said tartly. "You have quite a habit of casting yourself into the briars, Althea."

Thea took a chilled breath that did not go far enough toward steadying her nerves. "Of course I have," she said, surprised to hear her voice come out fairly evenly. "It is, after all, what I'm best at."

They tarried out on the terrace until the musicians had finished a country dance, the lively music coming faintly through the windows. Thea rubbed her arms and shivered, wishing she had a wrap. When she and Mrs. Wellins finally went back inside, no one paid them the least attention. Except for Trenwick, who had the audacity to wink at her, and Lord Wilford, who attached himself to her within minutes of their return and made Thea bristle with his hovering. Wilford seemed not to notice, too busy staring suspiciously — the truth be told, nearly pugnaciously — about the ballroom.

Thea spent the remainder of the night trying as much as possible to ignore her escort's inexplicable behavior and doing everything short of craning her neck after every blond head she saw. There were blondes of every stripe and stamp, but none of them wore peach.

That poor girl.

* * *

For the second night in a row, Hailstone stood back while Clary dashed pell-mell up the stairs. Ransley followed at a more sedate pace, swung the door out of the butler's lax grip, and pushed it gently closed.

Hailston dragged his eyes from the now-empty stairs. "Good evening, Your Grace."

He relieved Ransley of his hat, cloak, and gloves. And of the muff Clary had left in the carriage. The neighbors, were they watching, had enjoyed an entertaining display this evening. Ransley rubbed his hands together — they'd become chilled in the Ayleford's gardens and the ride home in a cold carriage had done nothing to warm them — and started up the stairs with a sigh. No point in dragging it out any longer than necessary, however much he wanted a drink.

Mariah, Clary's maid, was scratching at her mistress's door when Ransley approached. She looked up, dropped him an abrupt curtsy, and took herself off with such dispatch he could only stare after her. He hadn't thought he looked that much like a thundercloud. Perhaps she was merely grateful to escape the storm brewing in Clary's room.

Ransley knocked perfunctorily and went in. She hadn't thought to lock the door this time, thank heavens. He would not have appreciated having to cajole her into opening it. Not tonight. Clary had made herself perfectly disagreeable in the carriage on the way home, and Ransley was at the tag end of his patience.

His niece sat at her dressing table, her back to him, and pretended to survey herself in the mirror. "Thank you, Mariah," she said airily, "just leave my chocolate on the bedside table." She knew perfectly well he wasn't the maid; the dratted girl could clearly see him in the mirror.

"Watch yourself, girl. You're not too big to take over my knee."

Clary popped to her feet. "You wouldn't dare!"

"Wouldn't I?" He crossed his arms and leaned his shoulder against the bedpost. Her eyes flickered. Good. She hadn't mistaken the position for relaxed, nor failed to notice that he was not in any more pleasant a mood than she. He'd never laid a hand on her, and couldn't imagine he ever would, but he'd lost any patience he might have had when she'd finished ripping up at him in the carriage by calling him an unfeeling monster. Aware that the coachman and footmen could not help but overhear, he'd not deigned to respond then, but they would have it out now. "What have you to say for yourself, Clarissa?"

She glared, her chin quivering. For one irresolute moment, it appeared she would apologize for her infamous behavior. Then the chin firmed, her eyes blazed, and she cried, "It's all your fault!"

"My fault?" Ransley exclaimed, taken aback. "*I* didn't toss my drink at someone, then cross a ballroom like I was hacking my way through brambles."

Clary gaped at him. She whirled suddenly, plumped down on the chair before her dressing table, and burst into tears.

God save him from women's tears! Ransley couldn't think what had come over his ward; she never used to be so changeable. They'd rubbed along perfectly comfortably for years without need of more than the occasional correction on his part, which had always been taken with at least an appearance of equanimity on hers, even when she was eight. Now she couldn't seem to go a day without being overcome by some tempest or other. He'd initially blamed it on Lady Ashburne's influence, but had since reluctantly concluded that Clary had actually been calmer when that lady was around. He wished again that he'd waited until Lady Ashburne was able to help him keep Clary from these near-constant knocks to her reputation. The girl knew they were damaging her chances to make a good match, and the more they happened, the more tears she shed. Perhaps, were Clary in the soup less often, she'd be less inclined to emulate a thundercloud. And perhaps, were she less frequently overset, she'd be better able to stay out of the soup.

"I'm sorry," Clary gulped when he laid a hand on her heaving shoulder. A moment later, she'd buried her face against his chest and begun watering his waistcoat. Munson would not be pleased. "I don't mean to be so clumsy," she wailed.

"Clumsiness can be forgiven, Clarissa." Ransley patted her back gently until it appeared the worst of the storm had passed. "I doubt anyone would have noticed—" Except the recipient of her clumsiness, but at least Clary hadn't picked a dragon to run over. The tall, raven-haired beauty rose up in his memory, her eyes — as deep a blue as her gown — snapping with irritation, and he revised his opinion. Clary might well have picked a dragon, but at least it wasn't one who had any desire to take her head off. *Ransley's* head, on the other hand…. "—if you hadn't near-bowled people over on your way to the door." He set her away from him and fished in his tailcoat pocket for the handkerchief that had become an indispensible part of his wardrobe since Clary's come-out. "Whatever possessed you, child?"

Clary buried her face in the clean linen, lost in a fresh spate of tears. Anyone would think the girl was unfortunate in her upbringing and attempting to make her way in the world without the tutelage of the best governesses money could buy.

"All right. It's all right. I daresay no one will have made much note of it," Ransley lied. Heaven help him, but he was going to have to keep an even closer eye on his niece than he had to date. If she could forget herself so far as to panic over a relatively minor mistake, God alone knew what she'd do if she made a major one.

Clary subsided slowly into quivering sobs, patting at her face with the handkerchief. She turned about in the chair and straightened her shoulders a bit, as if to impress him with her maturity, the effort largely undercut by the broken sob that escaped her when she caught sight of her face in the mirror.

"Oh, I look awful."

"Most people do when they cry."

"Do you think Mariah can do anything about this?" She prodded the puffy redness around her right eye as if it belonged to someone else.

"It will fade by morning if you refrain from poking at it."

"Morning! Oh, but Uncle, I so wanted to go to Jennie Mackley's ball."

Ransley winced at the reappearance of not only the argument that had accompanied the first half of the ride home, but the wheedling tone that had driven him to bark at the girl, thereby guaranteeing that the second half of the trip was accomplished in a veritable downpour of tears. "I think it better that we not."

"But it's her come out, and we're special friends."

"You've only met her once."

Clary scowled at him in the mirror. "You said we could."

"That was before you—" Ransley saw her chin begin to quiver and quickly changed course. "—made your nose red with crying."

"But the lady in the garden said we could fix it up and go back to the ball right then and there. Surely Mariah could—"

"Miss Ravenshaw was wrong." Not least because Clary had clearly not finished emulating a thundercloud. Even if she steered clear of new trouble, Ransley wasn't certain Clary could keep her composure if some damn fool brought up her earlier faux pas. And her reputation would not be enhanced if she broke down in tears in some poor fellow's arms.

"You knew her? I didn't realize you knew her."

"Of course I didn't know her."

"Then—"

"That moonling, Wilford, called her by name."

Clary gave another sniff, one she'd learned from a matron with enough dignity to carry it off. "He seemed nice enough."

"It's easy to be nice when you have so few wits they rattle when you shake your head."

"Uncle Ransley! Don't you keep telling me not to say anything if I haven't anything pleasant to say?"

"Yes, I do."

She opened her mouth, and he glared until she closed it again. Clary huffed and returned to surveying herself mournfully in the mirror. Ransley patted her shoulder again, wondering how it could possibly be comforting. Yet it was what people did. Clary crumpled his handkerchief in her hands and rested her chin on them. "She might have helped," she said wistfully. "Miss Ravenshaw. She said she'd help."

Ransley was prepared to admit that he needed help. Specifically, a woman's help. What, after all, did he know about guiding a young girl through her come-out? He was already keeping his own rooms by the time his sister came out; he'd squired her to balls and picnics, but was in neither the position nor the mood to watch the process from the inner sanctum. And his other niece, poor little Amelia, had come out only in country society, and been in any case, a bird of quite a different feather from the half-sister she scarcely knew. Ransley's mood darkened. He had failed Amelia, his own decisions as much to blame for her death as the man who took her life. He would not, by God, fail Clary. She would have her London Season and she would shine as brightly as he knew she could.

But however much Clary needed a woman's touch, when Ransley thought of the raven-haired harridan who'd accosted him, he knew one thing absolutely. "Clarissa, my dear, any woman so unconcerned about her own reputation could hardly be a boon to yours."

Chapter Four

"My game, I believe." Josias Mallinson reached to take the pot, but a hand came down on his before he could do so.

"Hasty," Lord Alan Trenwick murmured, laying his cards on the green baize.

Mallinson sat back, his hands empty. He'd thought for certain he had that hand, and with it, the game. Damn Trenwick for pulling out a better one. He watched Trenwick pile the coins carelessly in front of him. They meant little enough to him, no doubt. The man was plump in the pockets and could afford to lose. Not that he often did. "Shall we go again?"

"Have you anything to wager?" Trenwick shuffled the cards with deft precision, his cool gray eyes on Mallinson's face.

Under the table, Mallinson's fingers clenched. The unutterable cheek of the man! A second son with no prospects, he had the devil's own luck, and gave himself airs with it. Mallinson would be a duke one day, but Trenwick would never be anything but a lesser lord, for all that Society insisted on giving *Lord* Trenwick honors, while making nothing of a duke's heir, just because his father had no title. Mallinson relaxed his hands with an effort and reached for the paper always left close at hand in Cocker's card room.

Trenwick gathered up his winnings. "I have never taken a gentleman's vowels. Good evening, sir."

Mallinson's hand curled into a fist on top of the table this time. Trenwick appeared not to notice. He walked casually away, Mallinson's money in his pockets. Damn the man and his airs and his luck! Mallinson rapped his fist against the baize and pushed himself to his feet. There were other wagers to make and other men to win money from. Men not too puffed up to take Mallinson's vowels. He was heir presumptive to one of the richest dukedoms in England, after all. When Ransley died….

Mallinson scowled. He took the glass off a passing waiter's tray and swallowed half the contents without tasting the fine brandy. The waiter was too well-trained to glare, but he stared at Mallinson a moment before turning about and heading back the way he'd come to get another brandy. Mallinson drained the glass and left it on a side table on his way to the billiard room. He was fortunate enough to come across Lord McAllister on the way. Considering himself a dab hand at the billiard table, McAllister was always willing to lay money on his non-existent skill. And *he* didn't object to taking Mallinson's vowels.

He was in the process of drubbing McAllister soundly for the second time when Wilford bumbled in.

"Oh! Hullo, Mallinson!" Wilford's unexpected hail caused Mallinson to miss his shot. He turned on the other man, who hadn't the imagination to quail at his expression and said only, "Pity, that," when McAllister proceeded to pot the red ball, winning himself three points and the game.

"How good to see you, Dart," Mallinson lied when McAllister had taken his money and gone, a satisfied smirk sitting awkwardly on his thin lips. "When are you leaving?" There were other gentlemen who could be convinced to test their skill at the billiard table, though few who'd bet so extravagantly on so little return as McAllister.

"Thought I'd watch," Wilford said, oblivious to the ruination of Mallinson's plans. Few would dare to play with Wilford in the room — he was widely considered to be bad luck, no doubt due to his tendency to speak at the worst possible moment.

Mallinson fished the balls from the pockets. "Very well, then. We shall play."

"Me? I don't play."

"I'll give you ten points," Mallinson said between his teeth. He handed Wilford a cue and pointed him at the table. "And we'll bet on the outcome."

Wilford smiled. "I bet I'll lose."

"Nonsense, Dart. Always bet on yourself to win." It was Mallinson who'd given Lord Arthur Furlong, who had not yet been the Earl of Wilford when they met at university, his nickname. Everyone had thought it a marvelous joke, even Wilford. Mallinson neither knew nor cared if Wilford realized it was a reference to his *lack* of anything resembling quick wits. "Put a guinea on it, there's a good fellow."

Wilford obligingly took a gold coin out of his pocket and laid it in the tray on the sidetable, and he obligingly lost it. He didn't hesitate when Mallinson suggested they play again, this time for five guineas.

Mallinson soon forgot his pique at Wilford for making him lose to McAllister. Wilford was such an appalling bad player that even if he knocked against Mallinson while he was shooting, it would still be a simple thing to best him. As it was, he was unusually subdued, and did nothing to foul Mallinson's game. Doubling the stakes each time, Mallinson soon raised the wager to eighty guineas.

He was sinking his ball for the winning point when Wilford laid his cue aside and wandered slowly — one might even say thoughtfully, were one talking about a different man — to the door. "Care to go again?" Mallinson said quickly.

"Haven't any more on me." Wilford plopped into a chair and began picking at the gilt arm.

"I'd be happy to take your note."

"Good of you," Wilford murmured. He patted his coat absently, as if he expected to find paper in his pockets, and didn't leave off despite his lack of success until Mallinson assured him they could settle up at the end of play.

Mallinson set about preparing the table, and nearly dropped his stick when Wilford suddenly exclaimed, "Demmed chit's a demmed menace," with uncharacteristic vehemence.

Mallinson cocked an eyebrow. "What chit?"

"Blasted girl spilled orgeat all down Miss Ravenshaw's gown, then took off across the ballroom. Miss Ravenshaw had to run her to ground to demand an apology, and I don't, I don't think the chit even offered one then! Can you imagine?"

"Indeed," Mallinson murmured. He offered Wilford the first round. When Wilford failed to drop a ball, he took over, listening with half an ear to Wilford fulminate against one useless female for ruining the dress, and apparently the night, and very possibly the reputation, of another useless female. To hear Wilford tell it, Bonaparte was less perfidious.

"And the duke! Standing there in the garden with Miss Ravenshaw as if her, her reputation meant nothing! I tell you, Mallinson, I don't think much of your uncle."

Mallinson missed the ball and came close to tearing the felt. "What the devil are you on about, Dart? Uncle Eustace has been dead these twenty years." And good riddance to the skinflinted old buzzard, who hadn't even left Mallinson enough to keep him in cravats.

"Not your Uncle Eustace." Wilford waved his arm about as if that would clarify matters. "The Duke of Ransley, whatever he is to you."

Mallinson set his cue aside with careful precision. "What about the Duke of Ransley?"

Wilford blinked. "What about him?"

Mallinson itched to take up the cue and use it on Wilford. He kept a careful rein on his voice and said, "You said the duke was in the garden with this Miss Ravenshaw?" Even thinking about it sent cold fingers crawling over his skin.

"Would never have happened if he kept that demmed ward of his on, on a closer leash. She needs to be brought to heel." Wilford firmed his jaw and pressed his lips together in an attempt, no doubt, to look fierce and resolute.

Mallinson ignored him. Oh damn it all! He knew it. The minute he saw Ransley standing in the middle of Cocker's like he belonged there, Mallinson knew things were about to take a bad turn. Starting with how hale and hearty

Ransley looked. And tall. Mallinson had winced under the man's firm handshake and rankled at having to look up to meet his eyes. In the nearly fifteen years since he last saw Ransley, he'd convinced himself that the man had only seemed so tall because Mallinson himself had been a boy at the time. Never mind he'd just come from university and hadn't grown an inch since. More to the point, he'd made himself certain Ransley must be ancient by now, bowed down with years and infirmity.

But Ransley had been disgustingly healthy and a great deal younger than Mallinson wanted to remember. Not at all a man who was preparing to stick his spoon in the wall and leave the title, the estates, and pots of money to his impatiently waiting heir.

That was bad enough, but to discover that Ransley'd set his sights on some female…. That was the outside of enough. Mallinson was Ransley's heir. His *heir*. Until now, Ransley had obligingly kept himself to himself and shown no sign whatever of even considering taking a wife. Any son out of Ransley, any pitiful little peep of a boy-child, and all of Mallinson's prospects went up in smoke.

He'd been trading on his inheritance for years — he could hardly be expected to get along on the pittance of an allowance Ransley gave him. He'd bought against it, borrowed against it, even taken out an obit loan from an obliging moneylender, payable upon Ransley's death. Everything hinged on Mallinson being duke one day. Were Ransley's name even so much as bandied about with some female's, merchants up and down Bond Street would be dunning Mallinson before the day was out. Not to mention the dozen, or three, gentlemen who held his vowels.

Something would have to be done. Mallinson had talked himself out of the danger when he'd met up so unexpectedly with Ransley. He'd convinced himself that there was nothing to worry about — the duke would quickly find a match for that blasted Seabrooke chit and go bury himself in the country again and everything would go on as it had before. Now he saw how foolish he'd been. Every minute Ransley remained in London, every ball he attended, every picnic or soiree or what-have-you he showed himself at increased the chance that he'd find some woman to marry. Some young woman who'd whelp out litter after litter of squalling brats. It was imperative that the man be returned post haste to the country, where he'd passed two decades without making a match and could be reliably expected to remain, still unmarried, until the happy eventuality of his death.

"How, how much do I owe you?" Wilford asked, startling him out of his thoughts.

"A hundred guineas," Mallinson said, blithely inflating the figure and ignoring the gold coins he already had in his pocket. If Wilford couldn't keep track of his blunt, that was his look-out. While Wilford sat down at the small table in the corner and obligingly began to write out a draft on his bank, Mallinson stepped to the door and closed it. "You haven't much use for Lady Clarissa, do you, Dart?"

Wilford looked up with a stricken expression. "Terribly sorry, Mallinson. I forgot she was a relation."

"Never met the girl in my life," Mallinson lied — he might have seen the chit when she was a child, but he couldn't remember and it didn't signify in any case. "I'm quite prepared to believe she's a jingle-brained widgeon if you say so."

"Don't know about that, but she's certainly cow-handed." Wilford scowled. "Gel ought to have punch spilled down *her* dress."

"Well, why don't you?"

Wilford gaped at him. "What, what are you—"

"It's quite simple, Dart. Next ball you're at, knock her arm when she's got a cup of something. Or spill your own on her. You can apologize very nicely, if it will make you feel better."

"But, but I don't—" He stopped, frowned in concentration for a moment, then shook his head. "No, I don't understand."

"You said yourself she'd deserve it for what she did to Miss Ravenshaw. Don't make the mistake of thinking she'll get what she ought from Ransley. I know him," Mallinson said with brash disregard for the truth. "He'll only coddle her."

"Oh, I don't think—"

"And you said this Miss Ravenshaw was in the garden with the duke?" That cold hand touched Mallinson's spine again. Ransley had never shown an interest in leg-shackling himself to a female of any persuasion, but the mere thought of it.... If anyone other than Wilford had happened upon them, Ransley — pattern card of propriety that he was — might well have gotten himself leg-shackled to save her reputation, and then where would Mallinson be?

"I'm certain it didn't mean anything," Wilford said, nervously fanning the draft he'd just written to dry the ink. "I shouldn't, I really shouldn't have mentioned it."

"Yes, but they *were* alone together, weren't they?"

"Not, not really. Lady Clarissa—"

"A schoolroom miss. Hardly a proper chaperone."

"Miss Ravenshaw was quite content to come with me. I, I think she was angry with him." Wilford's brows drew together. Mallinson took the draft away from him before his whipping it about could shred it to pieces. "She *did* ask rather a lot of questions about him."

"There you go." He folded the draft and tucked it in his pocket. "Better act quick, old boy, or he'll steal a march on you."

"You really think so?" Mallinson raised his eyebrows and Wilford flushed painfully. "But she won't accept my suit. I've asked her and asked her...."

Mallinson swallowed a cutting remark and said, "Well, she certainly won't be able to accept you if she's engaged to Ransley."

Wilford's distressed flush darkened. "But what am I to do, Mallinson?" He stuttered dreadfully over Mallinson's name, bringing back pleasant memories of days in university when he'd teased Wilford into stuttering so awfully he couldn't even manage his own name.

"We shall have to keep them apart, Dart. That's all there is to it."

"But how does spilling Lady Clarissa's drink help? She's not, she's not the problem."

"Yes, but she may be the solution. She's already blotted her copybook — her name is very nearly a byword as it is. Just one or two more little… incidents, and Ransley will have to take his ward back to the country to wait for the gossip to die down. And," he added, speaking slowly because Wilford still looked confused, "if Ransley's rusticating, he can't very well be setting his cap at your Miss Ravenshaw, now can he?"

"My Miss Ravenshaw," Wilford murmured and beamed. The smile faded quickly. "But how, Mallinson? I don't know what to do!"

Mallinson squeezed Wilford's shoulder reassuringly. "Don't worry, old friend. I'll help you."

Mallinson had been waiting for dead men's shoes all his life, impatiently looking forward to the day Ransley died and left him the title, the estates, and the money.

Ransley had dangled too much before him for too long to take it all back now.

Chapter Five

"THERE they are," Thea hissed. "Do you go talk to him, and I'll—"

"Whatever could I have to say that would be of interest to a duke, my dear?" Mrs. Wellins' mild reproof didn't put Thea off one jot.

Keeping the Duke of Ransley and his ward in sight through the swirling throng of dancers with no little effort, she said, "Talk about the weather, Aunt! You can talk about your health for all I care, just—"

"Althea Ravenshaw, you go too far."

Mrs. Wellin's remonstrance was quietly voiced, but Thea wasn't fool enough not to take it seriously for all that. Reluctantly, she turned her eyes from her quarry and gave her aunt a rueful smile. "My apologies. Enthusiasm carried me quite away."

"Enthusiasm will carry you to a spinster's grave, if you're not careful."

Thea forced herself not to grimace. Mrs. Wellins was a dear lady, quite devoted to her, and Thea could wish for no better companion to lend respectability to her solitary path through Society. It was a matter of some comfort to her that she was able, in return, to offer her aunt a security that Mr. Wellins, a poor curate, had been unable to bequeath. But Mrs. Wellins never left off worrying that Thea's determination not to blindly bind herself into some new servitude would ruin her chances at making a match. It was natural, Thea supposed, for any woman who'd been happily wed to believe it the ideal state for every woman. She patted her companion's hand. "I've not set out to ruin myself, I promise. I merely need to speak to Lady Clarissa for a moment. Without her guardian."

For the better part of a week, Thea had searched every entertainment for Lady Clarissa and her uncle. She had thought she saw them at a hugely-attended musicale with an unfortunately shrill soprano, but as she'd been unable to make her way across the crowded room to them, it was difficult to be certain. There were an astonishing number of young ladies with Lady Clarissa's gleaming blond tresses. However, Thea had yet to espy a gentleman with hair anywhere near as pale as His Grace's. She'd begun to wonder if, having seen it only by moonlight, she searched ballrooms, routs, musicales and theatre audiences for a man with the wrong shade of hair.

At first, Thea had kept an eye out for Lady Clarissa out of concern and curiosity. *Not*, she told herself, because of the unfortunate wager with Lord Trenwick. Agreeing had gotten her safely off the terrace without ruining her reputation, but to pursue it in any way would be the outside of enough. The more she thought on it, the more she thought... *hoped* that Trenwick had merely been playing with her. Surely he didn't mean to follow through on the bet. He was a rake, it was true, but surely not lost to all propriety. And if he did press the matter.... Well, if he did, she would have no choice but to forfeit the wager. The damage to Thea's reputation occasioned by waltzing with Trenwick would surely not be so great as the damage she'd escaped by wagering with him in the first place. Or the damage such a wager would cause Clarissa, should it become known. Thea would survive.

However, as the days passed without any sign of Lady Clarissa, Thea began to worry less about Trenwick and more that the girl's cold-hearted guardian had packed her off to the country, ruining her chances not only in this Season but possibly for the future. Gossip did eventually die, but one's successes and failures in previous Seasons inevitably became fodder for the next year's rattling tongues. A faux pas might be forgotten, buried in a throng of other events, but a faux pas followed by an immediate dash for the country would never leave the true gossip's repertoire. When she became aware of the growing rumors about Lady Clarissa's half-sister, tongues wagging more fiercely than they had when Ransley was dredging it all up in the House of Lords, she feared the worst. As the gossip mounted, Thea's heart bled for the girl, who appeared doomed to be sacrificed to an event ten years in the past.

Althea Ravenshaw was no stranger to gossip. Tongues had wagged fast and furious when she first entered Society. How dare she, a woman well past her come out, make her way through the entertainments of the *ton* as if she were not so firmly on the shelf that she'd long since been shoved to the back and covered with dust? Worse, she was a woman of some substance and no little beauty who managed to turn the heads of men who had multitudes of caps set at them, dragging their attention from the marriageable misses to herself, never mind she wasn't interested. Thea knew what it was like to hear your name bandied about in the vilest of terms, to see those you most want to impress lift their noses and turn away, to sit at home waiting for invitations that never came. She had been strong enough to hold her head high and sail on determinedly until all but the sharpest of tongues fell still and the *ton* pretended that they couldn't remember a time they had shunned her, nor any reason they might have. Pray heaven Lady Clarissa could do the same, though Thea was by no means convinced she could manage it with no support but that of her top-lofty uncle.

Thea very deliberately did not let herself think that the better Lady Clarissa was able to weather the storm of gossip, the safer she herself was from Lord Trenwick. She had made it through her own trial by fire, it was true, but she had no desire to go through that again, nor any certainty, should she fall from Society's good graces, that she would ever be able to find her way back in. But she did not wish Lady Clarissa well purely out of selfish motivations — surely that, and the fact that she'd wanted to help even before she ran afoul of Trenwick's sense of humor, counted for something.

Thea gave up attempting to convince Mrs. Wellins to help her get the girl aside and settled for keeping an eye on the chit in between dances. Thank heavens Lord Wilford had made himself scarce of late — there was no one, tonight, to put off the gentlemen who sought Thea out, and she chatted pleasantly with her partners while managing to keep her eye, most of the time, on Lady Clarissa. The young lady danced frequently and well — the gossip had not gone so far, yet, as to prevent any except the highest of sticklers from asking her to dance — while her guardian glowered on the edges of the room, his eye always on her. On one occasion, when Thea looked across the floor after Lady Clarissa, her eyes accidentally met the duke's. She looked quickly away, feeling unaccountably flushed.

When her chance came, Thea nearly missed it. The musicians were just drawing an energetic country dance to a close when Thea, who was dancing nearby with Lord Fenton, noticed Lady Clarissa murmuring something to her partner, a callow young man with an extraordinarily high collar. He flushed, offered her his arm, and nearly before Thea realized what they were about, they began to wend their way toward the refreshment room.

"A pleasure, as always, Miss Ravenshaw," Lord Fenton murmured, bowing. He was a pleasant fellow and an excellent dancer, but never seemed much inclined to flirt. Thea rather thought he danced with her because he missed doing so with his wife, who had passed some years previous.

"Likewise." She dropped him a curtsy, her eyes demurely downcast. "I wonder if you might escort me to the refreshment room, my lord. I find myself quite parched."

"I would be delighted."

As they made their way across the ballroom, Thea responded to his light conversation in kind, her thoughts on what she would say to Lady Clarissa. She must first know whether the girl desired her assistance. Recalling the chit's wide-eyed response in the garden, Thea rather thought her help would be welcome, but she shuddered to think of taking on the Duke of Ransley only to discover that Lady Clarissa wanted nothing to do with her. But it was not a conversation that could be had with their respective dancing partners hovering solicitously nearby. Perhaps Thea could suggest visiting the retiring room.

The question became entirely moot not five minutes after Thea and her escort entered the refreshment room. Lord Fenton had gone to get her a glass of something — Thea sincerely hoped it would not be orgeat — leaving Thea free to look about for Lady Clarissa. She spied the young lady, a glass in her hand and her dance partner at her shoulder, speaking with a small woman wearing a huge turban, its enormous feathers bobbing violently with the vehement motions of her head. Or rather, *she* was speaking at them. Lady Charyls, a veritable dragon of Society, never let any conversation turn into an *exchange* of comments. Thea had come under that matron's beady eye and sharp tongue on more occasions than she cared to remember.

The ballroom was quite overheated, and the refreshment room correspondingly crowded. Thea inched her way closer to her quarry, knowing she couldn't move far or Lord Fenton would be unable to find her. He was too good-natured to get testy about it, but that was no excuse for abandoning him. Lady Charyls was apparently holding forth most entertainingly, for lords and ladies were crowding in around her unwilling audience, making it impossible for Thea to clearly see what happened next.

Lady Clarissa jerked forward suddenly, her glass flying out of her hand. It described a perfect arc, liberally distributing its contents across Lady Charyls' face and dress before shattering on the floor. Thea winced in the sudden silence. Oh Lord, not again.

Impossible to reach the girl's side with any speed. As Thea attempted to make her way across the refreshment room, Lady Charyls' hectoring voice boomed out over the assembly. The dressing down she gave Clarissa could no doubt be heard in the ballroom, even over the musicians, assuming they hadn't stopped in shock at the first blast of Lady Charyls' voice. Thea could make out Lady Clarissa's voice picking up a minor counterpoint made up primarily of, surprisingly, buts instead of apologies. It was, it seemed, the only word she could squeeze in, and it wasn't doing anything to appease the enraged lady.

Nor was Lord Wilford helping. God alone knew where he'd come from, but he was hopping around Lady Charyls in an excess of nervous energy, brandishing a handkerchief with which he didn't dare to do more than dart abortive dabs at her dripping gown. She was having none of it, and in fact ceased her incensed litany long enough to tell him to stop bouncing about like a Barbary ape and take himself off.

Thea had very nearly reached Lady Clarissa's side, though she had no idea what she'd do when she got there. She was on no friendly terms with Lady Charyls, and chances were good that her support would only further enrage the woman, but she had to do something. Lady Clarissa was not helping herself — her attempts to explain matters to the dripping dragon not only continued to inflame her, but kept them from moving to someplace more private. A prompt apology and quick retreat were, perhaps, the best strategy, could Thea but effect them. However, before she could put her tenuous plan into motion, the Duke of

Ransley loomed up behind Lady Clarissa, taking her arm in an uncompromising grip that squeezed off her protestations.

"My sincerest apologies, Lady Charyls," he said in a firm, clear voice that cut her off mid-spate. "There is, of course, no excuse for such an accident, and I am quite certain my niece desires only to apologize for her part in it."

Lady Clarissa stared at him for a moment before snapping her eyes back to Lady Charyls, from whose nose a large drop of liquid hung, swaying violently with her every move. "I am, Lady Charyls. So terribly sorry. I don't know what happened—" She was quite clearly about to add something else, and Thea had a very good idea that the next word would have been "but." Instead, she broke off with a tiny gasp and glared at her guardian, whose fingers were visibly compressing the pale skin above her elbow.

"Again, Lady Charyls," Ransley said smoothly, "my sincerest apologies. Please have your modiste send me the bill for a gown to replace this creation. Which, if I may say so, beautifully becomes you." He was good, Thea acknowledged, as she watched Lady Charyls lift her chin, a sort of glow coming into her damp face. Never mind that she looked like a stick wrapped in a yard of silk. "Good evening." Ransley bowed more deeply than necessary and moved away, Clarissa clamped tightly to his side.

A knot of tutting women had formed around Lady Charyls, and a similar knot of twittering attendees around Lord Wilford, who appeared to be recounting the incident at length. Thea glanced from them to the door, wondering if she should follow the duke and his ward, and was unpleasantly startled to see Lord Trenwick standing nearby. His eyes met hers for a moment. Then he winked at her, a sardonic smile curving his lips. Making a snap decision, and forgetting Lord Fenton, who might never make it back through the madly chattering crowd with her drink in any case, Thea followed the duke and his ward.

She entered a long hallway just in time to see Ransley guide Lady Clarissa into a room Thea would not have dared to enter herself, as it was clearly private. She hesitated outside the door only long enough to hear Lady Clarissa sobbing.

The room was a library, and there was a fire burning in the hearth. The Duke of Ransley was standing before it with his hands clasped behind him, deaf to his niece's sobs. She was huddled on a settee in a tumble of skirts, her face buried in her hands.

"Good evening, Your Grace," Thea said, closing the door behind her. He turned to stare at her through eyes that had only a little more color in them than they'd shown in the moonlight. She dropped him a carefully correct curtsy and turned to the young lady, who looked up, her tears vanishing in her surprise at Thea's entrance. "Lady Clarissa."

Much to her surprise, the girl immediately dissolved into tears again.

Ransley sighed. "Do leave off the waterworks, Clarissa."

Forgetting he was a duke and a stranger, Thea glared at him and went to sit next to the sobbing young woman. She touched the shining hair, which had come out of its pins and was strewn wildly across the girl's shoulders, and was nearly knocked over when Clarissa threw herself into Thea's arms and began raining down tears on her bodice.

Ransley had the gall to look amused.

Thea scowled. "You might make yourself useful," she snapped. "Have you a handkerchief?"

"Of course I have a handkerchief. I have a watering pot for a niece." He handed her the square of linen and watched, a cynical curl to his lip, while Thea coaxed Clarissa into using it instead of her dress to sop up her tears. While Thea murmured reassurances and rubbed the girl's shuddering back, Ransley crossed his arms over his chest and leaned against the mantelshelf, for all the world as if the girl's distress was nothing to do with him.

"What in heaven's name have you been saying to the poor girl?"

His eyebrows went up. "I fail to see what business it is of yours."

"It's my business when she falls into my arms in hysterics."

"Had you not intruded, madam, she would not be in your arms."

Thea willed down her flush at the pointed remark. "No. You'd have let her cry herself silly without lifting a finger to help her."

Ransley sketched a mocking bow. "You know me so well, Miss…?"

Thea's cheeks grew hotter. "Althea Ravenshaw, Your Grace. As you well know."

"Not having been formally introduced, I hesitate to admit it. And you, of course, already know who I am." His coldly sardonic tone deepened, as if there was some shame attached to her knowing who he was. Thea bristled. She may have been putting herself forward, but it was for Lady Clarissa's sake, and Ransley had no call to treat her like some encroaching mushroom. "Yes, yes, Clarissa," Ransley said in response to a fresh spate of tears, "we all know you didn't mean to."

"No!" Clarissa pulled herself out of Thea's arms, having someone on her side giving her the courage to glare at her uncle. "No, I didn't do it."

"Half the *ton* saw you fling your orgeat at Lady Charyls."

"Oh, but!" Clarissa bit her lip and turned to Thea, as the only sympathetic ear in the room. "But someone ran into me and bumped my arm."

"Who?" Ransley was, for some reason, staring at Thea.

She realized suddenly why and flushed again, this time in anger. How dare he accuse her of such a thing! And what did he think she could possibly hope to gain from it in any case? "I was too far away to see who was nearest your niece, Your Grace," she said, refraining from biting off the words only with the greatest of effort. "There were a great many people about."

"And it's no use asking me," Lady Clarissa said mournfully, apparently unaware of her uncle's unspoken accusation. "I didn't see him at all. Just my orgeat going flying."

"Him?" The duke's attention shifted to his ward, and when his pale eyes released her, Thea sagged despite herself. The man was a menace. "If you don't know who did it, how do you know it was a man?"

44

"I felt his sleeve brush my arm. Oh," she moaned, showing signs of descending into fresh hysterics, "oh, but everyone thinks I did it on purpose! Even you don't believe me."

"Of course no one thinks you did it on purpose," Thea said in a firm tone she hoped would strengthen Clarissa's wilting backbone.

"No one would be fool enough to deliberately douse Lady Charyls," Ransley muttered, which definitely didn't help matters.

Thea went back to rubbing the girl's back, overwarm through her dress, while she sobbed into the handkerchief. She didn't hesitate to glare at the Duke of Ransley, who had the unmitigated gall to look surprised that his niece had begun wailing again. At this rate, the girl was going to work herself into a state.

"Enough now." Thea set Clarissa away from her, her hands on the girl's shuddering shoulders. "Wipe your tears and compose yourself. You can't go back into that ballroom looking like a colicky baby, now can you?"

"Go back?" Clarissa drew in a shuddering breath. "But I, I can't! Can I?"

"Of course you can. Ring for a maid, if you would, Your Grace." Thea said as casually as she could, well aware that she was issuing orders to one of the highest peers of the realm. "I'm certain one can be found to repair the damage to Lady Clarissa's toilette." Though she was very carefully not looking at him, she was aware of Ransley inclining his head toward her in a manner that could only be accounted mocking before going to tug on the bellpull.

Clarissa straightened up a bit, pulling her shoulders back. Thea released them with a gentle squeeze. "I don't know if I can show my face," the girl murmured.

"You can and you must," Thea told her. "It was an accident, in which you were as much a victim as Lady Charyls. You must hold your head high and make a reappearance, or people will assume it is more than that."

"But what am I to do? What shall I say?" Clarissa twisted to face her guardian. "Uncle Ransley?"

His eyes flicked to his niece, then returned to Thea. "Well, Miss Ravenshaw?"

He was clearly determined to be of no help whatever. Seething with irritation that a young lady's reputation rested in such callous hands, Thea took Clarissa's warm fingers in her own and said, "You must let the maid fix you up, and then you must go back into the ballroom as if nothing happened. If anyone is so lacking in manners as to bring it up, you will say that you're frightfully upset at having been so clumsy and you only hope Lady Charyls will forgive you." Ransley gave an inelegant snort, which Thea ignored. She was relieved when a footman tapped at the door and the infuriating man turned his attention from her in order to ask the man to send in a maid.

"But—"

"No," Thea said firmly. "I know someone bumped you, my dear, but you mustn't say so. Continuing to protest your innocence will only make you look all the more guilty. You must appear contrite and apologetic and distressed."

Clarissa sniffed mightily and gave Thea a watery smile. "I shan't have any problems with that last."

Thea patted her hand. "You'll do fine. Just don't look *too* distressed."

"She means," Ransley said from the position he'd retaken before the fire, "that under no circumstances are you to go back to weeping and wailing."

Thea scowled. "You might show a little sympathy."

"Why? You seem to be offering quite all that's needed." There came a scratching at the door and Ransley called for the maid to come in without turning his strange, pale eyes from Thea. "Here's a maid, my dear, come to make you presentable."

Thea hesitated. She ought to be getting back. She'd spent entirely too long away from the ballroom as it was, and Mrs. Wellins would be getting worried. Besides, she really ought not be seen exiting the library in the company of a man, even with his niece in tow. On the other hand, she'd been looking for an opportunity to offer her assistance for the better part of a week now. She'd much rather have talked to Lady Clarissa alone first, but it seemed unlikely she'd get another chance. Besides, it was now perfectly clear to her not only that Clarissa needed all the help she could get, but that her guardian wasn't about to go looking for any, assuming he even admitted that help was needed.

She turned to Lady Clarissa. "If you wish, I would be quite willing to help smooth your return to the ballroom."

Clarissa's eyes grew round and her whole face lit up with enthusiasm. Ah, the resilience of youth, Thea thought, quite forgetting that she herself was hardly a crone, for all that Society thought her past marriageable age. "Oh, would you?"

"Of course. I would be happy to."

"I'm certain you would," Ransley drawled. "However, that will not be necessary."

It was no less than she'd expected, but Thea felt a pang in her chest when she saw how Clarissa deflated. "Your Grace, surely you can see that your niece needs—"

"As her guardian, Miss Ravenshaw, I am perfectly aware of what she needs. Thank you for your assistance," Ransley went on in clear dismissal. "Your help has been... indispensible."

It was said in such a mocking tone that Thea bristled despite herself. She forced down her irritation and focused on assuring Lady Clarissa that she would do perfectly fine for herself and to keep her head up when she returned to the ballroom, getting very little more than that out before the duke showed her — with perfect and very firm politeness — to the door.

It was only after she was back in the hallway, fulminating against the stubbornness of cold-hearted noblemen, that it occurred to her to wonder which of the men in that crowd had caused Lady Clarissa to spill her drink on Lady Charyls. It could most certainly have been a simple accident, and the man in question too cowardly to admit to it, even though an innocent girl suffered for his actions. But when Thea thought of Trenwick standing there after Clarissa and the duke left, and having the audacity to *wink* at her....

"Oh, blast the man," Thea muttered, startling a passing footman, who gave her a very odd look before disappearing down the hallway. She'd thought better of Trenwick than that. Served her right for having any faith in the honor of a rake. "Well!" She smoothed her dress and tucked an escaped curl of hair behind her ear. "If he's taking a direct hand, then I shall certainly have to, whether the duke likes it or not."

Chapter Six

DAMN the heartless woman, hanging on Clary's tear-soaked handkerchief in an attempt to attach herself to his coat-tails!

Ransley opened his newspaper and shook it flat, barely noticing the footman who jumped to remove his empty breakfast plate before the paper landed in it. However he tried, he could not keep his mind on the page. Miss Ravenshaw was a beauty, true enough, but never had so appealing an exterior concealed so calculating a heart. A fortune hunter or a title hunter or both. Ransley was familiar enough with the type, but he'd never met one quite so brazen. All that censure about Clary's tears and his cold-heartedness toward them, when the woman was using those self-same tears and her oh-so-volubly demonstrated compassion for the girl to set her cap at him. Althea Ravenshaw was as heartless as they came.

Ransley hadn't known quite what to make of her when she first pushed herself on him in the garden. It had been far too coming of her, certainly, but he'd been willing to accept that she might merely have been concerned for Clary. Overly so, to have been so utterly unconcerned about her own reputation.

But it was made quite clear last night that neither a lack of concern for her reputation nor a surfeit of concern for Clary's had brought her into the garden. She'd been hoping to be caught out there with him, alone but for a chit barely out of the schoolroom who could not be accounted a proper chaperone, thinking he'd have no choice but to offer for her to avoid damaging his honor and her reputation. How unfortunate for her that it was Lord Wilford who stumbled upon them and not some high-stickler of the *ton*. Wilford was hardly likely to bring down the censure of Society on her, especially as he was so clearly sweet on her himself.

That having failed, Miss Ravenshaw had obviously decided a less direct approach was necessary, though it was still possible that she hoped to be caught out with him. The library was no more a suitable place for her to speak alone with him than the garden had been, and Clary no more an appropriate chaperone than she had been the previous week.

But he could see now that Miss Ravenshaw had a more devious plan. She would use Clary's recent difficulties and her need for a female confidante to get close to the girl, and through her, to him. She would show him how sweet and loving and motherly she could be, how helpful to his niece. And if she could not, through such means, bring him up to scratch, she doubtless believed she had his sense of honor to fall back on. At some future date, she would surely either intimate that he had made certain implicit promises to her or arrange for them to be found in some compromising position. Well, if she expected him to propose, she would be much disappointed. He might have, had anyone other than Lord Wilford stumbled upon them in the garden, but his eyes were opened now.

The woman was absolutely without shame, and if she hoped to bring him about with her attentions to Clary, she was sadly mistaken. Just thinking of how heartlessly she intended to use poor Clary made him seethe.

Though he did have to admit, it had been hugely amusing to watch the woman struggle to keep her temper when he refused to fall for her manifest charms. Her feigned compassion for Clary was very well done, but she had not managed to preserve the proper tone with him, becoming quite sharp indeed when he failed to react as expected. Were it not that Miss Ravenshaw's designs would ultimately harm Clary, Ransley would be tempted to let her continue, if only for the entertainment of thwarting her.

He turned the page, though he didn't remember a word from the previous one, and gave the newspaper a snap. But however he tried, he could not seem to stop chewing over that blasted woman's behavior as if it were a tough piece of gristle. His jaw even worked, from time to time, and he twice had to stop himself from grinding his teeth. And the worst of it was, he'd very nearly *liked* Miss Ravenshaw when she was only a misguided woman in a garden. He wanted to like her yet, proof of her perfidy notwithstanding.

"Blast!" Ransley said aloud, and threw down the unread, though well-thumbed, paper.

"Your Grace?"

"I'm sorry, Hailston," Ransley said, startled less by his butler's sudden appearance than by the man's uncharacteristically harried look. "I didn't see you there."

"No, Your Grace. I mean, of course, Your Grace. I mean—" Hailston broke off, shook himself visibly, and blurted, "It's Lady Clarissa, sir. She's gone riding."

Ransley closed his eyes and squeezed the bridge of his nose hard. "Please tell me she was wearing a riding habit." He'd confiscated the breeches she was in the habit of riding in at Tynesfield and forbidden her to bring any such thing to London. Or go about in such a matter ever again at Tynesfield, for that matter.

Given Clary's recent talent for plunging herself directly into the soup, however, he was very much afraid that such steps were insufficient.

"Yes, sir, but—"

"And she didn't go out alone."

"No, sir, but—"

"But? Did she take a groom with her or didn't she?" Not that a groom alone would suffice to protect the reputation of a girl in her first Season, but it was a damn sight better than nothing. He looked at the angle of the sun coming through the windows and winced. It was early yet, but some of the less layabed of the *ton* might be up and about, and might see Clary gallivanting about on a horse with only a groom for escort. He threw his napkin down on the table and rose. Munslow would still be in his bedchamber, tidying up. The valet would frown at having to get his lordship into proper rig for riding so quickly, but it had to be done; he'd do no one's reputation any favors going out half-dressed. He headed out of the breakfast room and toward the stairs at a brisk clip.

"Yes, Lady Clarissa did take a groom with her, Your Grace," Hailston said, in a tight tone more formal than he typically used outside the presence of company. "The undercook's youngest son."

Ransley stopped with his foot on the lowest stair and turned slowly toward his butler as the words sank in. "Youngest son? How old—"

"Ten, sir."

"Hell and damnation! Get my horse saddled." Ransley took the stairs two at a time.

* * *

Thea took a deep breath of the chill morning air and let it out gratefully. It was too early yet for much of anyone to be out and about, which was how she liked it. It was no easy thing to rise early after dancing half the night, but well worth the effort. Especially on this particular morning. She'd spent far too much of the previous night watching fruitlessly after Lord Ransley, Lady Clarissa and Lord Trenwick, then fussing over the situation when she ought to have been sleeping. She needed a good ride to clear her mind.

She turned to Ned, who rode half a length behind. "Ready?"

He grinned. "Yes, miss."

She touched her heel to her horse's side, and the mare obligingly picked up the pace. She was a taking thing with a smooth gait, much better than Thea had any right to expect from a hired horse. Her pockets were not so flush that she could afford to keep a horse herself, but she'd lucked into an excellent hiring stable that amply suited her needs when she was in Town. She was also lucky in the Neds — footmen typically had little need and less use for riding ability, but the Neds had grown up in the country and both brothers were comfortable in the saddle. Thank heavens, as she had neither the money nor the desire to hire a groom along with the horse.

In no time, they turned into Hyde Park, quiet at that hour but for the grooms of wealthy households exercising horses and the occasional early-rising member of the *ton*. Thea rode through the greenery, taking in the quiet with a sense of relief. She enjoyed the Town's entertainments, and would not choose to give them up in favor of rusticating year-round, but there was no denying that one needed a break, every now and then, from the endless social whirl.

Especially this year. One would have thought, after nearly four years of dealing with Society, she would have enough sense not to get herself into such a bumblebroth. She'd been so very cautious of her reputation when she first came to Town; she couldn't afford not to be. And perhaps her growing acceptance by the *ton* had made her complacent, for she couldn't think how she'd managed to run afoul of not one but *two* powerful lords.

No, actually, she could think how she'd done it quite easily. And she could wish that Lady Clarissa had seen fit to spill her orgeat on someone else. It all went back to that, really. That and Thea's general unwillingness to let a girl's clumsiness ruin her. Though it must be said that if she hadn't followed Lady Clarissa out into the garden, she'd be much calmer in her mind at present.

"Careful, miss," Ned said suddenly, dragging Thea out of her brown study just in time to avoid being run down by a large gray horse carrying an empty sidesaddle. Thea's fingers tightened instinctively on the reins, curtailing her mare's nerves before she could shy too violently. "Miss?"

"I'm fine, Ned," she assured him, patting her horse's neck. "See if you can catch that horse. Someone will be wanting him, no doubt."

He gave her a doubtful look, but went anyway, while Thea turned her horse's head in the direction the runaway appeared to have come from. Somewhere down amongst the trees there, she thought, and was proven correct a moment later when she spied figures through the greenery. She gave the mare a nudge and started in that direction.

Before Thea had closed the gap by more than a few hundred yards, someone in the trees gave a high-pitched whistle. A moment later, the gray came dashing past her again, this time with a snort that unsettled her own mare so that Thea found it necessary to tighten up on the reins to steady the horse and herself. Ned arrived a moment later, and the proximity of her stable-mate calmed Thea's mare down instantly, thank heavens. Thea liked riding, but she had not been born into the saddle like some.

Speaking of… Once her mare was calmer, she nudged her into motion once more, and she and Ned made their way into the trees. It was with a strangely fatalistic lack of surprise that Thea found Lady Clarissa there, bogged down by her heavy riding habit and trying to remount the gray with the help of a too-short stump and a too-young boy.

Thea reined up and sat watching for a moment, the other two too distracted by their struggle to notice they had an audience. Lady Clarissa was closer to making it back into the saddle than many women would be in her situation, and grimly determined to succeed, but the stump didn't give her enough height, and there wasn't anything else around tall enough to serve. The boy was too small to give her the boost into the saddle that she needed most, or even hold the horse's head and the stirrup at the same time. Thea glanced around, but saw no sign of the Duke of Ransley. However cold he was to her difficulties, were he about, he surely would not have left Lady Clarissa to her own devices. And he could not possibly have had so little sense as to let the young woman out with only a small groom in the first place. Though perhaps she gave him too much credit.

"Good morning, Lady Clarissa," Thea said.

Clarissa's head jerked up. She overbalanced and fell off the stump in a froth of skirts. Thea winced. She held out her hand for Ned's reigns, and the footman gave them to her before slipping quickly off his horse to offer his hand to the young woman.

"Good morning, Miss Ravenshaw," Lady Clarissa said, once she'd regained her feet with Ned's help. She gathered up her skirts, showing rather more ankle than she ought, and walked over to stand smiling up at Thea. "It's so lovely to see you here!"

"I wish I could say the same," Thea said, and nearly wished she hadn't been so severe when Clarissa's pleased glow vanished abruptly. "Whatever are you doing out here alone, child?" she added in a much softer tone. Clarissa bristled, and Thea regretted sounding quite so motherly. She couldn't help it, however. No matter that she was only a dozen or so years older than Clarissa, the girl was just so *young*.

"I'm not alone," Clarissa objected. "I have Jeremy with me."

The boy holding the gray horse ducked his head at Thea in what might have been a bow, but looked more like he was shying away from a blow. Ned walked over to take the boy in hand, speaking quietly to him and leading him through a careful check of the gray gelding, running their hands over its legs and flanks to check for any injury.

"Oh, they needn't do that," Clarissa said. "I've checked Gunpowder over already. He's quite well. He was just spooked by that stray dog."

"Gunpowder?" Thea said faintly. It was quite a name and quite a horse for a chit barely out of the schoolroom, but Lady Clarissa seemed quite at home, despite having lost her seat. Given the leaves in her hair, she must have been thrown altogether, but she seemed not only uninjured but unconcerned. Indeed, she seemed more confident and at home than she had at any time Thea had seen her.

"Oh yes," Clarissa said, turning her eyes, gleaming with excitement, back to Thea. "I raised him from a colt, and Uncle Ransley let me help with all his training. I even slept in the stable with him when he had the colic."

"Did he now?" And the blasted man had the nerve to be surprised when his ward failed to observe even the simplest rules of Society? "And what does he think of your riding neck or nothing through Hyde Park?" Admittedly, she hadn't seen Lady Clarissa on the horse yet, but Thea had no illusions about how this brash young woman was liable to ride a horse called Gunpowder. Especially when she'd managed to escape the oversight of her guardian and even that of a proper groom.

Lady Clarissa flushed and glanced away. When she looked back, some of the excitement had dimmed, but her lips were compressed in a determined line. "He doesn't know. He refuses to let me ride Gunpowder as he ought to be ridden. Gunpowder wasn't made to walk around like a broken-down nag."

"So, rather than chafe at the restrictions of riding Gunpowder in Rotten Row at the fashionable hour, you decided to bring him out in the morning and give him his head?"

Lady Clarissa's chin came up. "Yes."

"Without a proper groom."

"Jeremy—"

"Is doubtless an excellent groom, but too young to preserve your reputation, my dear." Not that any groom could have. Given the chancy state of Lady Clarissa's reputation, she ought not be allowed out of the house without her guardian or a female companion of mature years. Riding with just a groom was well enough for a woman in Thea's position, but did little for a chit in her first Season. The boy was nearly worse than nothing.

"But that's ridiculous! I rode by myself at Tynesfield all the time."

"What you did in the country, where no one of moment would see you, is one thing. What you can do here—"

"But there was no one around!"

"Perhaps not." And pray heaven Clarissa was right about that. If they were seen now, it might turn a few heads, but Thea's presence would help to preserve the girl's reputation. However, if she'd been spotted on her own earlier... Seeing that Clarissa was unconvinced, Thea gently asked, "How many people do you think would have been in the park by the time you managed to remount? Assuming you could." With only the boy to help her, Thea doubted Clarissa could have made it back into the saddle. Which would have left her walking home with the horse at her heels and her riding habit dragging. She'd have found herself back at Tynesfield, wherever that was, within a day and stuck there until the rumors subsided. And it would have been significantly more than a nine days' wonder.

Lady Clarissa bristled at that. "It's this ridiculous habit and that blasted sidesaddle! If I had my breaches—"

Thea smiled despite herself. "I think it best that you refrain from mentioning your breaches in public. And from swearing." The minx had clearly raised herself with little help from the duke, and heaven help Thea for finding her more amusing than shocking. "Come," she said, when Lady Clarissa chewed on her lower lip in lieu of a response. "We must get you home."

"Oh, but I've only just started my ride and—"

"The duke will be worried." He ought to be, at any rate, assuming the blasted man had even noticed his ward's absence.

Clarissa turned a rather alarming shade of red. "Oh," she said in a very small voice, and now the blood drained away from her face, leaving her disconcertingly white. "Oh please, he's going to be so angry. Please can you come with me and help me explain—"

"If you expect me to explain what possessed you to ride in the Park without a proper chaperone, I shall be hard-pressed to come up with anything reasonable," Thea said tartly. Clarissa turned blue eyes swimming with tears up to her, and she found herself relenting. "My dear, I can hardly call on a duke with only a groom to lend me respectability. I would ruin myself—" She managed to catch the words *as surely as you seem determined to* before they escaped and finished somewhat weakly, "and my companion is still home abed."

"Could I…" Lady Clarissa said hopefully. "May I come take a dish of tea with you, please? I'll make my own explanations to Uncle Ransley — he's not such a dragon as all that, and I shouldn't have asked you to help. I'll be fine, but… perhaps in a half-hour or so?"

Thea sighed. Well, she'd wanted to speak with the girl alone. Perhaps Lady Clarissa would know of a way that Thea could offer her assistance that the duke might accept. Trying to think of a method of overcoming his resistance had been a large part of what kept her up most of the night. It was an absolute necessity that she lend her assistance, now that she knew Trenwick wasn't above helping Lady Clarissa blot her copybook. But she could not attempt to discuss the subject with Ransley at a ball again — anyone might overhear, and they were lucky no one had on the previous occasion — and a respectable lady did not invite herself into the home of a man. Nor did she think Ransley would respond to an invitation to call upon her — if he were that accommodating, she wouldn't be in this mess to begin with. And even with Lady Clarissa in tow, she could hardly show herself into a duke's residence without so much as a by your leave. Home it was. "Very well. Let Ned help you back on your horse and we shall go home together. Jeremy? Go on back and inform the Duke of Ransley that Lady Clarissa will be taking tea with me." She gave the boy her address, and he took off nearly before the last word was out of her mouth, hauling himself up on a shaggy pony that had been placidly cropping grass nearby and trotting briskly off. At that rate, he'd be home in no time, pouring the tale into the ear of his master. Who was doubtless still abed, like most of the *ton*, and completely unaware of the trouble his ward had been getting into. They'd have plenty of time for a pleasant coze before he showed up.

With Ned there to toss her into the saddle, Lady Clarissa was mounted in a minute, and settled onto the horse's back like she was made to be there. Thea waited until Ned was remounted before leaving the shelter of the trees with him in tow. Lady Clarissa rode quietly at her side, as graceful on Gunpowder as she was awkward in Society, and managed to conceal any signs of chafing at Thea's moderate pace, a fact Thea had reason to be grateful for when they emerged from the copse of trees.

Traffic had picked up considerably, and there were now several dozen gentlemen of the *ton* out taking the air and exercising their mounts. None, thankfully, appeared to pay overmuch attention to the two women and their groom. Gunpowder sidestepped suddenly, thankfully not into Thea's mount. She glanced over and saw Lady Clarissa loosening her grip on the reins, which she'd clearly taken up a bit too tight at the sight of the others. The girl's eyes were downcast, her expression subdued.

Good, thought Thea, she's got enough sense to recognize what kind of position she'd put herself in. After the fact, at least. Now if only the girl could be brought to think *before* she acted.

Speaking of…. What the deuce was Thea going to say to the Duke of Ransley once she got him alone?

If she'd hoped to think about it on the way home, that hope was dashed a moment later when she was hailed by a familiar and most unwelcome voice.

"Oh, bother," Thea said under her breath, and turned to face Lord Trenwick. She'd like to have said something a great deal stronger, but she could hardly swear in front of Lady Clarissa after having scolded the chit for doing so.

"My dear Miss Ravenshaw," he said, reining his sorrel gelding in to prance alongside them. "How lovely to see you!" Trenwick took off his high-crowned Beaver and stood in his stirrups to sweep them a bow that was surprisingly graceful, for all it was done from the back of a horse. "You ladies are looking blooming this morning, if I may say so."

"It would be better if you did not," Thea told him tartly, appalled to hear Lady Clarissa giggle in response to the compliment. She prayed it was merely nerves. It would be wholly unsuitable for Clarissa to have even a nodding acquaintance with the rake, and was singularly inappropriate for him to have addressed her at all, even as indirectly as he had. Lady Clarissa's guardian might not be awake on all suits, but he was surely at least sensible enough to ensure that a man like Trenwick had not been introduced to his niece.

Not one whit abashed, Trenwick put his hat back on his head and smiled lazily at Thea as they jogged along. "What are we to talk about, then, if I'm not to compliment you?"

"I was not aware that it was necessary for us to talk at all," Thea returned. Were Lady Clarissa not present, she could have bearded him about taking a direct hand in winning his bet and his infamous treatment of the chit to that end. She could hardly do so at any ball or entertainment where they might be overheard. And she could certainly not do it in front of the girl, which left her precisely nowhere.

"You wish to ride in silence?" Trenwick said, willfully misunderstanding.

"We wish to ride alone," Thea said repressively. She heard a faint gasp from Lady Clarissa and turned to see the girl watching with wide eyes. Blast. She knew how impressionable young ladies could be, and how easily their heads could be turned by compliments and the impression that a fellow was bearing up bravely under a cruel injustice. The last thing she needed to do was turn Trenwick into a romantic figure in Lady Clarissa's eyes. Swallowing her sigh, she turned back to Trenwick. "You are too kind to offer, Lord Trenwick, but we are merely on our way home and wouldn't think of taking you out of your way."

"It would be no hardship at all to ride with two such lovely ladies," Trenwick said gallantly, his eyes twinkling. The blasted man was enjoying himself at her expense again. "However…" He tipped his hat. "As my services are not needed, I shall take myself off. I do believe my horse would appreciate the opportunity to run."

He put his heels to the sorrel's sides and was off like a shot. For a moment, Lady Clarissa's great gray horse quivered as if he might take off after Trenwick's, and Thea was not entirely certain the girl wouldn't just spur him on if he did. She nearly put her hand out to grab Lady Clarissa's reins. However, the chit showed a modicum of sense and stayed put, though her eyes remained on Trenwick until he and the sorrel gelding were out of sight. Then Clarissa sighed with such a wealth of hopeless yearning that alarm clamored in Thea's breast. The last thing any of them needed was for Lady Clarissa to develop a *tendre* for the blasted man.

"Oh, I'm *hopeless*," Clarissa said.

It was only with significant effort that Thea kept her relief hidden. It would not do to appear happy about Lady Clarissa's social inadequacies, however much an improvement they were over inappropriate connections. "Not at all," she said bracingly. "You're merely young."

"Alicia Stanhope is a year younger than I," Clarissa protested, "and she doesn't have these difficulties. *She* knows how to talk to men."

If Thea recalled who Miss Stanhope was aright, her predilection for flirting was nothing Clarissa ought to aspire to. Before she could say so, however, Lady Clarissa continued in a perfectly glum tone.

"I thought I was over it when I found it so easy to talk with Tony. I didn't care a button what I said when I spoke with him. But being able to speak so freely with him hasn't helped at all! Half the time when some gentleman compliments me, I just sit there, mute as a fish. And the other half, I say something totally unsuitable."

"Who is Tony?" Some relation, Thea assumed.

"Oh! Lady Ashburne's brother, of course," Clarissa said, as if it were obvious.

Not a relation, then. "It were best," Thea said carefully, "if you would not call gentlemen by their Christian names. Especially when they are not your kin."

Far from being downcast by the correction, Lady Clarissa seemed to brighten. "I told you. I'm hopeless." She turned to appeal to Thea. "Oh, Miss Ravenshaw, I do so need your help. Please say you'll help me."

"That is certainly my intention," Thea told the girl, who looked overjoyed. She only hoped she could figure out a way to make the duke as pleased with this state of affairs.

Chapter Seven

THE stairs creaked alarmingly as Ransley descended them three at a time. It had seemed to take forever to change into buckskin breeches and boots; surely Munslow wasn't always this slow. He found Hailston in the entryway, unaccountably calmer than he had been earlier and speaking with a round-faced boy who looked vaguely familiar.

"Gloves, Hailston," Ransley prompted. "Where are my gloves? I presume my horse is ready?" Hailston looked up, his expression somewhat dazed, and Ransley forced himself not to snap at his butler. "Is my horse ready? God alone knows what kind of trouble Lady Clarissa's gotten herself into."

"Actually, sir," Hailston said, then paused to clear his throat. He shook himself slightly and suddenly became quite businesslike, retrieving Ransley's gloves and hat for him. "Actually, she seems to have gotten herself rescued."

"Rescued?" Ransley paused in drawing on his gloves to peer back up the stairs. Surely he'd have heard her going up to her room?

"Yes, sir. Jeremy here — the undercook's youngest, sir, if you remember — has just informed me that a Miss Ravenshaw sent him to say that Lady Clarissa is taking tea with her at—"

"Oh, she is, is she?" Ransley stuffed his hat on his head and headed for the door, which Hailston barely reached ahead of him. "Come, Jeremy," Ransley ordered as he started down the outside steps. A groom waited there, holding Ransley's bay horse and a shaggy pony that looked a bit the worse for wear. Becoming aware of how the boy dragged at his heels, Ransley turned to find Jeremy looking quite as disconsolate as the pony. "Buck up, boy. You're not in trouble." Though god knows, he ought to be for going out alone with his mistress. But Ransley knew just how stubborn Clary could be when she had the bit between her teeth, and it would be wrong to rip up at a child for failing to rein her in when there were times Ransley himself despaired of it. "You're just going to take me to your mistress and hold the horses when we get there."

Jeremy brightened. "Yessir!" He scrambled up on his pony while Ransley mounted, then took off ahead of him, glancing back twice to be sure his little mount wasn't leaving his master's in the dust before settling in to lead him to Miss Ravenshaw's townhouse.

Miss Ravenshaw… Ransley's lips tightened and he closed his teeth on a few choice curses. Of all the clever, beautiful, designing females for Clary to run afoul of, Miss Ravenshaw was the worst. Taking advantage of Clary's predicament to drag her off to her townhouse, then sending for him as if he were an errand boy at her back and call. All, no doubt, with the intention of trapping him in a compromising position in which she thought he'd have no choice but to offer for her. Well, he would give her reason to think again.

The pony's shorter legs, and the fact that the poor beast looked like it'd been ridden from pillar to post already that morning, kept Ransley from pushing the pace. Which was just as well. He was no longer a young buck who'd be excused for riding pell-mell through the streets of London, and he wouldn't help Clary's reputation by becoming the focus of gossip himself. Still, the pace chafed and gave him far too much time to think, and he was in a particularly foul mood by the time they reined up in front of an unprepossessing house on an unfashionable side street.

He jumped down and handed his reins to Jeremy. He didn't have to ask if this was the right place, as Clary's Gunpowder was standing in front of the house, along with a placid mare and a gelding that had the unmistakable look of hired horses. They were held by a strapping young groom who nodded respectfully to Ransley. It was a fortunate thing that the street was quiet, or the number of horses now standing in front of Miss Ravenshaw's townhouse would be getting quite in the way.

Ransley took the stairs to the front door at a brisk pace, stripping off his gloves as he went. He had a moment's confusion when, in response to his knock, the door was opened by the groom who'd just nodded to him. He looked back, but the fellow was still down in the street. Upon second glance, he realized that the one who'd opened the door was dressed as a footman, but otherwise there was as little difference between the groom and the footman as between a brace of pistols. The effect was disconcerting, which he blamed for the fact that he forgot to demand the return of his niece and merely said, "Miss Ravenshaw?"

"Of course, Your Grace," the footman replied, showing him in and taking his hat and gloves, though Ransley was by no means inclined to linger. It was hardly a surprise that the footman knew who he was, given they had his ward in the house. However, it acted as a salutary reminder of Miss Ravenshaw's ulterior motives. The footman was prepared for him and would naturally show him into the drawing room, where Miss Ravenshaw doubtless waited alone to receive him.

Ransley's scowl was quite as dark as it ever got by the time he was shown into the townhouse's small drawing room.

"Your Grace." Miss Ravenshaw rose at his entrance and dropped him a curtsy. She was, surprisingly, still attired in a riding habit — he'd have expected her to put on a fetching morning gown before sending the boy for him. Though perhaps she knew how charmingly the deep burgundy of her riding habit went with her dark hair and lent her cheeks a rosy hue. Or perhaps, he reminded himself savagely, that was merely justified embarrassment at her heartless machinations. "How pleasant to see you."

"And what a surprise too?" Ransley said coldly. "Where is my niece?"

"Good morning, Uncle." Clary rose from the chair next to Miss Ravenshaw's and curtsied to him as well, something she hadn't done since she was eight. He blinked at her, wondering how he could have overlooked her in the small room.

"We were just about to take tea," Miss Ravenshaw said. "Will you join us? Another cup for His Grace," she said to the still-hovering footman, as if it was inevitable that Ransley would accept the invitation.

Ransley waited impatiently for the footman to leave. "I will not be staying for tea and neither will Lady Clarissa."

The blasted woman merely seated herself placidly and began to pour the tea standing ready on the small tea table before her. "You'll have to excuse us for being somewhat unprepared, Your Grace," she said mildly. "You arrived more precipitously than expected."

"And what else should I do when notified that you have my ward? However…" He bowed mockingly. "My sincerest apologies for not giving you more time to arrange matters to your satisfaction."

"It is no trouble, sir," Miss Ravenshaw said, as if his apology were genuine. "Merely that we have not had the opportunity for the coze we were looking forward to." She paused briefly when the footman returned with another cup, waiting until after he'd left to say, "Though it's unfortunate that my companion, Mrs. Wellins, has not been able to join us yet."

"Most unfortunate," he agreed. And most certainly planned. "Especially as we shall not be able to stay until she makes an appearance."

"That would be too bad. We have much to talk about."

"I must beg to disagree." He turned to his ward, who was still standing irresolutely between Miss Ravenshaw and himself. "Lady Clarissa—"

"I should like to stay, Uncle Ransley," Clary said, her voice quiet and her eyes downcast. What the devil? Clary surely knew he was angry with her — he had cause to be; anything might have happened to her, out on her own with only a boy for protection — but in his experience, she was more likely to rip up at him (or weep all over him) than cower. "If you'd kindly give your permission?" Her eyes flicked up to his, then quickly away.

That stung. She'd never acted afraid of him before. What kind of nonsense had Miss Ravenshaw been putting in his ward's head? He stared at Clary a moment, nonplussed, and Miss Ravenshaw took advantage of his silence to draw Clary's attention to herself, passing the girl a dish of tea.

Ransley gathered himself and said, "We will not be staying." He thought he did a fairly credible job of keeping his voice calm. The words emerged coldly, but were at least not seething with the rage he felt at that blasted woman. "Come, Lady Clarissa…" He held his hand out to her.

"I'm afraid I'm quite done in after the morning I've had, Uncle," Clary said, still not raising her eyes to his, "and shall need a few moments to collect myself." She pushed the dish of tea into his hand, gathered up the skirts of her riding habit, and seated herself in the chair next to Miss Ravenshaw.

Leaving him standing there, holding tea he did not want and wondering quite when he'd lost control of the situation. And quite possibly his temper, given that the next words out of his mouth were, "As the morning you've had started with a solitary jaunt in the park, it's not a wonder that you're done in; it's a wonder that you're not done altogether. Another such outing and I'll have no choice but to send you back to Tynesfield."

It was nothing less than the truth and needed to be said, but had he more control of himself, he would not have said it so bluntly. Clary gasped, and the cup Miss Ravenshaw had just handed her rattled on its saucer. Softer words hovered on Ransley's lips, but before he could utter any of them, Clary flared, "I did *not* go out alone! I had a groom with me."

Well, at least that put paid to the show of meek timidity. Thank heavens. He couldn't bear Clary as a milksop, however much her forthrightness might hamper her in Society. "He's all of ten, and even were he half a hundred, a mere groom would not have been sufficient to protect you. Hells bells, girl; if you gave half as much thought for your reputation as you do for—"

"Miss Ravenshaw had only a groom herself," Clary said pugnaciously.

Ransley stopped himself from responding with an effort and somehow refrained from pinching the bridge of his nose again. His head was already beginning to ache, no point in making it worse. How in damnation had he come to this? He'd had no intention of airing the linen in front of Miss Ravenshaw, who must be truly enjoying the show.

"Now Lady Clarissa," that woman said into the silence, "who accompanies me on my rides is neither here nor there when it comes to what you must do. I'm a dozen years your senior, and what's acceptable for me is not for a girl in her first season."

For a moment, Ransley was grateful for her support. Then he brought to mind his encounters with Miss Ravenshaw so far, and said, "That you should hold yourself up, madam, as the pattern-card of propriety Lady Clarissa should be emulating is farcical, especially given your tendency to push yourself on me without a chaperone."

Miss Ravenshaw's eyes fairly blazed at him. It took her a moment to recollect herself, during which he frankly rather enjoyed how anger animated her face. "I beg your pardon, Your Grace," she said finally, "but perhaps it has escaped your attention that it is *you* who are in *my* drawing room?"

Now that was the outside of enough! How dare she imply some impropriety on his part when his being in her drawing room was precisely the result she was aiming for when she dragged Clary back to her house? Ransley strode to the empty hearth and put the unwanted cup of tea on the mantelshelf before he could give in the desire to dash it into the hearth. He took a moment to compose himself, then turned back to the ladies.

"Clarissa, go wait in the hall."

"Really, Your Grace—"

"Uncle Ransley, I'm really far too tired—"

Ignoring Miss Ravenshaw, Ransley stared at his ward until she quailed. "The hall."

"Yes, sir." Her eyes downcast again — appropriately so this time — she rose, curtsied, and went out, leaving him alone with Miss Ravenshaw. While he had no doubt that was the state of affairs she'd been angling for all along, he was determined that she would find the experience far from comfortable.

"Now, Miss Ravenshaw," he said, turning to her. When their eyes met, he had the satisfaction of seeing her draw back in her chair. "It's time for some plain dealing. Cease your importunities and machinations. Cease attempting to work your way into Lady Clarissa's affections and my good graces. You will not induce me to offer for you, no matter what position you put me in nor what stratagems you employ."

The blasted woman had the nerve to look startled. "Offer for me?"

"Yes, blast you, offer for you. I won't."

"I wouldn't accept you if you did."

Ransley laughed. "You expect me to believe that?"

She stood and met him squarely, her eyes blazing even brighter than before. She really was quite ridiculously striking when she was livid. "I don't care a fig what you believe."

Before he could respond, the door opened and a small woman in a drab green morning gown bustled in, her cap set slightly askew on her faded brown hair. "I'm so sorry, my dear," she was saying as she entered. "I came as soon as I could; is the duke—" She caught sight of Ransley and gave a small gasp.

"No apologies necessary, Mrs. Wellins," Miss Ravenshaw said with every appearance of calm. Ransley was unwillingly impressed; he'd never have known how angry she was if she hadn't just a moment before been glaring daggers at him. "You've arrived in good time. My apologies for getting you up before your morning chocolate."

"Think nothing of it, my dear," Mrs. Wellins said quickly, glancing at Ransley and coloring slightly. She sat in the chair Clary had been in, tucking her skirts neatly about her, and poured tea into Miss Ravenshaw's unused cup.

Bemused, Ransley looked from the little woman to Miss Ravenshaw and saw her take a visible breath. "Now, Your Grace," she said, gracefully re-seating herself and folding her hands in her lap, "if we may speak about Lady Clarissa?"

"We may not." Why could the blasted woman not leave it alone? Recognizing that he'd have better luck preaching abstinence to an Irishman, and having no desire to continue beating his head against a wall, Ransley started for the door.

"Surely it's become clear to you that your ward is in need of the guidance of someone experienced with the *beau monde*."

Ransley stopped with his hand on the door and turned back. "Surely you're not suggesting that *I* don't know how to make my way in Society."

"I would not be so bold, Your Grace."

"Wouldn't you?" Ransley muttered. He came back and planted himself on the rug, his hands clasped behind him. "What, then, if I am not lacking in the social graces?"

For a moment, he thought she would disagree with him on that, and certainly he had made no effort to do the pretty with her. The last thing he wanted was to encourage her aspirations. But all she said was, "Lady Clarissa is not you."

He smiled, genuinely amused. "Of that, Miss Ravenshaw, I am singularly aware."

"Then why not admit that you could use some help? That between us, Mrs. Wellins and I can lend Lady Clarissa some much-needed support and assist her in safely navigating Society's entertainments?"

"And why would you do such a thing?" he asked slowly. He was willing to admit that he'd misjudged her — if it were her intention to get him into a position where she thought he'd have no choice but to propose marriage, she could hardly have resisted taking advantage of being alone with him. Yet if that was not her goal, what was? In his experience, few people acted altruistically, especially where money and position were concerned. What did she gain by helping Clary?

"Because no girl deserves to have her name made into a byword, simply by virtue of a few innocent mistakes. Or ruined by events a decade ago in which she had no part."

The oblique reference to Clary's half-sister, Amelia, touched his heart with ice. He'd failed Amelia, and she died because of it. Because of his stubborn unwillingness to see the dangers that threatened her. Was he doing the same now? And did Miss Ravenshaw represent a threat or protection against one?

"Why now?" he asked her. "Why Lady Clarissa? There are always girls making a hash of their come out."

She shrugged. "She needs help and… I suppose I need to provide it."

Because of something about the girl that appealed to Miss Ravenshaw, Ransley wondered, or because Lady Clarissa was the niece of a duke? He began revising his opinion of her. She might well be playing a deeper and cleverer game than he'd given her credit for. Was she looking for the social advancement provided by being seen regularly in the company of a duke? Or was there some man she had her cap set at whose jealousy she thought to pique?

"Your Grace." She leaned forward, as if she might impress her urgency upon him. "Lady Clarissa is fortunate in her guardian. But she needs more than a guardian. She needs a friend and confidant."

"And you propose yourself for that role?" he said, suspicion making his voice icy.

She sat back with a huff of frustration. "For pity's sake," she snapped. "How do you expect the girl to get by when her only support is a fire-breathing dragon, wreathing her in flames every time she turns around?"

Clasped behind him, his hands clenched. "Thank you, madam," he said stiffly. "But we will do quite well without you." He stalked to the door, pausing with it under his hand to say, "I'll thank you to cease interfering with my family."

The door was yanked suddenly out from under his hand, and Clary barged in, her face a virulent shade of red and her eyes swimming. "You can't! You can't tell her to go away. She's the only one who's trying to help! You don't understand and you don't care! I'm hopeless and I'll never be able to manage and it's all your fault!"

She stamped her foot and stormed back out, leaving him staring helplessly after her.

Miss Ravenshaw said quietly, "Are you quite certain you do not need my help?"

* * *

Thea waited until she'd heard the front door close very firmly behind the Duke of Ransley and his tempestuous ward before putting her head in her hands and massaging her temples.

"That went well," Mrs. Wellins said brightly.

"Please, Aunt; don't cut up at me as well." Thea sighed. "I'm not up to it."

For a moment, the room was silent but for the soft sounds of Mrs. Wellins wielding the teapot and a spoon. Then the rim of a saucer touched Thea's arm. "Have some tea, dear," Mrs. Wellins said.

"Thank you," Thea said. She made herself sit up properly and sipped gingerly at the tea before realizing that it had grown lukewarm during the confrontation. That came to her a moment before she realized she must be drinking out of either Lady Clarissa's or the Duke of Ransley's cup. The thought of her lips touching the same cup as the duke's sent an unsettling heat flickering through her. *Ridiculous!* she thought. *Stop being such a widgeon. He didn't even drink from his cup. Nor would it matter if he had.* And blast the man for upsetting her so. A more cold, stubborn, pig-headed man she'd never met. She sighed again. And yet, there had been moments when he'd looked nearly human, even hurt. She'd rather liked him then.

"Now," Mrs. Wellins said comfortably, "would you care to tell me what exactly is going on, Althea? Even dimwitted children learn not to put their head into a beehive after the first time."

Chapter Eight

"DO you see him?" Thea asked quietly, surreptitiously scanning the crowded ballroom while she fanned herself with a lovely creation of ivory and lace that was totally insufficient against the overwhelming stuffiness of the ballroom. The Greenhow's ball was rumored to be *the* event of the season — everyone who was anyone was there. Which as far as Thea could tell only meant that there were far too many people in far too small a space.

"No, dear," replied Mrs. Wellins, who scarcely seemed to be looking. Thea hoped she was just being circumspect and not— "Really, Thea, I don't think much of this plan of yours."

"Pray, don't start again, Aunt. We talked this over and decided—"

"You decided," her aunt said tartly.

"As I'm the one most affected...." Thea sighed. She realized she'd begun fanning herself briskly in her agitation and forced herself to slow down. "Please, let's not discuss this here."

Mrs. Wellins made a small sound that might have been either agreement or disapproval, but at least didn't restart the argument. Thea sighed again. She hated being at odds with anyone, especially her dear aunt. She knew Mrs. Wellins only had her best interests at heart, but wished she could make her see that this was really the only option. It was Thea who had made the wager with Trenwick, never mind it was under duress; it was therefore Thea who must needs pay the price.

If she could not get the Duke of Ransley to let her help his ward — which she was manifestly unable to do, the man being as stubborn as an ox — she would have to approach the problem from the other end. Trenwick must be convinced to stop making things worse for poor Lady Clarissa. The girl got into enough trouble on her own; she certainly needed no assistance from him. And if Thea could not convince him to release her from the wager, she would waltz with him and put an end to the bet that way. It would do her reputation no good, but surely would not be more than a nine days' wonder. She could withstand it. And it was much smaller price than Lady Clarissa would pay if this continued.

Now if only she could find Trenwick.

She'd come to her conclusion two days ago, after Ransley and his ward left. Her argument with him had convinced Thea that he would never accept her help, no matter how much Clarissa needed it, nor how much he cared for his niece — and she was convinced now that he did. Much good it did Clarissa, with Ransley as unmovable as a mountain. No, he would clearly never permit Thea to help Clarissa directly.

No matter how her heart sank inside her to consider the consequences of waltzing with Trenwick, it was what she must do. Now she simply wanted to get it over with. But she'd searched for him at every event she'd attended since, with no luck. The blasted man was playing least in sight when she most wanted to find him. And in the meantime, more rumors about Lady Clarissa's sister, speculations about the lady herself, and two more unfortunate incidents reached Thea's ears. While she doubted Trenwick could be blamed for Lady Clarissa laughing immoderately at some dance partner's witticism, that she'd had another mishap with her drink — this time a glass of ratafia that had ended up distributed liberally between her supper partner's waistcoat pockets — could probably be laid at his door. Thea really had thought better of him. These pranks were beneath even a schoolboy.

She caught sight of shimmering hair in the swing of the dance and smiled. Lady Clarissa appeared to be enjoying herself. Her partner was young Lord Peregrine St. George, who looked rather smitten with her, his eyes shining almost as brightly as his red hair. Lady Clarissa was nearly as graceful in his arms as she was on a horse, a blessing, as she would certainly not be able to rise above her many *faux pas* if she were ungainly in the dance as well as in the supper room.

If Lady Clarissa was here, then naturally the Duke of Ransley would be as well. Yes, leaning against the wall not thirty feet away… and staring at her. Thea looked quickly away and began fanning herself vigorously. It really was quite a bit too warm in the close room. Even though she wasn't looking at him, she was certain she could feel his pale eyes on her. She remembered how they'd blazed when she called him a dragon and shivered a little in the heat. How, she wondered, did such a pale gray burn so vividly?

She concentrated on watching Lady Clarissa wend her way through the figures of the dance. She didn't dare look about the room for Trenwick, as she had been doing. She had the completely unwarranted feeling she would only find herself looking at Ransley again, even if she kept her eyes away from where he was standing. It wasn't likely that he would move, yet she was afraid to take her eyes off Clarissa for fear that she'd meet his burning gaze wherever she looked.

The music came to a close and the dancers bowed and curtsied, the rigid pattern of the dance breaking up as men escorted their partners back to guardians and chaperones. Thea's gaze broke from Lady Clarissa just as she and her partner reached Ransley. She went back to scanning the crowd for Trenwick's brown hair and pleasantly handsome face.

After a few minutes, during which the musicians plinked quietly on the dais, retuning their instruments between dances, Thea became aware of a rush of attention toward the side of the room where Ransley and Lady Clarissa stood. Though she didn't know what was wrong, something clearly was. Thea rose instinctively to see if she could help, even if only by diverting attention, and only then noticed that Allen Wetherald had nearly reached her side. He was a pleasant gentleman and rather a favorite of hers, as he danced particularly well, but she could not, at that moment, be happy to see him.

She dropped him a quick curtsy and said, "If you will excuse me, Mr. Wetherald…" then walked away before he could do more than bow in response, mild surprise in his eyes. What else could she do? If she gave him the chance to ask her to dance, she would either have to accept or plead exhaustion and sit out the rest of the ball.

Thea moved toward the growing commotion and was ruefully unsurprised to find that it did indeed surround Lady Clarissa and her guardian. She increased her pace slightly, taking care not to walk too fast. It would not do to be seen rushing toward them; whether taken as prurient curiosity or a dash to the rescue, it would do neither Thea's nor Clarissa's reputation any good. As she neared them, she saw that the Duke of Ransley was drawn up to his full and considerable height, his face that impassive mask she knew quite well by now — the one that hid a towering rage. Lady Clarissa was shaking her head, looking on the point of tears. Facing them were a young man whose name and title Thea couldn't at the moment bring to mind, though she seemed to remember he was the youngest son of the Portemaine family, and a man she recognized with surprise as Lord Wilford.

Wilford was holding forth, rather too loudly, as was his wont. "…don't see why I should step aside for young Portemaine. I was promised this dance, after all."

"But I didn't—" Lady Clarissa broke off with a slight wince, and Thea guessed Ransley was squeezing her arm again. It didn't do any good, as Wilford responded as if she'd finished what was clearly meant to be a denial.

"You most certainly did. You promised me this dance, and now you're claiming you didn't because you've decided you'd rather dance with Portemaine instead."

The young man in question, who had begun to slide away, flushed, bowed to Ransley, and walked quickly away. Thea didn't blame him for making a prompt exit. Not only did Ransley look ready to breathe fire, but Wilford's behavior was bordering on the infamous. Self-respect would keep most men from publicly airing such a grievance; as bad as it painted the woman who tried to manipulate her beaus in such a manner, it was no boon to a man's reputation to be supplanted by another. Though he could be quite dense, Wilford was usually more aware of the proprieties than this. Thea recognized his mulish expression, however; she'd seen in on both occasions he'd bulled through her attempts to redirect him and insisted on proposing to her. She winced. He certainly wasn't going to stop on his own, and while Ransley was formidable, she doubted his ability to defuse the situation gracefully, assuming he could even get a word in edgewise. She began making her way around behind Wilford, who was holding forth at length and without his usual stammering.

It was with relief that Thea finally reached him. "My lord?"

Wilford broke off mid-word and swung towards her. He blinked twice quickly and said, "M-miss Ravenshaw?"

"I wondered where you'd got off to, Lord Wilford," Thea said with a smile that hopefully did not look as forced as it felt. "I believe I promised you this dance?" She heard a faint titter from somewhere nearby, but there was no way of knowing whether the amusement was at her having to remind Wilford of their dance or at the idea of him mistaking Lady Clarissa, with her shining hair and pale seafoam-green dress, for Thea's dark, emerald-clad self.

He blinked again. "I, I, yes, I suppose," he said vaguely, and took her gloved hand. As she'd hoped, he could not pass up an opportunity to dance with her. They'd danced a set earlier in the evening, and this was the first occasion she'd let him lead her out twice. Not only could her feet not take the punishment, but dancing two sets in the same evening would imply a depth of regard the tattlemongers could hardly resist. And the Lord knew, Wilford didn't need any encouragement. However, needs must…. She would just have to make certain it didn't happen again.

Her eyes met Ransley's briefly, and she received a rather startled nod from him. Well, he *should* thank her for her sacrifice — her toes still throbbed from her previous dance with Wilford — but she was pleasantly surprised that he actually acknowledged it. Thea refrained from smiling as Wilford led her over to make up the set for a country dance; it wouldn't do to appear pleased by any of this. A moment later, any inclination to smile left her when she spotted Trenwick leaning negligently against the wall nearby, smiling sardonically. Oh, blast the man, finally showing himself when she was utterly unable to go to him! And blast him for looking so demmed smug. It wasn't like he could take credit for—

Thea's thoughts slammed to an abrupt halt. Just so had Trenwick looked after Lady Clarissa spilled her drink on Lady Charyls, and Thea was as certain as she could be that he was the cause of that mishap. But how could he possibly have encompassed this? She'd thought that Wilford was merely being his confused and oblivious self; would he really assist Trenwick to win his bet against her? She looked at his vague, moon-shaped face and thought, *no, but he might be led to do so, not realizing he was being used.*

"Lord Wilford?" she asked when the movement of the dance brought them into speaking distance. "Is there any particular reason—" She broke off, belatedly remembering they were surrounded by listening ears. There was no possible way to ask that question that would not cause the very scandal she was sacrificing her feet for. Luckily, he made nothing of her interrupted question because, at that moment, his left foot came down hard on her right, and he doubtless thought that was what caused her to stop talking. It was certainly what caused her to bite her lip and suck in a sharp breath.

Wilford was so used to trampling his partners' feet that he merely muttered an apology and continued dancing, like a delivery boy who continuously calls "excuse me" while shoving his way through a crowd. Thea smiled gamely as he took her hand and led her around and back through the line of the country dance, and thanked the heavens that the figure of the dance separated them before he could tread on her foot again. As she came about, however, and saw that there was now an older couple standing where Ransley and his niece had been, her heart sank. Oh, pray heaven he hadn't dragged her away again! The girl could hardly redeem her reputation if every time something went wrong, her guardian spirited her away for the rest of the night.

Thea had to stop them before they left, if they hadn't already. But there was no way to extricate herself from the dance without causing tongues to start wagging again, especially not as she'd made such a point of claiming the dance in the first place. And even once the country dance was concluded, there would be the second dance of the set to get through. By then, the duke and his niece might be long gone, and Thea's feet, she thought as Lord Wilford's foot trod upon hers again, would be beyond saving. She and her feet were rescued, however, in the last figure of the dance, when Lord Wilford somehow managed to tread upon the hem of her dress, which gave way with a distinct sound of ripping fabric.

The music came to a halt and she curtsied to her partner, who was already stuttering, "I'm, I'm terribly sorry, M-miss—"

"Pray, think nothing of it, Lord Wilford," Thea murmured, her soft tones in contrast to his overloud apology. "I shall merely have to effect repairs. No, thank you, sir," she added when he appeared determined to escort her to the retiring room, "I see Mrs. Wellins over there." And she did, standing in a nearby doorway with an urgent look upon her face. "She'll be able to assist me." She lifted her skirts slightly, so the damaged portion would not drag, and hurried toward Mrs. Wellins.

"Oh, my dear," her aunt said as soon as Thea joined her in the doorway, "your dress...."

"Yes, yes, but sacrificed to a good cause." If only the cause of not being lamed by continuing to dance with Lord Wilford. "Where did they go?"

Mrs. Wellins didn't bother to pretend she hadn't followed Ransley and his niece. She had made it perfectly clear, after all, that she would much rather Thea tackled that part of the problem than stain her own reputation by being seen overmuch with Lord Trenwick. "The retiring room at the end of the hall."

"Good. Given the state of my gown, it won't look odd for us to repair to the retiring room ourselves." She slid her arm through her aunt's and urged her down the hallway.

"Oh!" exclaimed a pert little maid when Thea pushed open the door of the retiring room. "Oh, miss, you'll want the room at the other end of the hall. There's a gentleman—"

"I'm aware," Thea said, stepping through the doorway with Mrs. Wellins close behind her. "My dress is in need of repair. Have you a needle and thread?"

"Oh, yes miss," the maid said, much relieved to see that Thea was accompanied by an older lady. She scurried away to retrieve the tools always available in a retiring room to repair the ravages brought on by too many people trying to dance in too small a space. Thea stepped farther into the room. Lady Clarissa's voice could be heard coming from behind the brightly-painted screen that separated the room proper from the door. She sounded mulish and defiant. Thea followed the sound to its source and found Lady Clarissa sitting on a florid fainting couch, glaring up at her uncle, her face splotchy with what might have been tears, but given her expression was more likely to be anger. The Duke of Ransley stood over her, somehow managing to look thunderous and helpless at the same time.

"How could you possibly think I'm goose-brained enough to—"

"Come now," Thea said, making her voice brisk and business-like and raising it to be heard over Clarissa before the girl put her uncle into a temper, "take a damper, child. If you continue like this, it will take twice as long to make you presentable enough to return to the ballroom. What in heaven's name are you in such a taking about?"

Ransley stepped away from Clarissa when Thea approached, and said nothing as she seated herself on the fainting couch next to the girl. "Oh, Miss Ravenshaw," Lady Clarissa wailed, listing sideways into Thea but thankfully not beginning to cry, "I'll never be able to show my face again. Never!"

"Certainly not if you keep carrying on like that," Thea admonished.

The duke snorted. Thea ignored him. She thanked the little maid, who had returned with needle and thread, and sent her off after some cool cloths. There was time enough to fix her dress after steps had been taken to begin the repair of Lady Clarissa's appearance. First things first, however; there was a dragon to beard. Putting her arm around Clarissa, who was positively quivering, though Thea couldn't tell if it was nerves or rage, she turned her attention to Ransley and found his pale eyes already upon her. Heavens, even the retiring rooms in the Greenhow house were overwarm! Thea controlled the desire to employ her fan and girded herself for battle.

"Surely, Your Grace, you can now see that—"

"We need your help," Ransley said in his deep voice, leaving Thea feeling rather as if her horse had balked at a jump. Ready for battle and unprepared for his instant capitulation, she gaped at him. The corners of his mouth twitched in what looked for a moment like it would become a smile, but turned instead into a grimace. "*Clarissa* needs your help."

"I'm relieved to hear you say so," Thea managed after a moment. She was aware of Mrs. Wellins pulling over a small stood so she could sit comfortably while repairing Thea's skirt, but could not seem to pull her eyes away from the duke's.

"Yes, well." He speared a hand through his white-blond hair, further rumpling a style that was already somewhat unruly. He looked rueful, and for the first time, entirely, approachably human. "I can manage four country estates, a Town home, and I don't know how many hundred servants and tenant farmers, but it appears I cannot keep Lady Clarissa from landing herself in the briars with great regularity."

"But I didn't—" Lady Clarissa protested in far too elevated a tone.

"Of course you didn't," Thea said, before she could get into even more of a taking. She was startled to hear Ransley saying precisely the same thing at the same moment. When she raised an eyebrow at him, he raised one of his own.

"Clary's many things," he said, "not least a regular watering pot and a veritable ninnyhammer, but she's not fool enough to think she could get away with a trick like that."

Even as she drew breath to scold him for such callousness, part of Thea's brain was gibbering that she could on no account speak like that to a duke, even if he *had* admitted to needing her help. And even if she had, in fact, already spoken to him precisely like that on several occasions. Thankfully, before the words could escape, Lady Clarissa took in a shockingly deep breath and sat up straight to glare at her guardian. He glared back, and Thea let out a soundless sigh, both at having avoided the bumblebroth her tongue had been about to get her into and at finally being released from Ransley's burning gaze. For a moment, neither of them moved, then Clarissa slumped back down with a sigh that sounded like it had come from her toes, and Thea admitted to herself that Ransley did, at least, have *some* idea how to handle his niece.

"Be that as it may," Ransley went on, as if there'd been no interruption. "It has become clear, much as I might wish to deny it, that I cannot keep sufficient watch on Lady Clarissa myself to avoid these kinds of mishaps. Miss Ravenshaw, you were determined enough to offer the assistance of yourself and your companion earlier; do you still?"

"Of course," Thea said, "I shall be glad to."

He looked for a moment as if he were about to say something else, but then his lips firmed and he nodded sharply. Thea dragged her eyes away from him and turned to Lady Clarissa.

"Come, my dear, we must make you presentable again. You can't miss out on dancing at the event of the season, now can you?"

"But how can I go back after that?" Clarissa asked plaintively. At least she was no longer raging at her uncle, though it would take the cold compresses the maid would hopefully return with soon and a little time to remove the blotches of anger on her fair cheeks. "It'll be breakfast conversation all over the *ton*."

"Don't worry about that, my dear," Thea said, patting her hand. "It's far more likely that they'll be laughing about how poor Lord Wilford could have managed to forget who promised him the dance than thinking it was any error of yours."

The maid returned then with the cold compresses, and Ransley took himself off while Thea and Mrs. Wellins made Lady Clarissa presentable again. The retiring room felt much more comfortable once he'd gone — it was amazing how much room one person could take up — and Thea was able, for the first time in more than a week, to take a comfortable breath. Ransley had admitted he needed help and even agreed to accept her assistance.

Things were looking up.

Chapter Nine

JOSIAS Mallinson was extraordinarily irritated.

Every attempt to drive Ransley back to his country estate had failed. Mallinson had worked tirelessly, dripping poison in accommodating ears, making certain the biggest gossips in the *ton* knew the story of Amelia Holgate's murder, knew that she was half-sister to the Seabrooke chit, and thought the very worst of both girls. The tattlemongers ate it up. The story was all over Society, Lady Clarissa's name on every tongue, and still Ransley kept to Town. No matter how the rumors swirled; no matter how cow-handed Lady Clarissa acted, gaining a reputation for clumsiness unbecoming in a young woman of the *ton*; no matter what Mallinson tried, Ransley and his ward swept through Society like none of it touched them. Mallinson wasn't even certain Ransley was entirely aware of the extent of the rumors. Certainly none of it had conspired to prevent the blasted man and his blasted niece from being invited everywhere. Ransley's title and money bought a lot of forbearance and the girl's stunning beauty a great deal of forgiveness.

It gave Mallinson occasion to wonder if he was going about this wrong. If the point of Ransley's residence in Town was to get the chit married off, perhaps the quickest way of getting him to leave would be to get the girl affianced. But by the time he thought of that, he'd already sown quite a few rumors that, coupled with the girl's tendency to blot her copybook, would make most of the acceptable gentlemen of his acquaintance think twice about courting her. Of course, he wasn't on bosom terms with many men who were entirely within the pale. Of the men he knew who might be encouraged to set their caps at Lady Clarissa, most would be uninterested in a milk-and-water miss, and the rest would never be acceptable to Ransley.

He'd considered getting someone to compromise her — either she'd marry the man in question or Ransley would have to take her back to the country, her reputation in tatters. But none of the men he knew who might be talked into ruining Lady Clarissa could be trusted to keep their mouths shut about it afterwards. And if Ransley ever discovered his heir was behind such a trick, Mallinson could be perfectly assured that he'd never get the title. Ransley'd marry and sire an heir just to spite him.

Mallinson had half a mind to offer for her himself. But marrying the chit, though tempting from the standpoint of purely physical gratification, would not fix his problem. It would bring him whatever fortune she had in her own right and the generous dowry Ransley had settled on her, but not bring him one whit closer to the title. He deserved that title after all the years he'd waited for it. Besides, he'd have to woo the gel, which would entail a great deal of irritating effort with no real certainty of success. He was sure that, if he compromised her himself, it would be far more likely that Ransley would wed at that point than he. Not least because he had a suspicion Ransley would call him out for it. He wished in passing that he'd spent more time at Ransley Manor practicing with a pistol. Dueling might be illegal, but if he could be certain of killing the man....

No. Ransley was almost certainly the better shot, and Mallinson didn't fancy risking his skin in any case.

As for risking someone else's.... Well, even if Ransley would allow his niece to marry the man who compromised her instead of killing him outright, Mallinson wasn't entirely certain that the engagement would get Ransley to leave. Who would have thought he'd cling so determinedly to Town? He'd certainly never shown any appreciation for it before. Mallinson could only think that Ransley's attachment to the Ravenshaw woman must be closer than he'd guessed... and growing steadily more dangerous.

Wilford, who Mallinson had at first thought a stroke of luck, had been less than useless. He made the perfect gull, for he was too stupidly principled to deliberately give away Mallinson's part in the plot, and if anyone caught him out, he merely looked foolish. More foolish. No one would think anything of his clumsily spilling some chit's drink, were he spotted doing so, nor of his part in spreading rumors, for he wasn't generally thought to be bright enough to realize the import of what he said. But the very sense of fair play that would prevent him from spilling Mallinson's name if he were caught also prevented Mallinson from being able to use him for more... mean-spirited efforts. There was only so far Mallinson could encourage Wilford to go without exposing his hand to the man, or causing him to balk. And his lack of brains, while making him easily led to act on Mallinson's behalf without even realizing it, also made him far too dim to do a proper job of ruining Clarissa. Witness that scene at the Greenhow's ball — the man had looked a proper fool, blathering about Clarissa owing him a dance. Given that he danced like a crippled cow, most people were less shocked at Clarissa's perfidy than in sympathy with the chit for not wanting to have her toes smashed.

All that little effort had done was to make Wilford look foolish. And then, to cap off the fiasco, his clumsiness had torn the Ravenshaw woman's dress and sent her winging directly into Ransley's arms. Mallinson winced to think of it. They'd been thick as thieves ever since. Ransley and his ward hadn't been seen at a single social event without Ravenshaw and her companion dangling along behind them. Such sudden affinity did not go unnoticed by the tattlemongers, and speculation about the Duke of Ransley's marriage intentions was now making the rounds alongside the rumors Mallinson had started about his ward. In fact, the more widely Mallinson's little *on dits* about Lady Clarissa spread, the more widely rumors of Ransley's possible attachment to Miss Ravenshaw were bruited, as talking about Ransley's involvement in the one inevitably led to talking about the other.

Things had gotten so bad that Mallinson's tailor was dragging his feet at making him even one more suit without receiving at least partial payment of his tab and half the gentlemen at Cocker's now refused to take his vowels. It was clear that something more drastic would have to be done, and that Mallinson would have to do it himself. One way or another, Ransley must be made to leave.

Accordingly, he dressed himself up to the height of fashion, had his valet pour him into his jacket and arrange his hair à la Titus with scented pomade, and presented himself at Ransley's townhouse on Grosvenor Square just as Ransley and that ward of his were on their way out to attend the night's social round.

He had timed his arrival perfectly and was just handing his hat and gloves to the butler when Ransley and his ward emerged from the dining room. They were both dressed to go out, and they were alone. "Mallinson?" Ransley said, looking startled.

"Your Grace." Mallinson bowed slightly lower than necessary to hide his expression, relieved to see that the duke's relationship with Miss Ravenshaw had not yet reached the point where she was invited to dine with him. "My apologies, Your Grace. I had hoped to have a few words with you about Ransley Manor before we attended to our social commitments, but it appears my timing is unfortunate." He took his hat and gloves back from the butler, ignoring the fish-eyed look the man gave him.

"What about the Manor?"

Mallinson turned back around, smiling. "Nothing vital, sir. Just some questions about the management of the estate farms. It can wait." It was the only excuse he could think of for showing up on the man's doorstep — he didn't want Ransley to realize he was angling for an invitation — though it did mean he'd be stuck in a bloody boring discussion about animal husbandry at some point. He'd already nearly put himself to sleep reading several months' worth of useless letters from the steward that had been gathering dust on his mantelshelf. He couldn't think of anything he wanted to talk about less, but he knew better than to use the subject as an excuse without being prepared to speak on it to Ransley when the man eventually cornered him.

"Very well," Ransley said. "You may call on me tomorrow at one."

Mallinson bowed again, hiding a wince. One was a perfectly unreasonable time to expect him to be up and about, but he supposed it couldn't be helped. Not if he wanted to stay on Ransley's good side. He'd already pushed it quite far enough by presenting himself at the duke's house without an invitation. And didn't that rankle — he, the duke's heir, not invited as a matter of course to visit and dine and what have you.

Luckily, pushing himself on Ransley just as he was going out worked precisely as Mallinson had hoped it would. Becoming aware of Lady Clarissa's wide-eyed curiosity, Ransley abruptly said, "Clarissa, this young man is my heir, Josias Mallinson. Mallinson, I believe you remember Lady Clarissa?"

Mallinson smiled and bowed over her hand. "Indeed I do, though you were just a little bit of fluff last time I saw you," he lied, having only the vaguest memory of the ragamuffin. "You've become quite beautiful, cos, if I may say so."

She stifled a giggle and curtsied, flattered. From there, it was inevitable that Ransley should invite Mallinson to join them, and he soon found himself sitting across from Lady Clarissa in Ransley's carriage. His plan was working perfectly so far. At this rate, it wouldn't be hard to ruin the chit, perhaps even within the night.

Things were looking up.

* * *

Thea did not have to look to know that Ransley had arrived at Lady Cathorn's ball. Indeed, she was beginning to find it nearly impossible to *not* know exactly where he was any time they were in the same room. The man seemed to have a nearly magnetic pull on her eyes, bringing them round to him wherever he happened to be. And even when she forced herself not to look at him, she could still feel his presence, like the warmth of the sun on her skin. It was… unnerving.

When she did glance casually toward the doorway, she was surprised to see that the duke and Lady Clarissa were accompanied by another man. While Ransley was as well-connected as any lord — after years of schooling and social events together, most of the *ton* had at least nodding acquaintances with each other — he seemed on the whole more isolated than any man she'd ever met. He appeared to have spent the better part of at least a decade rusticating, and while he must have friends in whatever part of the country Tynesfield lay, he appeared to have few, if any, in Town. Though appearances might be deceiving. Ransley played his cards so close to his vest that, unless one had angered him, one could hardly tell how he felt under that icy control. Perhaps he was bosom companions with many of the men he addressed so formally in public, though Thea somehow doubted it.

She studied the man with Ransley, wondering what made him different from the rest. For surely there was something about him to make Ransley bring him along and introduce him around as he was. The fellow was a good six inches shorter than Ransley, with brown hair and an overblown handsomeness. His clothing proclaimed him a dandy — tight enough to limit movement in nearly every direction, with shirt points so high she doubted he could turn his head without stabbing himself in the eye. The brightness of his green coat and canary waistcoat made Ransley's black coat and russet waistcoat look quite somber by comparison. Something about the set of the stranger's head seemed almost preening, as if he knew without doubt that he outshone every man in the room, but Thea frankly found both the looks and dress of the Duke of Ransley far more taking.

She and Mrs. Wellins had already taken up seats on one side of the ballroom, and her aunt's fingers were jumping in time with the lively country dance being played. Thea forced her gaze away from the duke and watched the dancers, knowing he would eventually make his way over to them. Though it was hard to wait patiently, she always let him bring Clarissa to her. It would not do to appear to be dangling after him.

As always, it seemed to take an unconscionably long time, and yet nearly before she knew it, Ransley was making his curt bow in front of her. She rose and curtsied to him, murmuring, "Your Grace."

"Good evening, Miss Ravenshaw. May I make known to you my heir, Mr. Josias Mallinson?" There was nearly no inflection in his voice as he made the introduction, and Thea could not in the least tell how he felt about his heir. At least the connection explained the man's presence, though not why this was the first time he'd put in an appearance. Mr. Mallinson's expression was easier to read — he appeared somewhat put about when Ransley said "mister," though Thea could not think why, unless he had some title Ransley was not using. That seemed unlikely, as Ransley was, in her experience, punctiliously correct. So long, at least, as one hadn't thrown him into high dudgeon by calling him a dragon.

"My pleasure, Miss Ravenshaw," Mr. Mallinson said, bowing far too low over her hand. Up close, she could see that he was older than his manner of dress had led her to suppose and that his dress was even more elaborate than she'd at first thought, having needlework designs pricked into his waistcoat in gold thread. And — she just managed to hold back a sneeze — he smelled impenetrably of pomade.

"Mr. Mallinson." She bobbed him a shallow curtsy and saw him grimace. Did he expect her to make him as low a curtsy as she did Ransley? He might be heir presumptive to a dukedom, but until he inherited the title, he was no higher in the social register than she. She drew her hand out of his grasp, which was overwarm, even through both their gloves, and indicated Mrs. Wellins. "My companion, Mrs. Wellins."

Mallinson bowed nearly as low over Mrs. Wellins' hand, and Thea told herself such unctuous behavior was clearly just his way. And if he was to be around more, being Ransley's heir and clearly in Town for the time being, it would do her no good to conceive a disgust of the man. Still, as he settled onto the chair next to Mrs. Wellins and set about charming her, Thea could not help but mislike it.

She began to chat quietly with Lady Clarissa, who was seated between Thea and Mrs. Wellins. The girl's sphere had been circumscribed by two of the three adults at every entertainment since they'd made their agreement, and so far, there had been no missteps or youthful oversets. At times, Thea caught a flash of defiance in Clarissa's eyes and knew that the young woman rankled at such careful supervision, but if pressed, even she would have to admit that it was better for her reputation.

As Thea chatted and fanned herself desultorily in the overwarm room, she was aware of Ransley's heat along her left side. He was standing nearby — though not as near as her skin told her he was — his shoulders against the wall and his eyes on the dancers. Though he appeared not to be attending, Thea was quite certain he heard every word. Between that certainty and the fact that Mallinson's eyes — a washed-out blue nearly as pale as Ransley's — were on her the entire time he spoke with Mrs. Wellins, Thea had a great deal of difficulty maintaining her end of the conversation. She was relieved when Mallinson bowed, first to Mrs. Wellins, then to Lady Clarissa, and asked the girl to dance. Lady Clarissa, who seemed not to find Mallinson's behavior florid or his hair oil overly perfumed, accepted after a quick glance at her guardian for approval.

Mallinson swept Lady Clarissa into the figure of the dance, and Thea found she could breathe a bit easier. Well, not easier, as Ransley was still nearby and his closeness played havoc with her insides. Still, she was happier.

She ought to have been happier still when, just before the next set of dances, Allen Wetherald came to beg the honor of her company. He was light on his feet and in his conversation, and she would normally have been most pleased to dance the supper dance with him. She accepted Wetherald's hand with no outward sign of the strange reluctance she suddenly felt. It was foolish. Lady Clarissa was engaged to stand up with the Portemaine boy, who had apparently not been put off by the ruckus Lord Wilford had made the last time she was promised to dance with him. He was a perfectly suitable companion for the dance and supper afterwards. Mrs. Wellins had found a friend in the chaperones and was chatting pleasantly away. And the Duke of Ransley…

Oh dear. Thea joined Wetherald in the quadrille and tried not to think too hard about the sudden insight she'd had into her own heart. She hadn't realized she wanted Ransley to claim the supper dance until Mr. Wetherald had done so.

Thea put Ransley from her mind as she danced two lively quadrilles with Mr. Wetherald and allowed him to escort her to the supper room and select a plate of delicacies for her. After an acquaintance of several years, he well knew what she liked and how to make her laugh, and she enjoyed herself. She did not look for Ransley in the crowded supper room, or try to see who he might have companioned in the supper dance, and she most certainly did not think of him again until Wetherald escorted her back to her previous place along the wall. Ransley was standing precisely where he'd been when she left, and she could feel his eyes upon her from some distance away. Unlike Mallinson's pale, dissolute eyes, Ransley's eyes were piercing, and though she at times felt that they looked right to the heart of her, she found his gaze less disturbing than his heir's.

Mr. Wetherald handed her back into her seat, bowed and thanked her for a lovely supper, and took himself off. Lady Clarissa was already back, smiling and chattering away at Mrs. Wellins, who passed Thea her fan. She'd forgotten it when she agreed to stand up with Mr. Wetherald, and she found herself immediately putting the little ivory creation to use. Though it had been crowded and stuffy in the supper room, it seemed even warmer here. Though that could have been Ransley's effect on her, which conspired to put her quite out of countenance. His proximity prickled along her skin, and she very nearly gasped when he suddenly pushed off the wall.

"Miss Ravenshaw," he said, bowing. "Would you do me the honor of this dance?"

Thea felt herself go both hot and cold at the same time.

The next dance was a waltz.

Chapter Ten

MALLINSON was feeling very pleased. He'd insinuated himself easily into the company of Ransley and Lady Clarissa for the evening and flattered himself into the good graces of both the girl and the Ravenshaw woman's companion, who appeared to be acting as a sort of chaperone for the chit. And what that said about the state of rapprochement between Ransley and Miss Ravenshaw didn't bear thinking on. He'd even been introduced by Ransley to men who were otherwise too top-lofty to acknowledge him. If it did nothing else, this little exercise would at least raise him in Society's estimation to nearer the position he deserved.

But he'd pushed himself upon Ransley's party for a reason, and after spending half the night getting the lay of the land, he was now prepared to set his plan in motion. He knew, from speaking with Lady Clarissa during their set of dances, how much the strong-willed chit rankled at her guardian's constant supervision. And also how dearly she wanted to waltz. The yearning on her face when she was forced to sit out the waltz earlier in the evening would have been obvious to a blind man.

All it needed, then, was someone fairly young, definitely handsome, and decidedly dissolute. An unprincipled rake who could ruin a girl in her first Season merely by dancing with her, let alone waltzing. Preferably also someone likely to accept if called out. It really was most clever. With the chit's reputation ruined, Ransley would have no choice but to return to Tynesfield with her. And if Ransley *did* call the man out, well, then he would either kill the fellow, and have to make a dash for the Continent to evade the law, or he would be killed by him, and Mallinson would inherit what he was due. However this played out, Mallinson won.

He'd taken stock of all the men in the ballroom and determined that Lord Trenwick was the perfect choice. During the first set of dances after supper,

Mallinson found him standing near the door to the supper room with a glass of wine and a look of insufferable boredom.

"Trenwick."

Trenwick looked him up and down before drawling, "Mallinson."

"I have come on a... delicate errand from a young lady. She would like me to convey to you her regards and her wish to make your acquaintance."

Trenwick raised an eyebrow. "Oh?"

Mallinson launched into his prepared story — how Lady Clarissa had conceived a *tendre* for Lord Trenwick and wished nothing more than to dance with him. He did not have to do a great deal more than that to imply that she was no better than she should be. While it was common for young ladies to use their male relatives as go-betweens — they could not, after all, show their favor to a man not already dancing attendance upon them — rakes like Trenwick did not receive the attentions of *virtuous* misses. As Mallinson continued to reel off Lady Clarissa's supposed blandishments to Trenwick, he found it difficult not to gloat over the success of his plan. How useful of Ransley to allow Mallinson to accompany him and his ward to the ball and thus make it eminently believable that he was in a position to know and convey the chit's desires.

"And how," Trenwick said when Mallinson had concluded, "do you suggest I pay my regards to the young woman with the Duke of Ransley standing guard?" There was a gleam of interest in his eyes as he looked over at where Lady Clarissa sat next to Miss Ravenshaw that was not quite hidden by his show of ennui. "You do not, I hope, expect me to believe that he would welcome my attentions to her?"

"You may leave that up to me. Do you ask her to waltz, and I will take care of the duke." He turned to follow Trenwick's gaze. It was all going to plan. He could see Wilford moving between the couples engaged in a contra dance and those seated along the wall. He'd reach the chaperone in a few moments, and surely even Wilford could manage to keep the woman distracted for a few minutes. Mallinson would engage Ransley in conversation, and he was certain some fellow or other could be relied upon to stand up with Miss Ravenshaw. He'd yet to see her sit out a waltz.

And really, he'd begun to think he'd been mistaken in his concern over Miss Ravenshaw. She'd given that prosy fellow, Wetherald, the supper dance, and Ransley had scarcely exchanged two words with her all evening. As he watched the duke push off the wall and turn to bow to Miss Ravenshaw, however, he felt his hands grow cold and his head hot. Hell and damnation, he was asking her to dance, to *waltz!* The tattlemongers would be full of the story by morning, and by the next evening, doors all over the *ton* would be closed to Mallinson.

He barely heard Trenwick say, "A waltz? The chit is bold, isn't she?"

Miss Ravenshaw rose and curtsied and put her hand in Ransley's. They moved out to join the dancers, and Mallinson was aware of a stir of interest passing through the assembly. There was no time to lose if he wished there to be more on people's minds than gossiping about Ransley and the Ravenshaw woman's prospects.

"Oh she is, I assure you, up to every rig and row," he said, his urgency hidden behind the same façade he used to cover his cheating at cards. "The tattlemongers don't know the half of it." One of the musicians had apparently broken a string, for there was a bit of scrambling on the dais. A reprieve. A moment or two while the situation was remedied and those already standing up for the waltz chatted quietly.

"With the girl your cousin," Trenwick drawled, "one would be inclined to think it unmannerly of you to confess such a thing."

Mallinson felt himself flush painfully. He managed at the last moment to make his expression look like embarrassment, rather than rage at the insult, saying, "Normally, I would not. However, as the chit sent me to speak for her and convey her regards…."

"You thought to overcome my reservations by setting my mind at ease about her virtue. Or lack of it."

"I would not put it so boldly," Mallinson demurred. The broken string had apparently been repaired, as the fiddle player was beginning the exacting process of tuning up. Urgency swept through Mallinson, but as with any gamble he undertook, only seemed to make his thinking more precise. "If you doubt me, or believe I've misunderstood the lady's desires, you have only to ask her to dance. If she accepts you…." He trailed off suggestively.

Trenwick smiled sardonically. "Well, then I shall know she's no milk-and-water miss, shan't I?" He handed Mallinson his empty wine glass as if he were the veriest servant, and started toward where Lady Clarissa sat with the chaperone.

Mallinson shoved the glass at a passing footman and moved off to another part of the ballroom, where he would have a perfect vantage without being obvious about it. He watched Trenwick approach and bow to Lady Clarissa, who blushed, fluttering her fan becomingly. Wilford was, for once, doing his part perfectly, staying far enough to Mrs. Wellins' right to keep her head turned away from her charge. Mallinson hadn't told Wilford why he wanted Mrs. Wellins distracted. He clenched his fists and prayed Wilford wouldn't give the game away when he saw Trenwick. But thankfully, he remained characteristically oblivious; Mallinson wasn't even certain the man noticed Trenwick was there.

And then Lady Clarissa was rising and putting her hand in Lord Trenwick's, and triumph flashed through Mallinson. Done and done. Merely standing up with him was sufficient to damage her reputation; dancing would just be the icing atop the cake. He'd been certain she would. Not only would she be flattered by Trenwick's attentions, but with her chaperone distracted, she could only refuse him by pleading exhaustion. And good manners would require her then to sit out the rest of the evening without dancing a single dance. A spirited chit like Lady Clarissa would hardly be able to imagine such a misfortune.

Little did she know.

* * *

The delay before the music began shredded Thea's nerves. She stood facing the Duke of Ransley, waiting, so aware of his eyes on her, of his hand still holding hers, that when he asked whether she'd enjoyed supper — doubtless to pass the time and put her at ease — she scarcely knew what she answered.

Finally, the plinking of the musicians turned into the strains of a delightful waltz and they began to move. Despite herself, she drew in a sharp breath at the touch of his gloved hand on her waist. She hardly knew if she was moving her feet, though she supposed she must be, for Ransley was guiding her gracefully through the figures of the dance. She felt as if she were half-asleep, awake only where the heat of his hands seeped through her dress and her glove.

"I did not know," he said, and his voice startled her, for all that it was little more than a quiet rumble, "that my cravat could be quite so enthralling."

Her eyes flew up to his. "I... Beg pardon, Your Grace; I was not attending."

Amusement danced in his eyes. "On the contrary, Miss Ravenshaw. You were attending perfectly... to my cravat. It is a lovely color, I'll grant you that — I'm quite fond of it myself — but I had not thought it tied so intricately as to require study."

She'd known his eyes could burn with anger and intensity. She'd never seen them melt before. It was like seeing the gray ice of a frozen pond begin to break up in the spring. She felt herself smile. "I was concentrating on the dance, Your Grace. I would not wish to tread upon your feet."

He smiled back and it transformed his whole face. "I should not mind if you did."

"I should mind," she countered. "I would not wish to, like Lord Wilford, go about dancing upon the feet of all those who partner me."

"If Lord Wilford were as graceful as you, his partners would escape all trampling."

His hand tightened upon her waist and she could feel a flush mount her cheeks. "You flatter me, Your Grace."

"Hardly, Miss Ravenshaw."

Now that she was looking into his face, she found that she was no more able to look away from it than she'd been able to drag her eyes away from his cravat. He was watching her in turn, and though he was no longer smiling, there was a softness about his mouth that was as good as a smile. It turned something vaguely unsettled in the pit of her stomach. She was taken, suddenly, with the desire to touch that softness, and the line of his jaw, and the small crinkles at the corners of his eyes that betokened a smile as much as his mouth did. And she wished to do it without a glove keeping her skin from his. The sudden warmth in her chest quite stole her breath away, and she looked away, afraid the disconcerting feeling would somehow show on her face for him to read.

"Your Grace, I—" Catching sight of Lady Clarissa nearby, she automatically looked to see who partnered her, and her heart fell through the floor. "Oh no! Oh my, we—"

"No," Ransley said, his hand tightening on her waist. He'd come about, and surely he could see as well as she did the disaster Lady Clarissa had come to.

"But that's Lord Trenwick, we must—"

"We daren't step in now," he said quietly, his voice as hard and as sharp as steel. "That will only make matters worse."

Yes. Yes, of course. Dragging the young lady and her partner from the dance would only complete her ruination. But to stand idly by...

Clarissa was dancing with her head up and her eyes shining, regal and gorgeous and utterly unaware of the whispers that spread around her like ripples across a pond. She was clearly badly taken with Lord Trenwick, and equally clearly had no idea that the dance she was so enjoying was effecting the utter ruin of her reputation. Thea looked cautiously about and was surprised to find that she and Ransley were the cynosure of quite a few eyes. Doubtless all waiting to see Ransley's reaction.

No one was openly staring at Lady Clarissa and Lord Trenwick, but it was clear that many people were aware of the scandalous dance. Thea had little doubt the story would make its way through the ballroom within minutes and the rest of the *ton* by breakfast.

She and Ransley danced on, but the enjoyment of it had curdled in her stomach. She kept seeing Clarissa's face, even though she could no longer look at her, for Ransley had turned them so he could keep the couple in view. Such simple joy in the girl's expression, so soon to be destroyed. And oh God, but there was the break between songs and the second waltz in the set to dance yet. She didn't know that she could.

It happened when the waltz was just beginning to wind down. Thea did not at first know what was about; she was only aware of a ripple of something moving through the assembly like a wave. She closed her eyes briefly and prayed that it was not somehow related to Lady Clarissa's scandalous waltz with a rake. But no. The attention of nearly the entire ballroom had shifted toward the door at the head of the room, the musicians jangling to a discordant halt when they realized the dancers had stopped.

Ransley took advantage of the distraction to tuck her hand into the crook of his arm and lead her toward where Mrs. Wellins still sat. It was frowned upon to leave when the dance was yet progressing, though at least departing a waltz before it was completed would not disarrange the formation of the dancers as it would a quadrille or country dance. He must have seen more of the disturbance that had attracted all eyes than Thea could, for he appeared quite assured that their departure would not be remarked. His path deliberately took them past where Trenwick and Lady Clarissa stood, still quite as close together as if they were waltzing. Lady Clarissa was looking into Lord Trenwick's face, and Thea couldn't help but think he was possibly the worst gentleman the girl could conceive a *tendre* for. Perhaps, then, it was for the best that he appeared to share the rest of the assembly's fascination with whatever had taken place near the door.

"Step away, Trenwick," Ransley said in a low and icy voice.

"But—" Clarissa quailed when Ransley turned his pale eyes on her and left the rest of her protest unsaid.

Trenwick looked for a moment at Ransley, and Thea held her breath. The duke's words were scarcely short of an insult, and his tone…. There were men who would call him out for less. However, Trenwick only bowed mockingly and strolled away.

Ransley put his hand in the center of Clarissa's back and steered her towards Mrs. Wellins. The musicians had started up again, but the dancers seemed not to have regained their appetite for the exercise, many being too busy whispering together to properly attend. Thea wondered what the deuce had happened — despite her height, she'd been unable to see whatever had transpired by the door.

When they reached Mrs. Wellins, she stood and curtsied low to the duke. "I'm so terribly sorry, Your Grace—"

"Not here," he murmured, bowing first to her, then to Thea. "Come, Clarissa."

Not giving her a chance to speak, he guided her away. Thea watched them pass along the wall to the back of the ballroom and slip out into the garden through one of the French windows.

Thea tipped her head at Mrs. Wellins to indicate that they would be following, and her aunt retrieved her reticule and moved to accompany her. There were still more people standing about talking than dancing, and as soon as they'd reached a less crowded area, where she could speak unheard, Thea bent her head nearer her companion's and whispered, "What was about to cause such a furor?"

"You didn't see? Oh, my dear, it was astounding. Lady Heatherton, bold as brass in a bright red gown, not wearing so much as a scrap of mourning. And her husband not three months dead."

"Oh my," Thea said weakly. She could scarcely imagine what kind of woman would act with such flagrant disregard for the dictates of Society and her own reputation. What could possibly cause any woman of the *ton* to deliberately call down Society's censure upon herself in such a manner? There were times Thea became impatient with the rules she must follow, and times she conducted herself with something less than the full caution she ought, but she couldn't imagine anything that would cause her to flout them so brazenly. That way lay disgrace and ruin.

* * *

Ransley looked up when he heard the French window open. Unsurprised to see Miss Ravenshaw and her companion, he gave them a nod and directed his attention back to his niece as they closed the window on the strains of a waltz and joined Clary and himself on the empty terrace.

"… now, if you would care to explain what possessed you to dance with a man to whom you had not been introduced?" he finished.

Clary was infuriatingly starry-eyed, and her inability or unwillingness to attend to him made him wish heartily that he could box her ears. "Well, how *could* we be introduced," she said airily, "when everyone was either already dancing or chatting?"

"This is my fault, Your Grace," Mrs. Wellins said stolidly, surprisingly direct and blunt for a woman who had, so far in his experience, seemed somewhat shy and retiring. She was clearly the sort of person who believed in shouldering the blame for her mistakes, but in this case, he could wish that she would not. Clary would never learn if the consequences of her actions were never brought home to her. "I should never have allowed my attention to be diverted. But Lord Wilford—"

"Wilford!" Him again. Ransley owned he ought to have expected it — he'd known that Wilford danced attendance on Miss Ravenshaw with surprising determination for someone so flighty. It was inevitable, then, that he should be around a great deal — but Ransley had somehow not anticipated tripping over the man constantly, nor how much it would irritate him to find the moonling making calf's eyes at Miss Ravenshaw at every turn.

"Yes, Your Grace. Lord Wilford asked after the health of my son, who is with the army in France. I fear I become quite distracted when speaking of him," she admitted with quiet dignity.

"This is not your fault, Mrs. Wellins," Ransley told her. "You should have been able to expect Lady Clarissa not to be so corkbrained as to accept an offer to stand up with a man she did not know." He turned to Clary. "You know better than that, girl."

"You were off dancing," she flared, "and I wished to waltz. And besides, he introduced himself to me when he asked me to dance."

Ransley closed his eyes briefly and mastered the urge to shake her. "And did Lord Trenwick happen to mention," he said through his teeth, "that he's one of the most celebrated rakes in the *ton*?"

Clary stared at him, her eyes quite as wide, and as wounded, as if he'd slapped her across the face. "He's… Oh!" She put her hands up to her reddening cheeks. Miss Ravenshaw took her by the arm and sat her down firmly on one of the stone benches that dotted the terrace.

"Now don't get into such a taking," Miss Ravenshaw said. "It's not as bad as all that."

Whether it was the stern words or the hard marble bench, which must have been cold even through the layers of her skirt and petticoat, Clary took in a sharp breath and somehow managed not to descend into a fit of the vapors. Her wide eyes turned from Miss Ravenshaw to himself, but he was quite unable to share that woman's rosy view of events.

"Perhaps you would care to explain, Miss Ravenshaw," he prompted.

She looked unaccountably surprised. "Well, not that what Lady Clarissa did was not damaging, and very foolish — I have no doubt," she told the girl, "that your guardian taught you a great deal better than that — but I believe her reputation has been saved by someone even more foolish."

Still at sea, he raised an eyebrow at her.

"Lady Clarissa's waltz with Lord Trenwick will hardly remain on the tongues of the *ton* for longer than it takes them to drink their morning chocolate. Assuming it makes it even that far. They'll be far too busy talking about Lady Heatherton's attendance at the ball to bother themselves over it."

"The lady in red who made such a memorable entrance?" Ransley frowned. "Now why does that name sound familiar?"

"Lord Heatherton was killed three months ago in a duel. Rumor has it, by Lord Trenwick."

Clary gasped, her hand flying to her mouth. Both Ransley's eyebrows went up and he pursed his lips in a soundless whistle. Miss Ravenshaw glanced away, looking unaccountably flushed. He supposed she was ashamed to be spreading gossip, though few members of the *ton* did not know, or share, the various *on dits* that came their way. It was one of the things he disliked most about Society. "Well, that'll put the cat among the pigeons."

"Yes. The connection with Trenwick might bring your name into it somewhat, my dear," she told Clary, "but the *beau monde* have something far more salacious to talk about than your waltz."

"Indeed," Ransley said. "You should count yourself fortunate, Clary."

"Oh, I do!" the girl exclaimed earnestly. "And I promise — I won't take a step without consulting you or Miss Ravenshaw or Mrs. Wellins."

"See that you do," Ransley said, though he knew better than to think even this experience would cause a permanent reformation of Clary's behavior. She meant her promise, and he knew she would do her best to keep it. He also knew, from far too much recent experience, that she would almost certainly forget herself sooner or later.

He had been far too lax, both in her upbringing and in his responsibility to bring her out safely in Society. He'd given the girl her own head at home and failed to notice that she was turning into a perfect hoyden, and when he brought her to London, he'd hoped to have it all done quickly and without fuss. But Clary deserved fuss, and not the sort she'd been attracting. She deserved his full attention.

Ransley had allowed himself to become distracted by Miss Ravenshaw. The woman was charming and poised, and beautiful even when she was ripping up at him. Perhaps especially then. Seeing her, as he had, so very much in Clary's company these last few weeks, he'd been forced to change his opinion of her. She had been all that was right and proper, had shepherded Clary through several touchy situations, and showed no sign that she desired anything more than to be useful to the girl. And if her consequence had gone up in the eyes of some members of the *ton* due to her being seen so often in his company, well, he could hardly begrudge her that.

Nor did he wish to. In fact, he'd been enormously chagrinned to discover that his primary feeling, upon admitting once and for all that Miss Ravenshaw did *not* have her cap set at him, was one of disappointment.

He'd found himself watching her dance, converse, eat, ride, and wishing nothing more than to continue doing so. To have an excuse to do so, even once Clary was matched up and wedded off. And this night, after watching her partner Allen Wetherald, who he remembered from school as a retiring lad with little to recommend himself, in two dances and at supper, he had been utterly unable to resist asking her to stand up with him for a set of waltzes.

He should have known better. The last time he'd done what he wanted, instead of what he knew was right, Clary's sister had paid the price. He'd matched Amelia up with Giles Ashburne instead of letting her have a Season because he'd wanted to ally his house and his lands with Ashburne's and because he had most emphatically *not* wanted to go through all the rigmarole of firing the chit off in Town. His decision to keep her close to home had ultimately put her into the hands of the man who killed her, and it was not something he would ever be able to forgive himself for.

He could not afford to make the same mistake again; Clary was relying on him. He'd accepted Miss Ravenshaw's offer of help because he had not felt himself up to the task of keeping Clary safe. It was a craven thing to do, attempting to share out the responsibility of watching over his ward that was solely and rightfully his. And influenced in no little part, he had come to realize, by his unacknowledged desire to spend more time with Miss Ravenshaw. She was genuine in her desire to help, he believed, but she was a distraction, and one he couldn't afford. Distractions could kill.

He'd allowed himself a moment of pleasure, and look what had come of it. It could not happen again.

Chapter Eleven

"…AND I don't believe you've heard a word I said, Althea."

Thea blinked and brought her gaze from back some middle distance to her aunt. "I'm sorry, Aunt Florence. I was not attending."

"Really? I hadn't noticed," Mrs. Wellins said tartly.

Thea blinked again and returned her teacup — which she'd only just realized had been hovering in the vicinity of her lips for some time, though she could not recall having taken a drink from it — to the saucer. For her aunt to show even mild asperity betokened serious irritation. Thea put her dish of tea on the table at her elbow and turned her full attention upon her aunt. "I really am terribly sorry, my dear. I own I've been distracted, but that's no excuse for not listening. I can see something's bothering you, pray tell me what it is."

"Never mind me," Mrs. Wellins said with a dismissive gesture, though now that Thea was paying attention, she could see a tightness around her aunt's eyes that meant she was worrying herself over something. "You've been in a brown study for two days. I've never known you to be so distracted, Althea."

"I can't help it. I've not seen the Duke of Ransley—" She saw Mrs. Wellins' lips twitch. "—or his niece — don't give me that look, pray — since that to-do at the Cathorn's ball."

"Nonsense," Mrs. Wellins said. "They were at Lady Edmonstone's musicale and I'm quite certain I caught a glimpse of them at Mrs. Tindale's rout."

"Yes, Aunt. A glimpse. Of late, we have done nothing more than catch glimpses of them, and that from a distance. They haven't been nearer us than twenty feet in two days and I—"

Miss them. Both of them — Lady Clarissa's bright interest in everything she came across was very engaging, and Thea had grown quite fond of the chit — but especially His Grace. Miss seeing him, tall and imposing and really quite ridiculously handsome. Miss speaking with him, listening to his deep voice and enjoying his sardonic observations about the foibles of Society. Miss dancing with him…

"—am growing concerned."

It had only been the one dance, she reminded herself sternly, and that cut short by Lady Clarissa's and Lady Heatherton's separate efforts to tarnish their reputations. Thankfully for Lady Clarissa, Thea's prediction had come to pass, and the *beau monde* was far too busy gossiping like geese about Lady Heatherton to pay more than passing attention to Clarissa's misstep.

"The young lady appears to be doing well."

Without you lay unspoken in Mrs. Wellins' mild remark. And indeed, whether because she was keeping to her word or because Ransley was not letting her out of his sight, there had been no Clarissa-centered contretemps since the Cathorn's ball. Neither of her own making nor of Trenwick's. Thea sternly reminded herself that that, after all, had been the point of the exercise. She had pushed herself on the duke and his niece purely to see to it that the chit didn't put herself entirely beyond the pale or fall victim to Trenwick's infamous determination to win that horrid bet. However, Trenwick appeared to have turned his sights elsewhere since Lady Heatherton broke her mourning. That being the case, if Clarissa was managing to stay out of the briars on her own, and so far it appeared that she was, that was all Thea could hope for. And yet she couldn't seem to stop herself watching Ransley and his ward from afar, holding her breath to see if he would bring Clarissa over, as he had during their short rapprochement. But not of late. Oh, he acknowledged her — not even the biggest tattlemongers of the *ton* could say that he had cut her from his acquaintance — but he kept his distance. And she could naturally not be seen seeking *him* out.

Nor should she want to. Since when did Althea Ravenshaw moon after a man's attention in such a way? It was indecorous and, frankly, rather lowering. Enough, then. She would stop, and upon the instant. Thea did not *pine*.

"Indeed she is," she agreed, her tone dismissing the subject. She leaned toward Mrs. Wellins and put a hand on her wrist. "Now really, my dear, what is the matter? You look as though you have not been sleeping. Tell me what is bothering you, do."

Mrs. Wellins turned her hand to clasp Thea's with fingers like ice. "Pray do not refine upon it. I've been in a bit of a pother, it's true, but—"

"What is it? Is it Gabriel? Have you received a letter from him?"

"No, and that's just the trouble. It's been more than a month." Mrs. Wellins sighed. "One never quite gets used to hearing little more than what the papers say about the army's progress on the Peninsula."

"And so much of that nothing but Banbury tales and nonsense. Pray, Aunt, do not fadge yourself. I'm sure Gabriel will write as soon as ever he can."

"I'm sure he will." Mrs. Wellins gave Thea's hand a squeeze and released her. "Now, shall I warm up your tea?" she asked, lifting the pot. "I fear yours grew quite cold while you were wool-gathering."

"I'm certain it has," Thea said, falling in line with Mrs. Wellins' attempt to buck herself up. "If you would be so kind, Aunt, I— What the deuce is going on?"

"Thea!"

"Apologies," Thea murmured absently, already standing and moving toward the door. She ought to be mortified at speaking so in the presence of her aunt, but the ruckus coming from the entryway was hardly more decorous than her vocabulary.

She had not advanced beyond the middle of the drawing room carpet before the door flew open and a whirlwind rushed in. Thea found herself with an armful of sobbing girl before she could even properly take in the four people who had invaded the room.

"Lady Clarissa!" Her arms were already around the girl, where she'd instinctively thrown them to avoid getting bowled over, and it was equally instinctive to begin patting the chit's heaving back. "What's got you so overset, child?"

Receiving no answer from the girl, Thea turned her attention to the other three people in the room. One of the Neds stood by the door, trying to look as if this sort of thing happened every day. He did not quite have the phlegmatic mien of the best butlers, but was doing a fairly credible job of it. There was a girl with him, who Thea took by her dress and the way she lingered in the doorway to be a servant.

And then there was Lord Wilford, standing upon the edge of her drawing room carpet and looking nonplussed. More so than usual.

"Lord Wilford, are you able to explain this state of affairs?" Thea asked, when he appeared quite ready to stand silently watching until the last trumpet.

"Don't know why the chit is in such a taking," he said, blinking quickly. "Found her wandering about Picadilly with her maid, looking quite lost. When she said she was on her way to see you, I, I offered to take her up in my carriage. Halfway here, she turned into a downpour." Suddenly realizing that they'd burst in so quickly Ned hadn't had time to take his hat, he snatched it off his head.

"Very well," Thea said, resigning herself to determining what was about from the girl herself, if she could manage to get her calmed down. The effort certainly didn't need witnesses, however. "Thank you, my lord, for delivering her safely. I'm certain you have quite a crowded calendar, but could you possibly do me the inestimable service of informing the Duke of Ransley of his ward's whereabouts?" Mrs. Wellins made a small sound behind her, and Thea knew precisely what her aunt was thinking. And she was right. It was really too much of her, turning a lord, even one as ineffectual as Wilford, into a messenger boy. However, as it would both save her sending a servant and get Wilford out of her drawing room...

"Oh, I-I-I... I'd be honored, Miss Ravenshaw... but really, I can't. I'm, I'm already late as it is."

"I understand. I hope the rest of your day passes more enjoyably," Thea said firmly.

Lord Wilford looked startled, as if he hadn't quite realized that if he was too busy to carry a message to Ransley, he was too busy to stand about in her parlor. After looking irresolutely at her for several moments, he bowed suddenly, popped his high-crowned beaver back on his head, and strode out the door.

"Coward," Thea said under her breath, and heard Mrs. Wellins draw in a breath that sounded very much like the prelude to a laugh. She raised her voice to call, "Ned," before her footman could follow Wilford. "After you've seen Lord Wilford out, please return to show Lady Clarissa's maid to the kitchens."

"Yes, ma'am," he said, and vanished after Lord Wilford.

"You *are* Lady Clarissa's maid?" Thea asked the pert little servant, just to be certain. Wilford was perfectly capable of getting hold of the wrong end of the stick, and given the incident with the boy-groom, Thea wouldn't put it past Lady Clarissa to come out with one of the parlor maids or a scullery girl.

"Yes, ma'am." The girl bobbed a curtsy. "Mariah, ma'am."

"Very well, Mariah. Ned'll show you to the kitchens, where you can have some tea and put your feet up while Lady Clarissa visits with me."

"Yes'm. Thank you, ma'am." She bobbed another curtsy. Lord, but Ransley's servants were formal.

When Ned returned, Thea directed him to see to the little maid's comfort and then send someone to the Duke of Ransley's residence to let him know his niece was taking tea with her. Hopefully, she thought as the door closed behind the servants, his visit would be more peaceful this time than the last.

She closed both arms around Lady Clarissa for a moment, worried at her continued sobbing and the overwarm feel of her through her thin dress. "Come now," she said, taking Clarissa by the shoulders and setting the girl away from her. "Sit and take some tea with us, and tell us what has you so overset."

"Oh! Oh, Miss Ravenshaw, I—" She bit her lip and did not quite stifle the sob that escaped. She collapsed into Thea's chair and buried her face — quite red with crying — in her hands.

"No," Mrs. Wellins said bracingly, and Thea rather thought she'd probably spoken to her own children in such a tone. "No more tears. Drink your tea and then explain. From the beginning."

Lady Clarissa sat up, and took the dish of tea Mrs. Wellins handed to her, and managed several credible sips before taking in a shuddering breath and saying, "Oh, it's too horrible! I'll never get off the tattlemonger's lips!"

"From the beginning," Thea said firmly to forestall another descent into hysterics, taking the seat on Clarissa's other side and putting a comforting hand on her shoulder.

Clarissa took in another shuddering breath. "Uncle Ransley's been perfectly disagreeable. He said... he said we'd been too much in your pocket and could certainly get by without your assistance. But he's wrong!" She put her tea on the table, and only Thea's hand on her shoulder kept her from burying her face in her hands again. "He's wrong and this proves it!"

"You appear to have been getting along quite well," Thea pointed out. *Until now.* She resolutely did not think on what it meant that Ransley had said they'd been too much together, or the confirmation that he had been keeping his distance deliberately.

"Yes, but I wanted to see you. And he forbade me to."

Thea sighed. So much for a peaceful visit. "So you determined to come anyway."

"I wanted to see you," Clarissa repeated stubbornly. "I brought my maid," she added, as if that helped matters. It did, in that at least this time she'd gone out with a slightly more suitable chaperone than a ten-year-old boy. But this tendency to flout her guardian's wishes and then draw Thea into it…. "But then I couldn't remember the way, and when Lord Wilford drew up and offered to bring me, I thought… Well, I had Mariah with me, and it was certainly better than wandering around lost, hoping to strike upon the right street. And oh, Miss Ravenshaw…"

She descended into another fit of weeping, leaving Thea very much at a loss. It was hardly unheard of for a girl to drive out with a gentleman, though it would imply a closer connection than actually existed between Lady Clarissa and Lord Wilford. But his head certainly did not appear to have been turned by it, so at least he was unlikely to have tried offering for her during the short drive from Picadilly. While that was the kind of experience that might overset the poor girl — for she could hardly have conceived a *tendre* for him and would likely have found it extremely embarrassing — Thea knew from personal experience what Wilford looked like after he'd made such an offer. And he had shown no sign of the self-satisfied glow he'd worn after the two occasions he'd offered for Thea, who'd been startled at the time to find that his satisfaction somehow failed to diminish at being refused. Besides, Lady Clarissa appeared primarily concerned about her reputation, and so long as she'd had a chaperone or maid with her, being seen in an open carriage with Wilford would bring no harm to her reputation.

"Lord Wilford wasn't driving in a closed carriage, was he?" Thea asked. She couldn't imagine him doing so on such a fine day, but she was grasping at straws.

"No!" Lady Clarissa wailed. And really, that was no help at all in understanding what was the matter. The girl turned and buried her face in Thea's shoulder once more. "And he turned down St. James's," she added, muffled but perfectly audible.

"Oh dear," Thea said. She wrapped her arms around Clarissa again and let her sob for a bit, exchanging a helpless look with Mrs. Wellins over the girl's head.

No woman of the *ton* was unfamiliar with St. James's Street. Some of the best modistes were located there. So were all the most prominent gentleman's clubs. Thus, while it was a fine thing to be seen walking or riding on St. James's earlier in the day, by this time in the afternoon, the gentlemen were about — strolling the street and sitting in the windows of their clubs commenting on passersby — and it was as much as a woman's reputation was worth to be seen in an open carriage on St. James's now.

So much for Lady Clarissa staying out of the suds. Though this time, at least, it could not be said to be entirely her fault. Nor Trenwick's, for once. Much good it did any of them.

Chapter Twelve

IT took the Duke of Ransley quite a bit longer, this time, to show up on Thea's doorstep, a delay she put down to his having to wait for his carriage to be made ready and brought around. She didn't know him sufficiently to know whether he would lower himself to take a hackney cab were he alone, but she doubted he would do so with Lady Clarissa in tow. She also felt, and scolded herself for doing so, that it said much about their improved relations that he was not in such a great tear to "rescue" his ward from her clutches as he was last time Lady Clarissa had made a precipitous visit. In the intervening time, Thea and Mrs. Wellins managed to get Clarissa somewhat calmed down by dint of commiseration, quiet conversation about the latest fashions, and the liberal application of tea, though she was still in quite a state when Ransley showed up.

He came into the drawing room like an enraged bear, but ground to a sudden halt when he caught sight of Lady Clarissa's tear-ravaged face. Had Thea not been looking so closely, she might have missed the bleak expression that briefly crossed his face, but she thought she should have noticed the slight slump of his shoulders in any case.

"Tea?" she offered, and his eyes flicked to her.

"Thank you." He waited while Ned brought a chair out from the wall, then sat down cater-corner from Thea with a nod of thanks to the footman. "Well," he said quietly when Ned had left the room and Thea had handed him a dish of tea, "what has happened this time?"

Lady Clarissa took in and then let out a shuddering breath, but did not speak. She seemed inordinately interested in whatever she saw at the bottom of her teacup, leaving Thea to say, "Apparently, Lady Clarissa and her maid determined to come visit me. However, being unable to quite remember the way, they became lost and accepted Lord Wilford's offer to take them up in his carriage and bring them here."

"Wilford," Ransley said in a curiously flat tone. He appeared about to say something else, but gave his head an odd twitch, as if flinging off some thought, and took a sip of his tea instead.

"Wilford," Thea confirmed, as if it had been a question. He'd said something similar, she remembered, when they were sorting out the chain of events that had resulted in Clarissa's inappropriate waltz. She wondered quite what Lord Wilford had done to get into Ransley's black books. He'd made a fuss about a dance with Lady Clarissa, of course, but no one had thought anything of that, it having been Wilford, after all. It was well known the poor man had his attic to let, and few members of the *ton* took him quite seriously. If Ransley was still angry with him over that, he would surely fly up into the boughs when he found out what the hapless fellow had done now. Thea swallowed, wishing she hadn't been left to pay the piper for something that had, after all, nothing to do with her, and continued. "It appears that Lord Wilford became confused after he picked the girls up in Picadilly, and took the most direct route here." She paused, but Ransley merely looked at her. "Which lies down St. James's Street."

Ransley returned his teacup to the saucer and set both cup and saucer on the table with a very precise care that Thea thought boded ill. She noticed that Lady Clarissa was darting him little looks out of the corner of her eye. He sat back in his chair and rubbed one hand down his face, then said, in an overly calm voice, "Am I to understand that Lord Wilford drove my ward down St. James's Street in an open carriage?"

"Yes, Your Grace," Thea said, matching her tone to his, "you are."

He closed his eyes briefly. "That's three," he said irrelevantly.

"Your Grace?"

His pale eyes pierced her. "That's three times Lord Wilford has conspired to damage Lady Clarissa's reputation." His lip curled unpleasantly when Thea could only stare at him, put all at sea by the unexpected accusation. "He has claimed Clarissa promised him a dance she did not, distracted your companion so that she would not stop Clarissa from dancing with a notorious rake, and now deliberately driven Clarissa down St. James's in the height of the afternoon," Ransley said, ticking the points off on his fingers as if she needed help in counting them. "In addition, he has been present at several of Clarissa's... less graceful moments, giving me to wonder if he's also been responsible for her inability to hold onto a glass for more than five minutes together before its contents end up on someone's clothing."

"But that..." Thea blurted, truly startled. All three of them were staring at him now, Lady Clarissa with a rather unattractively gaping mouth. "I don't think—"

"Neither do I. I know. I know some of the recent failings damaging Lady

Clarissa's reputation must be laid squarely at her door. And mine. But these others are clearly Wilford's doing."

Thea struggled mightily to gather her scattered thoughts. "While I do not doubt that Lady Clarissa is telling nothing but the truth when she says someone knocked her glass from her hand, and that someone has clearly been spreading malicious rumors, I truly don't think Lord Wilford is guilty of more than being a bit addlepated. I know him—"

"Yes," Ransley bit off, "you *know* him."

"—and while he's certainly bacon-brained," Thea continued, solely by virtue of the fact that her words had taken on a certain momentum; otherwise, she'd surely have stumbled at his sudden vitriol, "I've never known him to be mean-spirited. And you must admit, Your Grace, that the rumors and... and the waltz, assuming it could have been set up by some third party, are the work of someone both clever and malicious." Someone like Trenwick, though she'd never have guessed him to be so ill-natured.

"Doubtless you know him better than I," Ransley said coldly, appearing either not to have heard or to have instantly discounted her point about the intelligence necessary to encompass such a plan.

"As for driving down St. James's," Thea went on, resolutely ignoring the growing pain in her chest. She hadn't realized how far she'd let him inside her defenses until he resumed hostilities. "In my experience, Lord Wilford is more than capable of unthinkingly undertaking such an act, and he appeared most confused about the cause of Lady Clarissa's overset."

"I'm certain he did. And I am certain that you do, in fact, believe him innocent of any wrongdoing." Though the words were conciliatory, the iciness of his tone took all softness out of them. "It's natural that you should do so. He is, after all, one of your suitors. Lady Clarissa," Ransley went on without giving Thea a chance to respond, "we shall be going now." He stood and held out a hand to his ward, who instantly rose to join him, her eyes downcast. "Thank you for the tea, Miss Ravenshaw," he said formally.

"Wait," Thea said, her mind stumbling to catch up with events that seemed to be moving all too fast. She caught them at the door, having no idea whether he had in fact waited. She hoped she hadn't rushed at them — that would be entirely too unmannerly — though she was sure Mrs. Wellins would scold her for it once they were alone if she had. "Your Grace, I—"

"Go ahead to the carriage, Clarissa" he said. Clarissa nodded meekly, dipped a curtsey that appeared instinctive, and went out into the hall, where Thea saw her join her maid before Ransley softly closed the door. Much to her irritation, she found herself quailing at the impersonal courtesy of the expression he turned on her. "Miss Ravenshaw," he said formally, "thank you for your care of Lady Clarissa. However, your assistance is no longer needed."

"Surely this only proves that—"

"She needs a guardian? Yes, she does. Lady Clarissa needs someone wholeheartedly on her side. It is clear to me that you cannot be that person. So again, Miss Ravenshaw, I thank you for your assistance." He took her hand in his. He'd taken off his gloves when he came in, and she had never put any on — not intending to be "at home" for callers that afternoon — and the feel of his bare hand on hers was shocking, seeming to touch something far deeper than skin. "I own I have… greatly enjoyed your company and will miss it," he said, and was there a slight unsteadiness in his voice, or was that merely the beating of her pulse in her ears? He paused a moment, and the slight softness that had appeared around his mouth vanished. "However, that is now at an end. I will see to it that Lady Clarissa does not darken your door in future." He bowed over her hand — an inclination not just of head but shoulders, and far more than any duke owed a mere miss — and went out, leaving her gasping. Her hand had found its way to her heart, which thudded unevenly, not seeming able to separate the salute from the dismissal or know precisely how to feel about either.

She stared foolishly at the closed door, her world overset. Her heart wanted to sing at the words and the bow, sob at his mistrust and his departure. For the first time in her life, she understood what the poets meant when they talked of the glory and the pain of love, for she felt all three — glory and pain and love — and all so strongly, she could scarce tell them apart.

And the worst part of it was, she couldn't blame him for denying both this and her. There *was* someone acting against Lady Clarissa, and in protecting herself and not telling Ransley what she knew, Thea was also protecting Trenwick.

And for that, she ought to be shot.

* * *

Ransley's hand was warm in his glove. Warmer, he was sure, than the other hand. He forced himself to pay very careful attention to his driving, for otherwise, he would find himself again dwelling on how her hand had felt in his, cool and delicate and…

Dash it all! He took up the reins he had let slacken and gave them a bit of a slap to get the horse moving at a faster clip. One couldn't lollygag about in Town traffic if one didn't want to be run down, and he shouldn't be constantly letting his mind wander back to Miss Ravenshaw.

He'd only done what was needful. He'd already decided that Miss Ravenshaw was a distraction he could ill-afford, that for Clary's sake, he must cut the connection. And now he knew that she could not be relied upon to keep a level head about her when it came to Lord Wilford. And wasn't *that* a facer? There he was, thinking he'd had a close escape in separating himself from Miss Ravenshaw before his affections could become engaged, only to find that hearing her defend one of her suitors hurt quite as badly as breaking his arm had when he was a boy. So much for getting away heart-whole.

Damn the woman! Damn her for her unwillingness to see the harm in Wilford, for her gullibility, and for her connection to him, which Ransley was certain played somehow into the trouble he was causing Clary, though at the moment, he could not see quite how. Damn her for her stubbornness and her determination to help Clary, whether he wished to accept her assistance or not. And for her lustrous dark hair and statuesque beauty and vivid blue eyes, that a man might fall directly into before he even realized his danger—

"Uncle?" Clary said in a small voice.

"Yes?" He surfaced from under heavy seas and gave the reins another slap, not realizing until he did so that Clary had put her hand lightly on his forearm. He switched the reins to one hand and laid the other briefly over hers. "What is it, Clary?"

She let out a soft sigh, sounding relieved, making him feel unwarrantedly guilty for his distraction. The girl had flat disobeyed him, after all, and put herself in the situation Wilford took advantage of. She didn't deserve the damage to her reputation that was likely to cause, but she certainly deserved at least a touch of worry about his reaction to her behavior. "I'm sorry."

"Sorry you disobeyed me, or sorry about the result?" he asked wryly, being more direct than he would if they were in the presence of servants. They were alone at the moment, however, or as alone as one could be on the streets of London, which was to say nowhere they might be easily overheard. His cabriolet wasn't built to seat four, so he'd given his tiger some coin and directed him to hire a hackney and see the maid home.

"Both," she admitted, and he glanced over to see a small smile tipping the corner of her mouth. He found himself both irritated and relieved that she could smile about this — at least she was not likely to go into a decline over this latest disaster. "But you do see, don't you, why I had to go see Miss Ravenshaw?"

"Frankly, I don't."

"I needed someone to talk to."

"I see," he said, though he didn't. "And for some reason, I wouldn't do?"

She sighed again, this time as if she were quite as exasperated with him as he was with her. "There are just… there are some things a woman would prefer to talk over with other women."

That gave him pause. Less the sentiment than the fact that his little Clary saw herself as a woman. But then, wasn't that the whole point of bringing her out in Town — that she was an adult capable of making an adult attachment? Much as he tried, he couldn't bring himself to see it. However… "I can see we shall have to find you a proper companion."

"What do you mean? Miss Ravenshaw is a proper companion."

"No," he said heavily. "No, she is not."

"But—"

"Not that she isn't a perfectly acceptable chaperone," he hastened to add before she could think he meant anything improper. "But you need a companion wholly focused on you, and Miss Ravenshaw's attention lies… elsewhere." Much as it pained him to admit it.

Clary was silent for several minutes as they jogged through the late-afternoon traffic. Finally, she said, "Is this about Lord Wilford?" When he didn't answer, she said, with more perceptiveness than he'd given her credit for, "I don't believe she sees him as a suitor, like you said. In fact," she went on when he still did not speak, "she was really quite livid with him about... about today."

"I'm sure she was. But that is neither here nor there." No, what mattered was that Ransley couldn't keep his wits about him when he was in Miss Ravenshaw's presence, and he must do so, for Clary's sake. He'd failed to protect her sister, not realizing the dangers that threatened her. With Clary, he had had ample warning of the potential harm. Warning he would not ignore. "Whatever the reason, Miss Ravenshaw is often in Lord Wilford's company, and Wilford does not have your best interests at heart."

"Do you really think so?" She gave a little shiver and moved closer to him. "He didn't seem... He didn't seem to quite realize what he'd done wrong. I'm not even sure he meant to do it."

"Perhaps not," he allowed, not because he believed it but because he did not like to think of her shying at shadows, fearful that someone was out to do her harm. Even if someone was. She should not have reason to fear. And she wouldn't, going forward; he would see to that.

"And even if he did, he's not so much about Miss Ravenshaw as you think. Surely I can still continue to visit her and—"

"I think not."

"But—"

"No, Clarissa. It's not safe for you. In this, you must be guided by me." He was silent a moment while he tooled around a snarl of carriages and horses surrounding a wagon that had spilled its contents in the road. When it was safe to take his eyes off the road, he glanced over at Clary and winced at the stubborn set to her mouth. "We shall get you a proper companion and—"

"But I don't *want* a proper companion," Clary cried. "I don't want some Friday-faced old biddy who can curdle milk just by looking at it sideways and won't let me talk to anyone or look at anyone or have any fun—"

"Having *fun* is what got you into this."

"No," Clary snapped. "Having to sneak out just to go see Miss Ravenshaw is what got me into this."

"For God's sake, Clarissa!" Ransley hissed. He drew up outside his townhouse and, seeing that he was without his tiger, a footman dashed down the stairs to hold the horse. Ransley lowered his voice still further. "Even you must be able to see how close you are to putting yourself completely beyond the pale! Another mess like today's and I shall have to send you back to Tynesfield until the talk dies down. Assuming it's not already too late."

Clary looked at him, stricken, her eyes wide and brimming with tears. "Oh!" She jumped down from the carriage and dashed up the steps in an extremely unladylike manner, banging through the front door before Hailston could even get it open properly.

Aware of not only the footman at the horse's head but all the windows of the neighboring houses that overlooked his own, Ransley did not sigh and he did not put his head in his hands. He descended from the carriage, handing the reins over to the footman, and climbed the steps with a feeling very like that of a man walking up the hangman's scaffold.

Clary had already disappeared from the entryway, though it seemed to Ransley that the thunder of her feet upon the stairs still echoed from the walls. He went into the library and sat down in his chair before the cold hearth.

A moment later, Hailston entered. "Tea, Your Grace?" he asked, his voice as imperturbable as ever.

"There's nothing I want less," Ransley said, only just managing to keep his tone from being vicious. "Brandy."

"Yes, Your Grace." Hailston busied himself pouring the drink for Ransley, the fact that he filled the glass twice as full as he normally would the only indication he gave that he was aware of Ransley's mood. Not that he could possibly have missed it, or the cause for it, given Clary's demonstration of temper. He hardly needed even that, given that all Ransley's black moods of late could be traced to his ward.

Hailston handed Ransley the glass of brandy and stood for a moment, watching him drink, before clearing his throat and saying, "They're said to grow up eventually."

Ransley snorted. "Chance would be a fine thing," he said morosely, and drank his brandy slowly, staring into the black remains of the fire.

Chapter Thirteen

"WELL done," Mallinson told Wilford when he found him sitting by himself in the billiard room of Cocker's. It was early yet, and few of their set had made it to the club, or he would have been more circumspect. "I hear you drove the length of St. James's with Ransley's ward in your curricle."

"I, I did?" Wilford blinked quickly. "Oh! Oh, I suppose I did. No wonder the gel was crying."

"Indeed," Mallinson said, torn between amusement and annoyance that Wilford had somehow managed, without even trying, to do more harm to Lady Clarissa's reputation than Mallinson with all his scheming. "Come," he said, "play with me." He set about preparing the table.

Wilford didn't move. "I don't feel much like losing at billiards today."

"Then try to win for once, Dart," Mallinson said with blithe disregard for the likelihood of that happening. He was in the mood to win some money, and Wilford was just the man to oblige him. And indeed, when he finished setting up the table and handed Wilford a cue, the man took it and absent-mindedly put a gold coin in the betting tray on the sidetable, which he proceeded to lose quite definitively.

It wasn't hard to persuade him to wager again, and they continued to play, Mallinson raising the stakes with every game. They played without conversing, Mallinson lost in thought and Wilford lost in... well, whatever he used for brains. Mallinson didn't particularly care to know what precisely was so occupying the other man, though he nearly planted him a facer when Wilford bumbled into him when he was lining up a shot. However, as Wilford apologized and instantly conceded the game — the first one, in all the time they'd played, that he'd ever had a chance of actually winning, even before he fouled Mallinson's shot — Mallinson magnanimously forgave him.

He found playing billiards, especially when there was money to be won, enjoyable. Playing Wilford, and thereby making the winning of money a dead cert, was downright relaxing. At least *something* was going right.

His efforts to make Ransley leave London had, so far, been resoundingly unsuccessful. Due to an incident he could not have foreseen, his little trick with Trenwick had had no effect, and he didn't dare try it again. Whatever else might be said about Trenwick, there was no doubt that the man was awake on all suits and certainly smart enough not to risk dancing with Ransley's ward again. At least not under his nose. Lady Heatherton's appearance at the ball had thrown the cat decidedly in amongst the pigeons. In all likelihood, it had saved Trenwick from being called out by Ransley, and in so doing, had put paid to the best of Mallinson's plans so far. Even if neither of the men had managed to kill the other, there had been great odds of Ransley having to make a dash for the country, at least, if not the Continent, to escape the legal consequences of dueling. It had really been the most delightfully clever plan, and its failure had sent Mallinson into high dudgeon.

He ought, now, to have been celebrating either Ransley's departure from Town or his death. Instead, Lady Heatherton's outrageous behavior had scotched any chance of a duel, and everyone was so busy talking of it that no one had bothered to remember Lady Clarissa's scandalous waltz with Lord Trenwick. That they were also not interested in talking about Ransley standing up for the same dance with Miss Ravenshaw was small comfort.

In fact, the only thing to take any comfort in was the apparent cooling of relations between Ransley and the Ravenshaw woman. For the first time in weeks, they'd not been thick as thieves at every turning, and that was all to the good. However, as Mallinson had no idea what precisely had brought about that state of affairs, he did not think it safe to rely upon it. He absolutely must see to it that Ransley left Town entirely, with little likelihood of returning, and he was not certain just how he was going to bring that about.

"I'm sorry about your cousin," Wilford said suddenly, and Mallinson very nearly fouled.

He took a breath, lined up his shot again, and sank the ball before turning to Wilford and saying with, he felt, remarkable calm, "What cousin?"

"Lady Clarissa."

"Told you," Mallinson said, turning back to the table. "She's no relation of mine. Not directly. And what is it you're sorry about?"

"I shouldn't, I really think maybe I shouldn't…" He put his cue down and began pushing the, quite respectable by this time, pile of coins on the betting tray around with one finger.

"Shouldn't?" Mallinson asked impatiently, going to take the money away from Wilford before he had it all over the floor.

Wilford flashed him a quick, strained smile. And oh Lord, but Mallinson knew that face. Wilford had looked so just before he'd confessed all to the headmaster about the time he and Mallinson and several others had stolen the school carriages and raced them through the commons. Well, not all, precisely. Wilford was far too honorable to split on his friends, even when he'd decided that what they'd done was wrong, but he was also too stupid not to give the game, and all his fellows, away once he determined to confess. "Shouldn't have driven Lady Clarissa down St. James's, for one."

"Nonsense."

"No," Wilford said earnestly. "Really. It's one thing to spill her drink and, and, and…" He shook his head, and Mallinson couldn't tell if he was too embarrassed to mention the rest or simply couldn't remember what all he'd done. "But she didn't deserve that. And Miss Ravenshaw was angry with me," he added plaintively.

Recognizing that that was likely the real sticking point, Mallinson said, "But you didn't mean to do it, Dart. Surely Miss Ravenshaw knows that."

"I don't, I don't know. Perhaps." He brightened. "I could tell her I didn't do it on purpose. Not like the other things." He wheeled toward the door and Mallinson caught his arm.

"Perhaps you oughtn't mention the other things, Dart," he said carefully. If Wilford opened his books to Miss Ravenshaw, Mallinson was sunk. Wilford was too bloody noble to actually mention Mallinson's name when he was making a clean breast of things, but once he started talking, it wouldn't take much to make him slip up.

"Oh, but—"

"In fact, perhaps you oughtn't say anything at all about this to Miss Ravenshaw."

"But she—"

"*You* know and *I* know that she's clasped a viper to her bosom, but she still thinks well of Lady Clarissa, and she mightn't believe you when you tell her how lost to honor the chit really is."

"She is?" Wilford asked, nicely diverted down the path Mallinson laid before his feet.

"Of course she is, Dart. You saw how she was. The minute you distracted her chaperone's attention, she was off dancing with Trenwick, of all people." He put his arm around Wilford's shoulders and steered him to a chair. "Would a virtuous girl accept a dance with a man like Trenwick?"

"No," Wilford said slowly and a bit uncertainly. "But it was just a dance, Mallinson. It's not like she…" He hesitated, clearly wracking whatever passed for brains for something scandalous enough, "…snuck off down the Dark Walk at Vauxhall Gardens with him."

Now there was a thought. Mallinson investigated it quickly from every angle. Yes, that might suit very well indeed. "Are you quite certain she hasn't?" he asked.

Wilford blinked quickly at him. "I, I haven't heard anything…"

"Well, the chit *can* be rather subtle. Though you wouldn't think it to look at her," he added wryly. "But as you know, I'm much about the Ransley townhouse these days," he said, and it was not quite a lie, for he'd had to spend several deadly dull hours talking estate business with the duke, "and I overheard the chit making plans to meet Trenwick there tomorrow night." It was a risk, for he might not be able to arrange things that quickly. But then, Wilford would hardly notice if it came off the following day instead, and if he did, Mallinson doubted he'd have much trouble convincing the man he was remembering wrong.

"Lud!" Wilford exclaimed. "It's a masquerade tomorrow! Mallinson, you have to—"

"I've already told the duke all I know of the girl's plans," Mallinson said, and that wasn't a lie either, for there wasn't a plan. Yet. He shrugged fatalistically. "I don't know that he's going to do aught about it. I told you," he reminded Wilford, "he dotes on the girl and makes himself willfully blind to her failings."

"But this! Even a demirep would think twice about something so bold."

"Quite. So you see, it's as well you've been trying to show Miss Ravenshaw that the girl is lost to all propriety. If they continue to be seen together in the social whirl, who knows how badly the connection might damage Miss Ravenshaw's reputation."

"Oh. I, I hadn't thought of that." He sat back in his chair, blinking and looking, for him, thoughtful.

Mallinson left him to it. He had much to do.

* * *

"Is His Grace in?" he asked, handing his hat and gloves to the sour-faced old butler.

"He is not, Mr. Mallinson," the butler responded, as Mallinson had known he would. Though he'd remarked little Ransley had said in their far-too-lengthy discussion of estate business, he'd certainly picked up on the fact that the duke planned a trip to Tattersall's that afternoon, for he found it highly unfair that Ransley should speak of buying a horse as other men talked of buying a hat. It had been a simple matter to loiter in some out of the way place nearby and wait for the man to leave. The hardest part had been rousting himself out of bed before noon to be sure of seeing the man go, especially having foregone his usual night at the tables to spend much of the previous night going from one social event to the next looking for Ransley and his ward, without any luck. Either Ransley'd kept the chit home, or they'd been at some entertainment whose host was too top-lofty to invite a mere mister.

"How unfortunate," Mallinson said, contriving to look downcast. "Perhaps Lady Clarissa?" He had been careful from the first to speak a bit loudly so that he would not have to obviously raise his voice at this stage.

For, as he expected, the butler said repressively, "She is not at home to callers, sir."

Scarce had the words left the butler's mouth before the lady in question was opening the door of the morning room, from which she had clearly heard every word.

"Mr. Mallinson," she cried with every sign of actually being pleased to see him, which was something of a surprise — he'd expected her to see him out of curiosity, but not with this much interest. "Do come in. You're just in time for tea. Hailston, if you would, please."

It was not a question, and the old butler showed him in with a face like he'd been sucking on lemons. Lady Clarissa took Mallinson's arm and quite tugged him into the morning room. He waited until the butler had closed the door to give her his most engaging smile. "What's about, coz?" As much as it suited him to discourage any thought of a family connection when speaking with others, it suited him even more to play it up here.

"Oh, you *have* come in good time, Mr. Mallinson. My uncle is being a perfect beast and I'm in sore need of a friend."

"You have one in me," Mallinson assured her comfortably and settled in the chair next to her, glancing about the pleasant, airy room to hide the gleam of triumph in his eyes. He'd believed, after tipping the butterboat on each occasion upon which he saw her, that he would find her more willing to listen to him than not, but hadn't counted on her looking on him as some kind of confidant. What a lovely surprise. It would make things all the easier.

It was really quite difficult to contain his glee as Lady Clarissa immediately set about emptying her budget to him. He adopted a serious expression to prevent himself from smiling, which was just the right tactic, for the more downcast his response to her tale of woe, the more she felt him on her side and the more freely she talked. Ransley and Miss Ravenshaw were on the outs, Clarissa had been forbidden to visit the woman, and Ransley had indeed kept Clarissa home the previous night. A decision which had made her absolutely livid and led to a flaming row with Ransley, which in turn led to Clarissa having been sent off with only half her supper in her belly. Mallinson found himself amazed that anyone would dare to argue with Ransley; perhaps he had not bent the truth as far as he'd thought when he told Wilford that Ransley doted on his ward. Lady Clarissa's half-supper had clearly been augmented by a full portion of anger, the girl having hoped to see Lord Trenwick at the Duchess of Elward's rout. She was, it appeared, quite taken with the man, and especially his risking his life in defense of Lady Heatherton's virtue by dueling with her husband. Mallinson was hard put not to smile at *that* romantic drivel. If it was actually Trenwick who met Heatherton upon the field of honor and killed him, which was by no means certain, everyone involved having kept the affair very quiet to avoid the legal consequences, it was far more likely to be about Lord Heatherton's unpaid gambling debts than anything to do with Lady Heatherton.

Ultimately, it was no difficulty at all to bring the conversation around to the masked Venetian Ball taking place that very night at Vauxhall Pleasure Gardens.

A masquerade the young lady had naturally heard about and even more naturally wished to attend.

"But the way Uncle Ransley is acting, there's no chance of him taking me," Lady Clarissa said on a falling sigh. Really, the chit ought to take up acting.

"Perhaps you might go in any case," Mallinson suggested lightly, making a show of being more focused on his tea than his comment.

"Oh! But I couldn't!" There was a pause, during which Mallinson drank his tea and refrained from speaking. After several silent moments, Lady Clarissa said, "How could I?" And it might have been another statement that such a thing was impossible, had not her tone walked it very near to a request for details.

Mallinson acted as if she could not possibly have intended any meaning but the second. "You need only pretend to have the headache and retire early to your room. That way, you will have an excuse for not going to any entertainments the duke's planning to attend, or for being out from under his eyes, if he means to keep you home again. Then you will be free to go to the masquerade. I am quite certain, if pressed, that you will find you know a way to slip out of the house without being seen," he said with a teasing air.

"I don't know what you mean," Clarissa said, her virtuous tone quite at odds with her smile. Really, if he did not despise her upon principle, he might actually grow to like the conniving little baggage. "But... I was so angry at Uncle Ransley for not letting me go out yesterday, will he truly believe it when I find it necessary to cry off tonight?"

"He'll believe it all the more. Knowing how much you wished to do the social whirl yesterday, he'll know only the most putrid headache could prevent you from attending tonight." Or he'd think the chit was sulking. Either way, the ruse would serve.

"But..." Lady Clarissa appeared suddenly to realize that they were in the middle of the morning room and scooted her chair closer to his so that she might ask in a much-lower voice, "but I have no costume for the masquerade, and no chaperone, and how am I to get there?"

"And why wouldn't your very own cousin be chaperone enough?" Mallinson asked, pretending mild offense at being discounted. He then bent his head close to hers and whispered conspiratorially, "You must wait until nine and then leave the house unobserved."

"So late?"

"It will be easier to depart unobserved," Mallinson said. That would ensure that she'd be in Vauxhall after the *beau monde* had mostly retreated to their supper boxes, leaving the darkened pathways to wild young men, rakes, and the demimonde. "I'll be in my carriage, waiting for you at the end of the lane with a domino and mask for you to wear. Then you shall go off to the masquerade and no one but you and I will know you were there. But," he added, his tone serious, for it was a matter of the utmost importance, "you must promise to never tell

Ransley my role in this. Should it come out, I'm mortally afraid he would shoot me dead."

"No!" Lady Clarissa exclaimed, squeezing his hand fervently. "No, I should never whisper a word to anyone!"

"Good. Nine tonight; we are agreed?"

For a moment, he thought Lady Clarissa was going to waver, for she looked as if she were having doubts about the advisability of the scheme. Mallinson was about to remind her of Ransley's infamous treatment of her when it appeared she had reminded herself of it, for her lips firmed up and she nodded resolutely.

"Very well then." Mallinson rose and bowed to her. "I must take my leave of you then, Lady Clarissa. I have much to arrange." He straightened up and winked at her, making her blush, and somehow manage to restrain his smile until he was back out on the street.

Delightful, indeed.

He started down the street, scarcely looking at where he was going, making his plans as he walked. He needed to hire a carriage and rent a couple of dominos and masks. No, perhaps it would be best to buy the costumes outright, so there would be no chance of being connected in any way with the masquerade. He could buy the costumes without having to give his name. And the carriage could be hired from a little jobber he knew who cared not a whit for the name of his employer so long as he was paid in advance. This was going to take a bit of blunt. Good thing he'd won enough from Wilford to bankroll the thing.

He crossed the street, a little sweep clearing the mud and horse dung away before him, and walked on, ignoring the boy's shout at not being tossed a coin. Greedy little beggar.

The masquerade would be perfect. It was not quite the done thing, though there would be members enough of the respectable set there. Masks offered a freedom from constraint that few could resist, and provided an excuse — not that much of the *ton* needed it, hypocritical prating prigs that they were — for licentious behavior. And then there were the members of the lower classes who attended, for anyone with the price of admission could come. Those of good repute did visit Vauxhall Gardens and did attend masquerades there, but they were careful to keep to their own kind. And if Lady Clarissa kept near the supper boxes and the orchestra building, she might even escape ruin, though only if no one guessed she was there without chaperone or guardian. Mallinson meant to see that she did not.

It was not enough merely to get Lady Clarissa to the masquerade. He must needs ensure that her presence — unescorted and cavorting with the most unseemly of the attendees — became known. Thus, a costume for himself. No, two. One to escort her in and another for after he'd slipped away from her. He would lose himself in the revelers, change his domino and mask, pick his moment, and publicly unmask her. It meant additional expense, not only in the purchase of an extra costume but in the payment of the entrance fee — once for

Lady Clarissa and twice for himself. He would have to go in earlier in the evening and secret his costume in some dark corner. But it would be worth it.

Ransley would have no choice but to dash for the country with his ruined ward in tow. This was even better than his previous efforts. Those, he saw now, had been far too cautious, seeking only to send Ransley packing for the Season. But if he only made Lady Clarissa into a nine days' wonder, the duke would surely be back next Season, and Mallinson would have to go through it all again. No, he had to ensure that Ransley remained at Tynesfield for good. With any luck, this scandal would ruin Clarissa so completely that she would never get another Season. Ransley would have to marry her off quietly in the country to some bumbling squire who either hadn't heard the *on dits* or would overlook the scandal to take the niece of a duke, even if she was soiled goods.

Mallinson smiled and walked on.

Chapter Fourteen

"OH!" Clary said when she got her first look at Vauxhall Gardens, a fantasy of colonnades and archways, lush gardens and secluded arbors. At first, she tried to stop herself craning her neck to take in all the sights, though she wanted to stare about like the veriest country miss. It was only when she quailed as she passed up along The Grove between the supper boxes, fearful that someone might see her and carry word back to her uncle, that she remembered she was costumed and masked and, like everyone else there, unidentifiable. From that point, she didn't hesitate to look.

It was a fine, clear night, and the stars in the heavens seemed reflected in the trees of Vauxhall. There must have been thousands of lanterns, colored lights and mirrored lights and lights shaped like stars, all glowing amongst the trees, shining down upon the gravel walks.

And the *people*. Clary had thought herself quite jaded by the sad crush that was the hallmark of a truly popular event, but she had never, she thought, seen so many people in one place. They crowded into the Grand Walk, flitted back and forth between the supper boxes, and gathered around the orchestra building to dance as if they would never dance again. There were dominoes in every color with masks to match, some unadorned and some that made the mask and domino that Mallinson had brought her, bright blue with silver trim, seem positively dowdy by comparison. There were revelers in dress no different than would grace any ballroom (but for the masks) and others in costumes from the simple to the outlandish. Kings and queens, Romans and Harlequins, and some that defied all description.

There was music and laughter and gaiety, and oh, she didn't know what she wanted to do first.

"One moment," Mallinson said low in her ear and disengaged her hand from his arm. He darted into the crowd and reappeared before she could become worried by his desertion with two glasses in his hands. Clary was shocked to realize he'd snatched them from the table in one of the supper boxes, but the gentlemen and women around the table were laughing as if it was great fun, and Clary reminded herself that she was at Vauxhall — at a *masquerade* at Vauxhall — and she was no longer some schoolroom miss to be shocked at such things. "Here," Mallinson said, handing her one of the glasses.

She took a sip and gasped as it burned in her throat. "What is it?!"

"Arrack punch," he said and swallowed from his glass. His eyes glittered at her from behind his brilliant green mask, daring her to drink again.

So she did. It burned less this time, though she was not quite sure she liked the taste. Mallinson offered her his elbow, still keeping his glass in the other hand, and she tucked her hand around his arm, sipping sparingly from her glass as they strolled and trying to somehow take everything in at once.

The orchestra struck up a waltz, and Mallinson laughed, swinging her around into position and putting his hand at the small of her back. Her hand was on his shoulder and each of them still had their glass of arrack punch in the other hand. Clary became quite giddy with the turns and the music, loving the expansive feeling that filled her chest. No one could recognize her here, no one could scold her for some misstep or stare at her as if she'd run wild given just a moment's freedom, or blame her for anything she did. She was free.

Eventually, she tired of dancing, and Mallinson seemed to know it almost before she did, moving them slowly toward the edge of the crowd. He took her glass from her — when had she drained it? — set it and his on the table in another supper box, and once more tucked her hand into the crook of his arm. They wandered slowly down one of the walks, lanterns winking at them from high within the branches of the trees. There was a crush of people filling the walk, and Clary wished them all to perdition as fervently as she adored the wonderful variety they presented. In the crush, she could only catch glimpses of the follies and arbors tucked here and there about the place, and she could hear a waterfall somewhere that she couldn't see.

She tightened her hand on Mallinson's arm. She rather liked him, though his eyes were a bit too small, and he sometimes held her hand overlong when he greeted her. And she knew that her uncle didn't particularly care for him — it was never too difficult to tell when Ransley had taken someone into dislike — but at the moment, that was more a mark in his favor than otherwise. Remembering how Uncle Ransley had treated her of late, she scowled and clung all the closer to Mallinson.

She wasn't some child, needing to be locked in the nursery to keep her out of trouble. She needed someone to stand by her and help her out — like Miss Ravenshaw did — not scold her and order her about. And then to forbid her to see Miss Ravenshaw!

Clary stamped her foot, and only then realized they'd stopped walking. They were at the edge of another clearing, where a smaller orchestra played and yet more people danced. It was a bit less crowded here, and she felt like she could breathe more freely. She hummed and swayed to the music and wondered if Lord Trenwick was there. She'd like to waltz with him again when she wouldn't get into trouble for it. Uncle Ransley had said he was a rake, but he'd been acting ridiculously stuffy lately, and Clary suspected he'd simply taken the poor man into dislike. Just like Mr. Mallinson, and with as little reason. Trenwick hadn't acted at all like she thought rakes must act. He'd been nothing but courteous to her, more so than some of the "suitable" men she'd been introduced to. He hadn't looked her over like she was the prize cow at the village fair, but had chatted and flirted gently and made her feel so comfortable with him that she hadn't found herself tongue-tied even once. She hoped he was at Vauxhall. Perhaps she'd already seen him and didn't even know it. It must be nearly impossible to find anyone in this throng, all masked and costumed.

The costumes here, she noticed as her eyes followed the dancers, were lighter and freer. Some of the men went about in only their shirtsleeves, without coat or waistcoat or cravat, and there was something disturbingly vulnerable about their bare throats. Some of the ladies' skirts were slit partway up the side, their bodices immodestly low, and some… She wasn't entirely certain some of the women were wearing more than a shift under their dominoes, which clung to their bodies as if the silk had been dampened.

Realizing she was staring, Clary dragged her eyes away. She turned to her companion, and found him gone.

* * *

Thea rubbed her temples and wished she hadn't come out. She dearly loved the opera and had been engaged to attend with Lord Wilford for several weeks now, but she ought to have cried off, however much it would have been bad form to do so at the last moment.

She had wanted to stay at home with her aunt, but that lady had pushed Thea to go until she felt she had no choice. Mrs. Wellins had taken to her room after receiving a letter from her son's superior on the Peninsula. Gabriel had not returned from a recent scouting mission and it was unknown whether he was alive, dead, or captured. The least Thea felt she ought to do was stay with her aunt at such a time, but Mrs. Wellins had been adamant that she did not require Thea's company and that Thea should not, under any circumstances, send her regrets to Lord Wilford.

Thea had finally complied, not least because she was no longer entirely certain that her motives were pure. She'd believed that she was arguing the point because she wished to companion and support her aunt during so horribly trying a time, but had begun to worry that Mrs. Wellins' obliquely worded accusation that she was avoiding Wilford might have some truth to it. While she still did not believe Lord Wilford so ill-natured as to be the author of Lady Clarissa's misfortunes, she could not seem to stop herself from blaming him for being the cause of her estrangement from Ransley, albeit unknowingly so.

Still, Mrs. Wellins had insisted that Thea should go, she did adore the opera, and she had made promises to Lord Wilford. Therefore, attend she must.

It was surely not the fault of the reputedly excellent soprano that every trill seemed to arrow straight through Thea's brain, and by the break, she was in desperate need of an escape.

Lord Wilford had been most solicitous of her once she made her weakness known, and had gone away instantly to have someone summon his carriage. Thus it was that, well before the audience could be quieted down enough to begin the second act, Thea found herself being jogged about in Wilford's carriage on the way back to her house, her temples throbbing in time with the horses' hooves. She had neither maid nor companion, but her head hurt so dreadfully she couldn't worry herself over whatever Wilford, or any member of the *ton* that chanced to see her in a closed carriage with him, might think.

"Thank you, Lord Wilford, for escorting me home," Thea said, offering him a wan smile. "I'm sorry to so disarrange your evening."

"Oh, no trouble, no trouble at all. That caterwauling would give anyone the headache. Can't think why people like it," Wilford said, looking earnestly at her.

"If you do not like opera, why do you have a box?"

He looked surprised. "Everyone has one. Everyone who is anyone, anyway."

Of course. Like most of the *ton*, Wilford only attended the opera to see and be seen. Ah well, it wasn't like she'd truly expected him to have an appreciation of it.

Wilford shuffled his high-crowned beaver around in his hands, running the brim through his fingers. He'd nearly dropped it twice and seemed, on the whole, more nervous than usual. She'd thought Wilford too unaware of himself to be much inclined toward nerves, and it was disarranging to have him acting so. She rather thought his fidgeting had a great deal to do with the state of her own nerves tonight. She dearly hoped he wasn't working himself up to propose to her again.

"I really am, am most sorry you're unwell, Miss Ravenshaw."

"Thank you, Lord Wilford. I shall be well soon enough, thanks to your kindness in seeing me home."

He beamed for a moment, but in the next, the streetlamps that shone through the carriage windows showed his face drawn into quite the most serious expression she'd ever seen on him. "I hope, Miss Ravenshaw… I hope you know in how high esteem I hold you. You are all that is proper and, and gracious, and I—"

"Thank you, Lord Wilford," Thea interrupted him with a wince. He'd started off tentatively, but as he went on, his words picked up speed like a runaway train. Perhaps she could derail him? It would be too bad to have to deny him yet again. But Wilford kept on as if he hadn't heard.

"—I'm sure you know that I want only the best for you. Which, which is why I simply have to say—"

"Lord Wilford."

"—that I really think you ought—"

"Lord Wilford!"

"—not spend so much time with that chit." He took in a sudden breath, having been left nearly gasping by his plunging speech. "Yes?" he said, only then realizing that she'd been trying to speak to him.

Thea gaped at him. She ran his words back through her mind. No. No, she was quite certain they still made no sense. "Lord Wilford, perhaps you would care to repeat the last part of that?"

He blinked. Their carriage was momentarily stopped by some kind of traffic obstruction, and the light of a nearby streetlamp shone full on his face. He looked blank, and she wondered what precisely was going on behind that vacuous façade.

"You shouldn't spend so much time with that chit," he said when she'd nearly given up hope of getting an answer. "It's, it's not, not good for your, for your reputation."

Lord, she'd never heard him stutter so! He capped off the performance by dropping his hat onto the floor of the carriage between them. In reaching for it, his arm brushed her skirt, and she feared he was going to work himself into a fit, he stuttered so badly in apologizing.

"Quite all right," she said in the hopes of calming him. "Would I be correct in assuming that you're referring to Lady Clarissa?"

"Of course! I haven't seen you giving the favor of your, of your regard to any other member of the muslin company."

She was reduced to gaping at him again. This time, he appeared to actually notice.

"My, my apologies, Miss Ravenshaw!" he said abjectly. "I don't know what came over me. I shouldn't, I shouldn't have—"

"Used such a word to refer to Lady Clarissa," Thea reproved sternly. Good God! If Ransley heard him say so, he'd call him out for sure. And if anyone else did... "Honestly, Lord Wilford! It's unworthy of her *and* you. You could do permanent damage to the girl's reputation." She wondered if she'd been mistaken in him — a man who could call a girl like Clarissa little better than a prostitute might well be capable of extreme spite.

"No more than she's done to it herself," he surprised her by answering, an almost militant gleam in his eye. She wondered what the deuce Lady Clarissa could have done to Lord Wilford to make him so determined to think the very worst of her. "Even now, she's disporting herself at Vauxhall Gardens like the veriest barque of frailty."

"What in the world could possibly make you think such a thing?"

"Have it on good faith," Wilford maintained stubbornly. "Gel's far too coming, anyone could have told you that. Even though she's the niece of a duke. Miss Ravenshaw," he possessed himself of her hand, over which he looked earnestly at her, "you really, you really must protect yourself. I know you've done your best for the chit. A-and what does the ungrateful baggage do? Go off to a masquerade with Trenwick, of all people!"

"Trenwick," Thea said, her heart sinking within her. While she wouldn't trust Wilford not to be all about in his head where news of any importance was concerned, this had to be taken far more seriously if Trenwick were truly involved. She grasped Wilford's hand back, so startling him that he gave a little jerk. "You said she was with Trenwick? At the masquerade at Vauxhall Gardens tonight?"

"Yes. Yes, she—"

"Where did you hear this? Who else knows of it?" Pray God it wasn't widely known. They might yet keep Clarissa from ruin.

"I expect Trenwick does. For one." Wilford smiled with all the naïve pleasure of a child carrying off some witticism.

"Have your coachman take us to Grosvenor Square. To the Duke of Ransley," Thea directed urgently. "Oh, immediately, Lord Wilford. The girl's very future depends on it!"

Wilford's hand came up and he rapped upon the roof of the carriage with his cane, though his expression was the next door neighbor to confused, quite as if his body was acting directly on her orders without consulting his brain. In response, the coachman opened the trap in the roof and peered in.

"Grosvenor Square," Thea said when Wilford only blinked at the man. "Ransley House."

"Right you are, m'lady," the coachman said, touching the brim of his hat. The trap closed with a bang, and after a moment, she could feel the vehicle turn a corner.

"You must tell the duke everything you know," Thea told Wilford.

"A-are you quite certain he doesn't know already?"

"He should scarcely have allowed her to leave her room, did he know anything of this."

"If you say so," Wilford said doubtfully. They sat for a moment in silence, Thea fretting and Wilford frowning. He broke his silence to say, "I rather think the duke does not care for me."

It was said inconsequentially, almost as if it were the first thing that came to mind when he thought of Ransley and had nothing to do with the present circumstances. However, it brought Thea's eyes and her mind back to her companion and precisely what she was taking him to do. To say that Ransley didn't care for Wilford was a severe understatement. In fact, if they appeared on his doorstep with this story, and if it turned out to be true and Lady Clarissa not with her uncle (and Thea dearly hoped to find them either both at home or both out), it was not outside the realm of possibility that Ransley might call Wilford out, believing him to be responsible for Lady Clarissa's misfortunes.

"Upon second thought, Lord Wilford," she said quickly, "I think you could do Lady Clarissa, and myself," she added when he looked mutinous, "a greater service by traveling directly to Vauxhall Gardens and commencing a search for her. I shall inform the Duke of Ransley and bring him to Vauxhall."

"Miss Ravenshaw! That's not, I don't think that's—"

"It's the best plan," Thea said bracingly. "The duke has to be informed, but the search for his niece must not be delayed. I trust you to undertake it with all due discretion," she said with more hope than certainty. She must have sounded sufficiently convinced, for he sat a little straighter and rapped on the roof with his cane again.

"Pull over here, Coachman," he directed when the man opened the trap. The coachman complied as quickly as he could, but it was still several minutes before they had inched out of the flow of traffic. Thea had occasion to be grateful for her erstwhile headache — now vanished into a surfeit of nervous energy — for they were at least not being swept along by the flood of carriages carrying the *ton* home after a full night of entertainments. "Go wherever Miss Ravenshaw directs you," Wilford said to his coachman, who had kept the trap up to receive further instructions.

"Yes, m'lord," the man said.

Wilford made as if to step out of the carriage and paused with one foot on the step. "But how shall I—"

"You must hire a hackney, Lord Wilford, and have it take you to Vauxhall. The duke and I will follow as close as we may and find you once we get there."

"But you, you shouldn't, with Ransley, and—"

"There isn't a moment to lose in arguing," Thea said firmly. "Please, Lord Wilford, do me this service."

"Of course," he said. Stepping finally out of the carriage, he bowed to her from the street and closed the carriage door.

"Ransley. Grosvenor," Thea said firmly to the waiting coachman. He touched his hat brim and started working his way back into the flow of traffic again.

Thea sat back against the squabs and breathed a sigh of relief at narrowly escaping a confrontation between Wilford and Ransley. It was only then that she fully realized that she, now, would have to carry the whole story to Ransley, and likely bear the brunt of his bad temper.

"Oh heavens!"

Chapter Fifteen

"I'M here to see His Grace," she told the butler firmly when he opened the door.

He looked at her, then behind her, only to see she had no companion, nothing but the carriage waiting on the street, the horses stamping restlessly. His lips slightly pursed, clearly as near an expression of disapproval as he'd allow to break his impassive mien, he looked back at her.

"Please," she added, feeling humiliated and desperate. If Lady Clarissa was *not* in need of rescue, she would box Lord Wilford's ears when next she saw him.

"Of course, madam," he said, and stood back from the door to let her in.

"Miss Ravenshaw," she said, managing to hide her relief only with the most rigorous effort.

"This way, Miss Ravenshaw." He appeared to unbend slightly, making her wonder what was said of her in the servants' quarters of this house and whether the gossip came by way of Lady Clarissa's maid or Ransley's valet. He showed her into a sumptuous drawing room and bowed slightly. "I'll let His Grace know you're here."

"Thank you."

There was a fire in the hearth, and Thea went over to warm herself at it, feeling unaccountably chilled, though she was still wearing her wrap, which the butler had not offered to take. She tried to think through what to tell Ransley, but the words kept jumbling in her head. She was no closer to knowing how she was going to broach the subject when he walked through the drawing room door. He had clearly not been out to any formal entertainment, for he was wearing Hessian boots, buff trousers and a coat of blue superfine that lent color to his eyes.

"Miss Ravenshaw," he exclaimed, coming directly to her and taking her hands. "What's happened? What emergency has brought you to my doorstep?"

His hands were bare, and Thea wished she'd taken off her gloves, so that she might feel his skin on hers.

"We haven't time for explanations. Is Lady Clarissa at home?"

"Of course she—" But her urgency drew him up short, and without looking away from her, he said, "Hailston, send for Lady Clarissa."

"Yes, Your Grace," the butler said, startling Thea, as she hadn't realized he was still in the doorway.

"What is it you think's happened?" Ransley asked when the butler had left.

Realizing, suddenly, their position, Thea reluctantly drew her hands from his and stepped back, trying to regain some of her equanimity by shifting away from his disturbing nearness. "Let us first see about Lady Clarissa," she temporized. If the girl was at home, and pray heaven she was, then Thea need not get into the sordid details. She would just make her apologies and, she realized, still have to go to Vauxhall. For then she would need to find Lord Wilford and convince him of his error before he spread the rumor yet farther. She wished now that she'd brought him with her. For all that she thought Ransley's reaction chancy at best if Wilford was right, if he was wrong, there was nothing more suited to scotching his misapprehension than seeing Lady Clarissa in the duke's drawing room.

Ransley looked at her oddly, but appeared willing to be directed by her, for he did not pursue the matter, but only stood before the fire looking at her. She found the intensity of his eyes with the glow of the fire reflecting in them even more disturbing than his nearness. When he broke the silence after several minutes, she very nearly jumped.

"Miss Ravenshaw—" But she was not to know what he meant to say, for the butler returned just then with a face like a tombstone. "Yes, Hailston?"

"I regret to say," Hailston started, then paused as if gathering his courage. "I regret to say that Lady Clarissa is not in the house."

"Are you sure— No," Ransley answered himself, "of course you are. Miss Ravenshaw, would you care to explain?"

Whatever softness had been in his face a moment ago was gone. Thea took in a quick, stifled breath and began. She'd not managed more than a dozen words before Ransley swore shockingly and strode from the room. She exchanged a startled glance with the butler, who was so bowled over as to actually look shocked. As if possessed of one mind, the two of them followed the duke. They found him in the library. It was clearly where he'd been spending his evening, for there was a fire in the hearth and a book and glass on a table by one of the chairs. Ransley was at the desk with a pistol and other accouterments laid out before him.

He glanced up briefly when Thea and the butler entered, said, "My greatcoat, Hailston," to the butler, and then turned his eyes, which were flat and cold, on Thea. "Continue, Miss Ravenshaw."

"Oh, but—" Thea said, unable to draw her eyes from the pistol, which his hands were preparing with steady efficiency.

"Continue," he grated in a voice like an avalanche.

"He, it…" Thea stopped, took a deep breath, and gathered herself. "It appears that Lord Wilford believes she was going there to meet with Lord Trenwick. I don't know—"

"Wilford. And Trenwick." His voice was as flat and cold as his eyes.

"I don't know," Thea made herself continue, "that Wilford has the right of it, nor where he heard that they were together, but came here immediately to find out if Lady Clarissa was home safe and offer my assistance if she was not."

"Thank you." Ransley had finished loading the pistol and now stood with it and headed for the door. "You have done enough."

"On the contrary!" Thea followed him back out into the hall, where Hailston waited with the duke's greatcoat and beaver hat.

"Your wallet, sir," the butler said, handing it to Ransley the moment he had him in his greatcoat and before the duke even had his hat on. "I took the liberty of retrieving it."

"Thank you." Ransley put the wallet and pistol in one of the capacious pockets of his greatcoat with one hand and his hat on his head with the other.

"I have a carriage waiting," Thea said, feeling that the situation was running away with her. That earned her a measuring look. "Having another woman along will lend Lady Clarissa added respectability once you find her," Thea said, moving swiftly toward the door. She was glad now that the butler hadn't offered to take her wrap, for it meant she could hurry outside and the duke had perforce to follow her. She had no intention of permitting him to leave her behind.

"Isn't this—?" Ransley said when he saw Wilford's carriage with its coat of arms.

"We haven't time; get in! Vauxhall," she told the coachman. "As quickly as you can." She opened the door, reasonably certain that Ransley would hand her in if he did not have overlong to think on the matter. And so he did, and then followed her inside, looking bemused.

The coachman, taking Thea at her word, sprang the horses the moment the door was closed, throwing her against Ransley's strong chest. He caught her about the waist and set her back upon the seat, bracing her until she managed to grasp one of the straps. His hands were strong and hot through her wrap and dress, and she realized when he drew back that his butler had forgotten to give him his gloves. She felt warmth rise into her cheeks to match the heat that his fingers had left upon her waist.

"And where is Lord Wilford?" Ransley asked after she had stared helplessly at him for several moments.

"I sent him ahead in a hackney to begin the search for Lady Clarissa."

"You sent him…" Though his lips were pressed tight and bracketed with lines of concern, a bark of laughter escaped him. "And if he is the cause of all this? As well send the fox to guard the henhouse."

"Were he responsible," Thea said carefully, "I do not think he would tell me about it while there was still time to save Lady Clarissa."

"Perhaps," Ransley allowed, his mouth set in a grim line. Silence grew between them, filling the carriage until Thea thought she might scream at the tension. She knew he was fretting and could not keep from fretting herself. Clarissa was a ninnyhammer to even think of doing what she'd done, but she did not deserve this disaster. Thea found herself watching Ransley's face in the play of lamplight, first picked out in high relief, then thrown into darkness. He was looking out the window, and she jumped when he spoke. "You believe this situation can still be retrieved?"

Dear God! Was Ransley, of all people, looking to *her* for reassurance? "I think…" She hesitated and found herself reaching out to lay her hand over his. "I think it may yet not be too late. And… and if it is too late for her reputation, we may still be in time to rescue—"

"Her," Ransley finished. He turned his hand into her clasp, and it was an entirely different thing than it had been with Wilford. It was like holding a small space of hope between their two palms. "Yes," he went on. "Clary is far more than merely her reputation. The girl is… a handful." Lamplight shone off his quick smile. "But she is my niece," he said simply.

"She can have no better guardian."

Sharp laughter barked from him again. "There are those who have cause to doubt that. Myself included."

"She can have no guardian that would love her more," Thea said staunchly.

"Aye." He sighed. "I only wish that were enough."

There was nothing more Thea felt able to say, so she only squeezed his hand and did not complain when his grip tightened with each passing minute. By the time they began to slow near the gates to Vauxhall, she could no longer feel her fingers, so tightly did his hand cling to hers.

"Wait here," Ransley ordered, and leapt out before the carriage had quite come to a halt.

Startled, Thea did as she was told… for about half a minute. Then she realized that he was, in his usual high-handed way, leaving her behind. "The devil I will!" she said and began to climb out of the carriage.

The lack of a shocked gasp and stern admonition for swearing reminded her forcefully that she was alone, without the presence of Mrs. Wellins to lend her respectability. It came to her, so suddenly she missed the carriage step and nearly fell, that in her rush to save Lady Clarissa from being discovered alone at Vauxhall with a man not related to her, Thea was now alone at Vauxhall with a man not related to her. Her heart pounding, both at the realization and her misstep, she clung to the carriage door even after she had gingerly felt her way down to solid ground.

"Stop being such a ninny," she scolded under her breath, and forced herself to let go of the door and straighten her shoulders. She was there because Lady

Clarissa would soon find herself in dire straits, if she was not already, and because Trenwick's involvement in this disaster must be laid squarely at Thea's door. If she faced consequences for this, it was no more than she deserved. Thea was strong; she would survive.

"Are you all right, m'lady?" the coachman asked from his perch.

"Quite," she assured him and herself. "Please remain here until the duke and I return."

"'Fraid I can't." He gestured at the jam of carriages in the street. "I'll be rousted if I try to stay."

"Then come back around every twenty minutes or so."

"And if Lord Wilford hails me?" he asked, showing that he'd picked up at least part of her conversation with Wilford.

"Pick him up and tell him you must wait for me."

He was shaking his head. "Tell my employer where to go? It's as much as my position is worth, madam."

"I'll see you keep your position," Ransley said from behind her. Thea spun with a gasp, her heart pounding again. Ransley was looking at her from far too close, a fall of burgundy fabric over his arm and a scowl upon his face.

"Yes, Your Grace," the coachman said. "Thank you, Your Grace."

He seemed to have no doubt that Ransley could do as he promised, though the duke could hardly be said to be a bosom companion of Lord Wilford, with an attendant influence over him. Perhaps the coachman assumed that, being a duke, Ransley could do anything he said he could. He was probably right.

"I told you to wait in the carriage," Ransley said sternly.

"And I told you I would not be left behind."

Ignoring that, he thrust the armful of burgundy cloth at her. "Here, put it on quickly before you're seen."

It turned out to be a domino, not quite long enough for her, but sufficient to cover her dress and wrap, by which she might easily be identified by anyone who had been at the opera earlier in the evening. A gray mask that covered nearly her entire face completed her disguise. "Where did you get these?" she asked as she quickly donned them and pulled up the hood of the domino to conceal her hair.

"Bought them from a Cit who was leaving the Gardens," Ransley said shortly, affixing his own mask. He did not need a domino, for his greatcoat was as anonymous as any costume. The black half-mask he was putting on did not seem sufficient to Thea, for she felt she might have identified him as easily by the chiseled line of his lips as his pale hair and paler eyes, both washed even more colorless than usual by the silvery glow of the moon and the light of the lamps scattered throughout Vauxhall.

Touched by the care he was taking for her reputation when he must be beside himself with fear for Clary, Thea laid her hand on Ransley's arm. "I'm certain she will be safe."

"Trenwick is for it if she isn't," he growled in a voice that reminded her of the pistol in his pocket. "If I even find him with her, he won't escape a whipping." He drew her hand through the crook of his arm and led her through the gates of Vauxhall Gardens.

Under other circumstances, Thea would have found the experience enjoyable. She'd been to Vauxhall before, of course, but only with a large party, and she had remained near the supper boxes and orchestra building throughout the evening to avoid any risk that a stain should attach to her reputation. Walking through Vauxhall with Ransley was a different experience altogether. The duke moved through the crowd of revelers without checking his stride in the slightest, as if there was no doubt they would give way before him. And so they did, parting as a wave parts to go around a rock. Thea had seen the same thing happen in the ballroom. Previously, she had believed it the result of the natural deference shown to a peer of the realm, but now she rather thought it had more to do with the intensity of his glittering eyes.

"I wonder where Lord Wilford is," Thea murmured, scanning the crowd from behind her mask. She despaired of finding anyone in such an unholy throng.

"Did you honestly expect to find him here?"

Somehow, Thea did not think he was talking about the difficulty of identifying him amongst the masked revelers. "I had hoped to," she said evenly. "I had hoped he might have found her and be making his way out with her." She was careful not to let Lady Clarissa's name escape her lips where it might be overheard.

"Assuming he didn't simply forget why he was here, and assuming he could find her, and assuming—" He broke off and his lips thinned.

Assuming he wasn't responsible for this disaster in the first place.

Thea appreciated him not rejoining the argument. Not least because she was no longer entirely certain of her position. For a man not involved, especially one who was such a slowtop, Wilford knew a sight too much about what was going on.

They worked their way past the supper boxes and around the orchestra building. The orchestra, in their elevated position, appeared to be playing nothing but waltzes. Many of the revelers danced far too close, seduced into impropriety by the lure of the masquerade and an overindulgence in hot wine or Vauxhall's infamous arrack punch, which was reputed to be extremely strong.

Thea felt a fugitive moment of desire — to be once more in Ransley's arms, moving in time with the music — which she quickly quashed. She should not be thinking of the heat of his body and the feel of his hands on her when there were far more important matters to attend to.

"You might join one of the supper parties," Ransley suggested, sounding reluctant. She wondered if he was aware that he had brought his arm, and perforce her hand, in closer against his body. "And watch for her from a box."

"I should have to identify myself to prove that I'm not some encroaching mushroom," Thea said. "It is likely to become… awkward."

"Indeed," Ransley agreed. "But so is our next step. She's not here—"

"You're certain?"

"I'm certain," he said with finality. "Which leaves the walks and the less well-illuminated areas."

"Let us go, then."

"Out of the crowd and the lights, people's behavior is like to become more... licentious."

"I'm not a widgeon, Your— Sir," Thea said, her breath catching at the near-slip. If someone overheard her calling him "Your Grace," they would be well on their way to identifying him. There were not *that* many dukes. And his presence was like to make people wonder where his ward was. "I'm well aware of what we may see." It was something of a lie, for though she had heard rumors, she was not nearly so worldly as all that.

"Very well," he said. He drew her arm a little farther through the crook of his elbow, bringing her in even closer to him, and laid his other hand over her fingers where they rested on his forearm. To anyone catching a glimpse of them, they appeared lost in a romantic connection; only she knew how tense his muscles were. His arm felt like an iron bar under her hand. He bent his head toward hers, and she was lost for a moment in his eyes. "Where shall we start? Druid's Walk, Dark Walk, or Lover's Walk?"

"Lover's Walk," she heard herself say, utterly unable to draw her eyes from his.

Chapter Sixteen

CLARY was confused. The lights and the music and the dancers all seemed to be whirling around her, and she wanted to dance along with them, but she didn't have a partner.

She'd had one, she thought. A man in a brilliant green domino… Mr. Mallinson, that was it! But she couldn't see him anywhere. She turned around and around, looking for him, and for every turn she made, the gardens seemed to revolve a turn and a half. She stepped sideways to catch her balance and bumped into a tall man with all his shirt buttons open. Clary couldn't seem to draw her eyes away from how his shirt gaped around his neck or the wedge of skin and hint of hair revealed by the opening.

"Hello, pretty," the man drawled. "Aren't you a bit overdressed?" He wrapped his hands around her waist and smiled, showing too many teeth.

"Do I know you?" she asked peering at him, but his mask showed nothing she could recognize. He smelled of spirits and his hands were too warm at her waist, even through her domino and dress, creating damp spots that made her shrink reflexively away.

"Not yet," he said, and spun her around, making the lights whirl even more crazily.

She half-fell and managed to stagger away from him as he grabbed for her. She got all the way to the hedge before she dared turn and look, her heart pounding crazily. But he'd found a woman more to his liking and was holding her far too close. She appeared to be enjoying it, but then, perhaps she was just cold. Clary didn't see how she could not be, wearing so little.

There was an opening in the hedge near her, and Clary looked at it uncertainly. Was that the way they came in? It didn't look familiar. There were four other openings into the clearing where the orchestra played and the dancers spun about, and from where she stood trembling, she couldn't see a jot's worth of difference between them.

The dancers seemed to move faster. They were all smiling and laughing, and some part of Clary felt that she ought to want to join them, but something about their wild abandon frightened her. She wished she knew which path to take.

She was suddenly aware of a dark shape near her and spun to face it. The figure was cloaked and masked and gloved all in black, an ominous shade nearly swallowed by the night. Clary shrank instinctively from the black hand that reached for her, but it caught her anyway, tearing away her mask.

With a shriek, she ran.

She darted down the nearest path, the gravel biting at her feet through her thin dancing slippers, and ran blind, not seeing what was before her, so desperate was she to escape what was behind. She collided suddenly with something hard and unyielding, half-knocking the breath from her. When she fumbled to step away from it, it put arms around her to hold her in place. A scream caught in her throat, Clary pressed both hands to the man's chest and pushed as hard as she could, but only gained enough space to look up into his face. The scream died in her throat when she recognized Lord Trenwick's cool gray eyes behind his black mask.

"What the devil are *you* doing here?" he said.

Clary blinked owlishly at him, then smiled. "Didn't Mr. Mallinson tell you?" He must have asked Trenwick to watch over her when he was called away. Why else would the man be in just the right place to rescue her? She wondered muzzily why she couldn't remember Mr. Mallinson telling her he had to leave.

"Oh, he told me all right," Trenwick drawled, his arms loosening enough that she might have stepped away if she'd wanted to. "But I didn't get the impression your interest went beyond sharing a waltz to annoy your guardian."

"Bother my guardian," Clary said petulantly.

"Yes, I rather thought that was the point." There was amusement in his voice, and Clary had the sudden lowering feeling that it was at her expense. Well, she'd show him! She was just tall enough not to have to stand on tiptoe to brush her mouth over his.

He took in a quick breath and stepped back. "What the devil!" She giggled, shocked by his language. "Are you under the hatches?" When she only blinked at him, completely at sea, he took her by the shoulders and bent to peer into her eyes. "How much did you drink?"

"Only the one glass," she said airily. At least she thought it was only one. She wished he'd lean a bit closer so she could kiss him again. His lips had been fascinatingly soft.

"Of?"

"Oh…" She waved her hand. "Punch." She managed to get her arms around his neck, though he didn't make it easy, and clung there. He smelled very nice. She probably oughtn't be so close to him, but there wasn't anyone around to see.

"And I was starting to get a bit worried. There were all these people, and some of them were really… really not the thing. Did you know? What some of them were wearing…" She shook her head and noticed he was regarding her a bit quizzically. "And one of them tried to dance with me, and someone else grabbed my mask, and I was frightened. But then there you were! And you saved me, and I feel ever so safe now. You're wonderful. Just like a hero in a storybook."

His face underwent the oddest transformation. He looked, for a moment, as if someone had planted him a facer, and then his smile became a softer thing at the same moment he set her gently away from him, prying her hands from around his neck and holding them in his own. "You really don't know, do you?"

"Know what?" she blinked owlishly up at him.

Instead of answering, he asked, "However did you get *here*?"

"Shh. That's a secret," she whispered.

"And without a mask?"

"I told you: someone took it." Clary thought of the dark, looming figure and shivered. A moment later, something warm enveloped her. She looked down and saw Trenwick's hands tying the laces of his black domino, which he'd flung about her. "I'm not cold," she objected, trying to push his hands away. As well try to push Gunpowder when he wished not to move.

"Your domino is far too identifiable." He finished tying the laces, then took off his own mask and put it on her.

"But now everyone will know who you are," Clary said on a yawn. Her eyes were starting to feel heavy and the world seemed to sway a bit as it revolved around her.

"Better than everyone knowing who you are. Most of the sporting set know me even with the mask. And it certainly wouldn't do for you to be seen with me." He tucked her hand into the crook of his arm and began to walk, giving her no choice but to walk along with him. "That's worse than simply being seen here."

"I don't know why not," Clary said. "You're wonderful." He snorted. "Really! I can talk to you. Most people, I can't. Especially men."

"I haven't noticed that you have any trouble talking with your beaus."

"Oh, but I really am hopeless!" she assured him. "It's just that I get through by pretending I'm Lady Ashburne."

"Lady Ashburne," he said slowly. "Roger Ashburne's wife?"

"Silly," Clary scolded, tapping his arm with her free hand. "Not any more."

"Of course, right. Now that was a man riding for a fall long before he managed to tumble out of his carriage."

He continued to walk, moving steadily even though the path was very ill-lit. Clary began to think half the lamps had been turned out. Then she realized she was walking with her eyes closed and forced them open. It didn't get appreciably brighter. She leaned her head against Trenwick's shoulder. It wasn't easy to walk like that, but it wasn't easy to walk anyway, with her head so heavy. She yawned. "Where are we going?"

"Out," he said shortly, and when she peered up at him, she saw his jaw was tightly set. "We must get you back to your uncle before anyone else sees you."

"Bother my uncle," Clary said and stopped walking.

"So you've said. Where is he? The supper boxes?" When he realized he'd have to pull her along to make her move, Trenwick turned to face her.

They were directly opposite an alcove in which water cascaded down a series of rock ledges into a pool. It was very pretty. Something moved between Clary and the waterfall. She looked up and saw Trenwick's face. He was not smiling.

"Where is he?" he said slowly and clearly.

"You needn't talk like I'm a slowtop." Clary scowled. "He was home when I snuck out."

"When you..." Trenwick shoved his hand through his hair, tousling it. He closed his eyes briefly, looking pained. "He will shoot me when he finds me," he muttered.

"No! He can't!" Clary threw herself at Trenwick, fetching up against his chest, where he caught her with a grunt. "I won't let him! If he hurts you, I'll... I'll never speak to him again!"

Lord Trenwick huffed a noise that might have been a laugh. He patted her shoulder, then wrested her arms from around him and once more began to draw her down the dimly lit path. "Thank you, my lady," he murmured, his voice scarcely carrying even to her. "With such a staunch defender, how can I be anything but safe?"

Clary couldn't see what he thought was so amusing. She tried to stop again, digging in her heels, but this time he just kept walking, and she found herself trotting to catch up. "But I don't want to leave! Can't we stay? Just for a bit? I'm enjoying myself now that you're here."

"Trenwick," a man said heartily, looming up out of one of the cross-walks to stand much too near Clary. He was large and sweating under his black mask. "Lost your costume?" He barely glanced at Lord Trenwick as he spoke, but appeared to be trying to look through Clary's clothes. She moved instinctively closer to Trenwick.

"Ormsby." A smile grew slowly on Trenwick's face. "Oh, must have lost it somewhere," he drawled, as if the question could not possibly be of less interest to him. "Bit distracted."

"Indeed." Ormsby's smile, like that of the man back in the clearing, showed too many teeth. It put Clary in mind of a crocodile, and she shrank even closer to Trenwick, who disengaged her hand from his elbow and put his arm around her. "One of your pretty bits of muslin?" Ormsby said, his voice oily with implications Clary felt too muzzy-headed to grasp. "Bit overdressed, ain't she?"

"Not if you enjoy the unwrapping." Trenwick smiled and gave the other man a nod as he began to guide Clary away.

Ormsby winked vulgarly and took himself off, laughing in a way Clary didn't like. "Don't like him," she mumbled, yawning again. It was entirely too warm to be wearing two dominos, and then there was Lord Trenwick's arm around her. She rather liked that, though it made her even warmer and sleepier. She couldn't quite decide what to do with her own arm and wondered, her heart pounding at her daring, if she might slip it around his waist.

"Be glad he didn't recognize you. The worst quidnunc doesn't gossip more than Ormsby."

He was hurrying her along now, but Clary didn't want to walk anymore. They were coming closer to another orchestra, the sound of the music wafting through the darkness, and she wanted to dance. "Can't we—"

"Trenwick!" Uncle Ransley's shout was nearly drowned out by the explosion and burst of light.

* * *

"No!" Miss Ravenshaw clung to Ransley's arm, preventing him from getting the pistol out of his pocket. Another firework exploded overhead, drawing all eyes.

"Are you defending him?" Ransley hissed, struck to the heart by her betrayal. What the devil could she possibly see in the dissipated rake who currently had Clary tucked infamously close against his side?

"No!" she said again, this time sounding angry, rather than panicked. "But he is unmasked." Even though she was so close he could feel her breath on his face, he could scarcely hear her over the barrage of fireworks signaling the close of the evening. "And you, sir, are entirely too identifiable, even with the mask. If it gets about that you fought with him, it would be a short step from that to the most likely reason."

Bloody hell! The demmed woman was right; he didn't dare shoot the blackguard, now or later, for fear of causing the very scandal they were attempting to avert. Scarcely had he admitted the truth of it to himself than it became a moot point in any case, for Clary had flung herself at him with a cry. Between them, the women made it impossible for him to safely use the pistol, and he gave it up as a bad lot. Showing himself to be completely lacking in any sense of self-preservation, Trenwick swept him an elaborate bow, smiling sardonically, before walking away. Ransley growled, but did not go after the man, instead putting his arms around Clary to soothe her. She was clearly overwrought by the horrible experience, and as she sobbed against his chest, Ransley began to rethink his decision to let Trenwick go. First thing tomorrow, he'd hunt the man down and find some pretext to call the bastard out. If he made the reason public enough, the *ton* would have to at least pretend to believe it wasn't about Clary.

Then he realized what Clary was sobbing over and over — "Don't hurt him; oh please, don't hurt him." — and he growled again, wishing Trenwick to the devil.

"He won't, I promise," Miss Ravenshaw said soothingly, and Ransley wished her to the devil too for committing him. He did not stop to ask himself why he should feel in any way bound by her promises. "Come, sir," she added to him, "let us leave while everyone is still distracted."

It was excellent advice. Ransley offered Miss Ravenshaw his arm, took Clary firmly by the hand, and began the slow process of wending through the crowd toward the exit.

"Oh, but I was having such fun," Clary protested in precisely the same tone of voice she'd once used when asserting she was not the least bit tired when she was nearly asleep on her feet. He'd thought she'd outgrown that when she was ten.

"We will discuss your *fun* when we get home," Ransley said, and saw the parts of her face visible behind the mask blanche. And well she ought to worry. She was disheveled, a glow of perspiration upon her skin and the smell of arrack punch on her breath. Her identity was, thankfully, hidden beneath the black mask and enveloping black domino, which was so much too big for her that it nearly tripped her up. In fact, if Trenwick had not been bare-faced, Ransley was very much afraid he might have overlooked his ward entirely. The realization that he owed the man, even if only for being brazen enough to disport himself without a costume, did nothing to allay his temper.

The walk back to the gates was accomplished in silence. It would hardly have been possible to speak over the ongoing barrage of fireworks, and Ransley had nothing he wished to say where he might be overheard. The final blasts had sounded by the time they made it back outside the Gardens, which was just as well for the sake of the horses.

It was still necessary to wait another ten minutes before Lord Wilford's coachman made it through the throng, and Clary spent the time sulking, leaning sleepily against Miss Ravenshaw and scowling at him. She'd retreated to the other woman's side after Ransley scotched three attempts at conversation, none of which was suitable to hold in public.

He waited until they were all in the carriage — the coachman looked nervous at leaving Vauxhall without Wilford, but agreed to take them when Ransley promised to send a note of explanation with him for Wilford — to demand, "What the devil did you think you were doing?"

"What else was I supposed to do when you kept me home for days on end?" Clary countered, the color high in her cheeks. She'd removed her mask and cradled it against her, for all the world as if there was something special about it. "You won't let me do anything!"

"It's only been two days, girl, and that's no excuse for this. What in God's name possessed you?" He was aware of Miss Ravenshaw looking resolutely out the window, and her polite withdrawal filled him with shame for brangling with Clary in front of witnesses. He wished now he'd allowed the carriage ride to pass in peace. However, he appeared to have wound his niece up like some mechanical toy, for she launched into a drawn-out, convoluted story that made little sense. Although that could just be because she was clearly more than half-foxed, he spotted several holes in the story that clearly ought to contain another person. Someone Clary appeared to be protecting.

Trenwick again, he thought, and listened in sour silence to Clary's rambling account of being rescued and protected by the man. It was clear she'd built him into some kind of fairytale prince in her mind, and it was all Ransley could do not to bury his head in his hands. He was in dire need of a drink by the time they reached his townhouse.

Clary had lapsed into silence several minutes before they arrived, and Ransley hadn't prompted her, feeling nothing but relief that she'd finally talked herself dry. When she didn't stir at the footman opening the carriage door, Ransley realized she'd fallen asleep, the black mask still clutched securely against her chest. He gathered her up with grim tenderness and carried her up the stairs into the house.

"All is well," he told Hailston, who met him at the door, shock and fear draining all the life from his face. "She's just… tired." He would not say "drunk" with a footman hovering at his shoulder and one of the downstairs maids watching from the hallway, her eyes as big as an owl's. "Send her maid up, will you?"

He was halfway up the stairs when he heard Miss Ravenshaw's voice at the door, and his foot wavered a moment before coming down on the next tread. It was the height of rudeness to just walk away after everything the woman had done for him. For Clary.

"Hailston, is it?" Miss Ravenshaw said in her low and gentle voice. "I need to write a letter to Lord Wilford. Might I use His Grace's stationary?"

Ransley waited long enough to hear Hailston show her into the library before wearily climbing the rest of the stairs. He'd laid Clary on the bed and was stepping away when her maid rushed in.

"Oh, my poor mistress. Is she—"

Touched by her concern, he made himself smile at her. "Just burnt to the socket," he lied. "If you would put her to bed…?"

"Of course, sir." She dropped him a perfunctory curtsey, her attention already focused on her mistress, and he went out and back down the stairs, feeling ancient.

When he entered the library, Miss Ravenshaw was sitting at his desk, apparently just finishing up her letter. She had removed the mask and domino and draped them over the back of one of the chairs. After seeing her masked and cloaked for such a span of time, he had the oddest feeling that she now looked rather exposed. He took in her porcelain skin and the lock of dark hair that had escaped its elaborate styling and lay curled against her neck as she bent her head over her writing, and felt something stir in his chest. He took a steadying breath and removed his own mask, dropping it on one corner of the desk. After a moment, he took the pistol out of his pocket and set it down next to the mask. Miss Ravenshaw laid down her pen and capped the inkwell.

"What did you write?"

She smiled. "I thanked Lord Wilford for putting his carriage at my disposal tonight and commended his generosity." She sanded the letter, folding it as soon as the ink could reasonably be expected to be dry.

He found himself smiling back. "That should serve to keep the coachman out of the suds."

"I certainly hope so." She handed the letter off to Hailston, who was hovering discreetly nearby. "Could you have this delivered to Lord Wilford's coachman? He ought to still be outside. Ask him to wait for me a few more minutes."

"Hailston," Ransley said when the butler had taken it and bowed. He handed the man his wallet. "Give the man some money. Be generous."

"Yes, sir." Hailston bowed and went out, closing the door softly behind him.

Ransley took off his hat and greatcoat and laid them over Miss Ravenshaw's domino on the chair, knocking her mask to the seat cushion in the process. He picked it up absently and carried it with him as he moved to stand in front of the fire. It was scarcely flickering over the coals, but heat still radiated from the hearth, warming his legs even through his boots.

"Your Grace?"

Her voice seemed to come to him from far away. He took a breath and surfaced from contemplation of the lazy flames, or perhaps the gray mask in his hand. He set it on the mantelshelf and turned to Miss Ravenshaw, who hovered uncertainly an arm's length away.

"My apologies, Miss Ravenshaw. You deserve better of me." He found himself going to her, taking her hands in his, his heart so full of gratitude he could not remain unmoved or keep himself at a distance. "You have been... a rock. Thank you." He squeezed her hands lightly, wishing he could strip off her gloves and hold her fine-boned hands bare in his own.

"Where were you?" she said, hardly seeming to notice his gratitude. "You looked a million miles away."

He could see how weak his smile was in her pained reaction. "Not so far. Only a few hundred. Tynesfield."

"Your manor?"

"Yes." He made himself release her hands and step away before he could do anything he ought not. There was a traitorous warmth in him that had nothing to do with the fire and which made him a coward, for he could not look at her face as he said, "I shall take Clary back there tomorrow."

"Oh, but—!" She cut herself off, biting her lip as if keeping back further words that wished to be spoken. He might have smiled if he didn't find it so ironic that she should refrain from challenging him now, when she'd had no qualms about doing it before. *Now* she kept to the proprieties. *Now*, when he was so tempted to ignore them.

To distract himself, he answered her unfinished protest. "If even half the story Clary told is true — and I'm not so bottlebrained as to believe she wasn't lying quite a bit — then I have no choice but to get her away from Town for a time." He sighed and answered the question in her eyes. "She's got a blue domino on under the black." He'd seen it when he laid her on the bed.

Miss Ravenshaw made a small, pained sound. "So the bit about having her mask ripped off…"

"Is likely true. Someone there — many people, perhaps — will have seen her face. While I might hope they did not see her with Lord Trenwick, it is just a hope. And in any case, it's very clear that Clary is far too wild. I must take her away and keep her in the country until she will allow herself to be led by me, otherwise I shall never manage to keep her out of the briars."

"Please don't, Your Grace," Miss Ravenshaw said, coming to him and putting her hand on his forearm. "If you take her away now, the gossip will taint all her future chances. Keep her here. Between us, we can keep her safe."

Her touch burning through his coat, Ransley found a harsh laugh somewhere inside him. "How do you propose to keep her safe when you refuse to even protect your own reputation?"

She drew back as if he'd slapped her, and it was only the speed with which he put his hand over hers that kept it upon his arm. He squeezed her fingers when she would have drawn them out from under his hand.

"You are," he pointed out, far more gently than he'd thought he intended, "alone with me in my library, after having been alone with me in a closed carriage, in which you dashed off with me to Vauxhall without chaperone or companion."

She scowled. "Oh really, Your Grace! I'm not a green girl. I'm nearly thirty, and hardly need to be chaperoned at all times. Really, what could possibly have happened?"

Her dismissal lighting a fire inside him far greater than that in the hearth, Ransley drew her to his chest and said, "This," before bringing his mouth down upon hers and showing her as extensively and convincingly as he could.

Chapter Seventeen

THE rattle of curtain rings and a sudden flash of brilliant light upon her face woke Thea out of a sound sleep. She rubbed her face, yawning, and made herself sit up against the pillows so her lady's maid could settle her breakfast tray across her lap. She wanted nothing more than to lie abed another age, having gotten very little sleep the night before, but that would not be fair to Chloe. It would only result in the maid having to get a replacement breakfast when this one went cold.

So Thea yawned and munched on toast and drank her morning chocolate as Chloe bustled about the bedroom busily, arranging Thea's clothes for the day and the dressing table to her own satisfaction. Thea yawned a bit more and rubbed her hand over her face again — she'd arrived home not much later than she usually would after an evening's entertainments, but had chased sleep fruitlessly for hours. The thought of what had kept her sleepless, and the brush of her fingers over her tender lips, kindled something inside her, and she knew she blushed.

Thea wasn't entirely unaccustomed to kisses. She'd had her share of courtly kisses on the hand, daring kisses on the cheek, and even a few stolen kisses in moonlit gardens, though she'd been careful to severely limit those for the sake of her reputation. But not even the most ardent of suitor's salutes held the smallest of candles to Ransley's kisses. He had strained her close to his breast and kissed her as though he wanted to devour her, and she could only press mindlessly closer and wish to be consumed. She could scarcely breathe, or even want to, wanting only to everlastingly meet his mouth, his lips, as he taught her things about kissing she'd never before even suspected. She knew now why poets talked ever of lovers' kisses. It seemed to her last night, as Ransley's mouth covered hers, his lips and tongue strong and demanding, that between them, they made over the world to contain only themselves. And she had felt banished from that new world when he finally found the wherewithal to set her away from him. She ought to have been grateful for his control; instead, she just felt cold, just wanted to step back into the heat of his body. He had been hard against her, strong and unyielding: his arms, his chest, his thighs, his…

She hurriedly put her cup of chocolate down before she could spill it and pressed her hands against her burning cheeks. He had made her want to melt, to be somehow taken inside that broad chest and kept safe and protected. She was, she reminded herself sternly, an independent woman, with means of her own and no need for a man to make her life complete.

And yet.

And yet, last night was the first time in her life, she thought, that she had ever felt truly alive.

But he would be gone by this afternoon. It would take his servants longer to close up his townhouse, but Ransley and his ward need not wait for them. If he wished to be gone within the day, it would be easy enough for him to manage it. He would take his ward and retreat to the country, and Thea wasn't entirely certain she'd ever see him again. Whether or not Lady Clarissa's visit to Vauxhall became widely known, gossip about her disappearance in the middle of the Season would most certainly make the rounds. And those rumors would make it all the more difficult for her in her next Season. Thea suspected that, once back in the country, Ransley and Clarissa might well find it easier to look closer to home for a suitable connection than brave the wagging tongues of the *ton* again. And certainly Thea could not visit him at Tynesfield.

If Ransley were known for his house parties, Thea might hope to be invited to one, but he had no reputation for entertaining, and she doubted he was likely to begin now. If not invited as part of some larger group, she could not go. Nor, certainly, could she invite him to visit her.

Nor would it be safe to do so. Not when her body yearned and her face heated at the memory of his kisses, her heart throbbing with the fugitive desire for more of them.

No, he would be gone soon, and for the sake of her reputation, it was as well. Such pleasures could too easily turn her head, making her lose sight of virtue and propriety. And that she could not afford.

She made herself get out of bed before she could succumb to the desire to simply stay there. That all the blandishments of Town now seemed only cold and flat was neither here nor there. She would just have to move past it. Eventually, surely, everything would stop feeling so gray.

It was as well he was leaving. Perhaps, if she told herself that often enough, she might believe it.

* * *

Mallinson stumbled out onto Pickering Place from the latest of the gambling hells in which he'd spent the night and cringed away from the sun that pierced between two buildings and straight into his eyes.

"Damn! When the devil did it get to be morning?" he muttered, pulling his hat lower.

He looked consideringly back at the narrow doorway into the hell, the third or fourth he'd been in that night. If it had a name, he didn't know or care what it was. It was much easier on the eyes inside, and they had brandy — not very good brandy, it was true, but they weren't stingy with it like some clubs — and a man might play *chemin de fer* or hazard or faro, as the mood took him. But Mallinson had spent everything in his pockets during the course of his night of celebration, and the thought of having to cajole someone into accepting his vowels made his head throb more than the rays of the rising sun. They'd all be singing a different tune once news of the night's events had got round. Ransley had no choice now but to leave Town, and with him would go any doubt about Mallinson's inheritance.

He pulled his hat still lower, ducking his head and squinting against the slowly growing light, and headed down Pickering toward St. James's Street. Perhaps he might stop in at Cocker's on the way to his lodgings — see if any of the tattlemongers were about and whether they had the *on dit* about Lady Clarissa yet. He could also have himself a brandy to take the edge off his headache.

Mallinson turned in at Cocker's and stopped for a moment before the large mirror mounted in the entryway to straighten his lapels. His shirtpoints and cravat were in need of attention after the long night, but there was nothing to be done about that. He pushed his hat and cloak at the attendant, irritated that the man hadn't bothered to assist him with them as he would a *lord*, and went inside to look around. There was no one in the billiard room, and no one worth talking to in the first card room. Reminded that it was very late — or, depending on your point of view, very early — Mallinson snarled under his breath. He'd been near to jumping out of his skin all night, rapturously anticipating the moment the story became widespread. Certainly, he couldn't risk sharing it himself, for fear of the talk being traced back to him. But waiting for it to make the rounds and arrive back at his ears was torture.

It had all gone so wonderfully well. Lady Clarissa was naïve, wide-eyed, starved for amusement, and oh so trusting. It had been simplicity itself to get her down one of the secluded walks. Oh, the look on her face when he'd ripped off her mask! The whites had shown all the way around her lovely blue eyes, and she'd taken off like a banshee was on her heels. Mallinson had stayed long enough to see her run into the arms of a man who was quick to trap her in them. Unseen, he had tipped his hat to the fellow, may he have pleasure of her. Then, sure of his victory, he'd taken himself off to celebrate through all the clubs and gambling hells that would permit him through the doors.

But now... Now he needed to hear about the success of his clever plan. He rubbed his hands together in anticipation and went on into the second card room. There were a few more men there, but they were the same type of cardsharps he'd spent the last several hours with, not yet done gambling the night away and not interesting in anything outside the fall of the cards. They wouldn't know any rumors that hadn't already made it through all the rest of the *ton*. Disappointment filled Mallinson. He was exhausted, and his head throbbed, and he didn't think he could stand to go home to bed until he knew the gossips had the tale and his future was secure.

He grabbed a passing waiter. "Brandy." The man looked at him with an expression far too superior for a mere servant, then down at his hand, which was wrapped around the man's arm. Despite himself, Mallinson let go. "Brandy," he repeated.

"Yes, sir," the man said, but he didn't move. What the devil was he waiting for? Payment?

"Put it on my account," Mallinson said through his teeth.

"My apologies, sir," the waiter said and walked away. From his tone, the jumped-up lackey wasn't sorry and he wasn't going to bring the brandy. What the everlasting hell was going on? Mallinson had never had trouble in Cocker's before. Well, there had been some difficulty about his unpaid account when Ransley and Miss Ravenshaw were sitting in each other's pockets, but any talk of him paying his shot had ended when Ransley broke off contact with the woman.

"Mallinson," Wilford bleated from behind him, startling him half to death and sending a new pain through his head.

"Dart," Mallinson said, turning to face the other man. Though Wilford looked weary, he'd clearly been through the hands of his valet recently, for his shirt and cravat were knife-edged, making Mallinson feel positively wilted by comparison.

"You'll never guess what's happened," Wilford said in entirely too chipper a voice for the time of day. He was grinning from ear to ear.

"Why don't we sit down and you can tell me?" Mallinson said, taking Wilford's arm companionably and guiding him to a table in the dimmest corner of the room. "But first, be a good fellow and order me a brandy, would you?"

Wilford agreed readily, and didn't even fidget much when Mallinson turned it into two brandies before he felt equal to trying to get anything useful out of the other man. On both occasions, the waiter — a different one this time — set the brandy on the table in front of Wilford, even though it was clear that it was Mallinson who was drinking. He felt suddenly cold. The inveterate gamblers might care little for the latest *on dits*, but the owners of the various clubs kept very close tabs on the gossip so they might know who it was safe to extend credit to and who should be cut off. After his night's work, Mallinson ought to be treated nearly as well as if he were already a duke, but instead, the servants were acting as if he were a younger son with no prospects and his pockets to let.

What the devil had happened?

"Now," Mallinson said after drinking off his second brandy. He contemplated ordering a third, but decided it would be as well to keep his wits about him. Even if he scarcely needed two together to deal with Wilford. "What's about, Dart?"

"I've been trying to tell you! I think, I really think Miss Ravenshaw will accept my suit this time." He was so exalted he could scarcely sit still. Mallinson found him exhausting to look at. He began wishing he hadn't stopped at two brandies.

"With the *ton*, Dart. What is the latest news? I've been two days over the cards," he lied, "and feel woefully out of touch."

"The devil take that," Wilford said, shockingly direct and looking, for once in his life, not the least bit vague. "See here, the letter she sent me." He pushed the paper into Mallinson's hands.

Realizing he'd get no further sense out of the man unless he humored this odd start, Mallinson dutifully read the letter. Then he read it again. It was very businesslike, and though it warmly expressed Miss Ravenshaw's thanks for Lord Wilford's assistance, the language was quite deliberately formal. Mallinson smirked — the woman had obviously been trying not to encourage Wilford's romantic aspirations and had just as obviously failed. Something about it though... He laid the letter down on the table in front of him and tapped his fingers upon it. He misliked it. He misliked it strongly and didn't know quite why.

"You see?" Wilford said, beaming at him across the table.

"Indeed. Precisely what service," he asked off-handedly, "did you perform for the lovely Miss Ravenshaw, if I might ask?"

Wilford's foolish expression became even more stupidly moonstruck. "She *is* lovely, isn't she? I really, I, I, I really think this time, this time she won't—"

"Dart!" Mallinson interrupted sharply. Grimacing at Wilford's hurt expression, he made himself take a breath and speak more gently. "What did you do?"

"When?"

"For Miss Ravenshaw," Mallinson said slowly, holding onto his temper by his fingernails. While it was likely nothing to signify, he would feel much more equal to the occasion if he knew everything about Miss Ravenshaw. That female had already spiked his guns on several occasions, proving herself a veritable menace. And there was something about that letter....

"Oh! I took her home early from the opera. She had a putrid headache."

Mallinson somehow managed to refrain from rolling his eyes. If that woman had spent the evening at the opera with Wilford, it was small wonder she'd come away with a headache. "And?" he prompted, for that wasn't sufficient to require a letter of gratitude.

"And I lent her my carriage so she could go to Vauxhall." Wilford beamed, clearly not seeing anything havey cavey about a woman crying off an engagement with him by claiming a headache, then begging the use of his carriage to take her to another engagement.

At Vauxhall. A sudden pain stabbed behind Mallinson's right eye. "Why did she want to go to Vauxhall, Dart?"

"Strangest thing. I was only warning her to, to protect her reputation. But she insisted on dashing off after the chit. Lent her my carriage to do it and, and even went to Vauxhall myself to look for the girl. Spent the demmed night looking for the demmed gel. Never saw anyone I knew, not even Miss Ravenshaw. It's blasted hard to recognize anyone under all those masks," he said suddenly, as if it were some new discovery and not the entire point of a masquerade. Mallinson rubbed his throbbing temples. "Almost thought they were playing least in sight," Wilford said with the simple recognition that someone might wish to escape his presence that somehow never translated to either an understanding of it or any damage to his emotions. He beamed. "But the coachman came back with the letter. And I think, Mallinson, I really think—"

Mallinson stopped listening. He very nearly stopped breathing, his chest tight with anger. He'd like to have told Wilford to shut it, but was so elevated with rage, he couldn't speak. He glared at Wilford's perfectly tied cravat and thought about putting his hands about it, and the neck under it, and squeezing until the fatuous voice stopped. He'd forgotten that he told Wilford Clarissa would be at Vauxhall with Trenwick, and even if he *had* remembered it, he'd have thought it a great advance on spreading the gossip, given Wilford's tendency to have enough tongue for two sets of teeth. Mallinson would have drawn Wilford's cork himself if he'd had any idea the man might actually say something to Miss Ravenshaw. He prayed Wilford's bumbling hadn't scotched everything. But that letter...

That letter. He looked back down at it and smoothed it out where his clenching fingers had crumpled it. With a stifled exclamation, he snatched it up and held it to the light, wishing now that he hadn't chosen such a dark corner to sit in. Before he could get a better look at the watermark, however, Wilford plucked the letter out of his hands, tutting about his mishandling of it.

He was about to take it back from the man when someone dealt him a terrific blow on the shoulder, nearly knocking him from his chair. Mallinson stumbled to his feet and turned to find Ormsby beaming at him with no trace of amusement in his eyes.

"Mallinson, what a surprise to see you. Thought you'd be home drowning your sorrows."

"My sorrows?" He rubbed his shoulder, which ached from Ormsby's "friendly" clout.

"The Duke of Ransley and Miss Ravenshaw."

"Have not been seen together for a week," Mallinson snapped before he could stop himself.

"You haven't heard?" The gleam in Ormsby's eyes proclaimed him quite satisfied to be the bearer of bad tidings. "It's all over the *ton*. Ransley and Miss Ravenshaw were seen arriving together at the Venetian Ball at Vauxhall last night, and without that dowd of a companion. An announcement is confidently expected by all."

Ice swept through Mallinson. The destruction of his plans, the sudden reversal of his fortunes, so overset him that he could only blink at Ormsby, unable to find even the weakest of arguments. Both men ignored Wilford's protests that Miss Ravenshaw couldn't possibly have accepted Ransley's suit. After all, he had a letter.

Ormsby smiled unpleasantly. "I would remind you, Mallinson, that I'm holding a number of your vowels. And that there's no place in the *ton* for a man who doesn't pay his debts of honor."

Mallinson said something, he didn't know what, but neither Ormsby nor Wilford tried to stop him from leaving. He stalked back out onto the street, nearly forgetting his hat and cloak. The attendant at the door — the little toad — didn't even bother to remind him. Scarcely aware of his surroundings, Mallinson walked back to his lodgings in a black cloud and climbed the stairs to his room, his mind working nine to the dozen and not managing to churn out even a single coherent thought, let alone a plan.

It wasn't true. It couldn't be. But it didn't have to be, did it? Even the rumor was sufficient to scotch Mallinson's plans. Rumors... Mallinson croaked out a laugh. Hoist with his own petard, it seemed. What was he to do?

When he stomped in, his valet jumped up from where he'd been dozing before the fire. "Where've you been, sir?"

Mallinson scowled at his valet, an inferior specimen, but all he could afford. "What the devil business is it of yours?" He was gratified to see the man quail.

His valet hurried to help him out of his greatcoat and boots, then followed him into the bedroom to divest him of the remainder of his clothing. When he was down to trousers and shirt, Mallinson pushed the man away and threw himself on the bed. Perhaps by the time he awoke, the news of Lady Clarissa's presence at the masquerade would have eclipsed the stories about Ransley's.

Mallinson woke to a touch on his shoulder and a filthy headache. He rolled over and glared at his valet for daring to wake him. The man blanched, then stammered, "Boy came for you with a message. Seems it's urgent, like, and he won't leave until he gets an answer."

"What message?"

His valet handed it to him gingerly, then took himself off, which was just as well, for when Mallinson saw what it was, he wished mightily to box someone's ears.

It was a quarter-sheet of foolscap, folded and sealed carefully. Though the round, schoolgirl's hand on the outside was unfamiliar to him, it didn't take him but a moment to realize it was from Lady Clarissa, who begged him to see that the message within got to Lord Trenwick. Mallinson sat bolt upright, his heart pounding. Did the girl have not a shred of sense? Did she even consider what would become of him if her note fell into Ransley's hands? He snarled and broke the seal, pulling out and scanning the enclosed message to Trenwick.

A hysterical laugh rising in his throat, he crumpled the note in his fist and threw it to the floor with a strangled curse. Stupid chit! A damsel in need of rescue, according to her note, and Trenwick the only one to do it. Ransley was set on dragging her away and she begged Trenwick to prevent her from being buried in the country. If he loved her, he'd come straightaway to save her. Romantic fool.

Mallinson slumped on the bed and buried his head in his hands, muffling his shrill laughter. He'd finally done it; Ransley was retreating to the country. And if, by some chance, the man changed his mind, Mallinson held in his hand the leverage needed to force Ransley's hand. Proof that the girl was as absolutely lost to propriety as he'd made sure was rumored and had formed a connection with one of Society's most notorious rakes. She'd be the talk of the *ton* if this note came to light, and her reputation would certainly never recover if she did, by some miracle, convince Trenwick to take her away from Ransley's house.

And none of it made a jot of difference when the only thing the *ton* was talking about was Ransley's expected nuptials. Even if Ransley stayed away from Town, even if he and the Ravenshaw woman did *not* marry, the rumor would still be there, and Mallinson's prospects would ever be considered on shaky ground. But really, there was little chance of there not being a marriage. Ransley was stiff-rumped, top-lofty… and the very pattern card of propriety. Once he became aware of the rumors, he would almost certainly offer for Miss Ravenshaw to protect her reputation, even if he hadn't been at Vauxhall with her. An appalling thought struck Mallinson.

Cursing, he dove to scoop up the discarded note. Carrying it to his desk, he smoothed it flat and looked at it closely in the brilliant sunlight falling through the window. Half of a watermark was visible on one edge of the trimmed paper. He cursed again and rifled through the desk, looking for the quires of paper he'd taken away from Ransley's townhouse on his second visit. Ransley had funds enough to cover the loss, and surely owed his heir the use of some of the paper printed especially for the duke by an exclusive stationer. He found one of the purloined sheets, and laid it in the light, and tried to remember if the watermark — unique to Ransley's stationary — was the same as on the Ravenshaw woman's letter to Wilford. Much as he tried to convince himself it was not, the sinking away of his stomach said otherwise.

Mallinson sat back in his chair and tried very hard not to panic. If Miss Ravenshaw was writing letters on Ransley's stationary, then some, at least, of Ormsby's tale might well be true. At a minimum, it meant that there was some kind of rapprochement between them. He shivered as he remembered Wilford crowing about how he'd helped Miss Ravenshaw with Lady Clarissa. He was such a want-wit that if he hadn't already opened his budget to her, he doubtless soon would. Whether he meant to or not, Wilford would certainly give away

Mallinson's hand in this to Miss Ravenshaw. And given that she and Ransley had been seen smelling of April and May, whatever she knew, Ransley would soon know.

The jig was up.

Mallinson stumbled to his feet and went to pour himself a bumper of quite expensive brandy. Might as well enjoy it now; no tradesman would give him credit to buy even poor-quality goods in future. And not only could he no longer live on his prospects, but Ransley was likely to cut him off once he learned of Mallinson's scheming, if not call him out. Mallinson's hand shook as he brought the glass to his lips. He would be lucky to only lose his allowance and not his life.

Perhaps it wouldn't come to that. He drank off half the brandy without tasting it. Ransley did have a care for his reputation, after all, and it was bad form to murder your own heir. Or leave him without a feather to fly with. Surely…

He drank the rest of the brandy and put the glass on the mantle, then leaned his head against it and stared unseeing into the hearth. His valet hadn't bothered to make up the fire, lazy thing, and the room was chilled. Mallinson looked blankly into the grate, which was as black as his mood, and for a while, he stayed there, unmoving.

Gradually, however, light began to penetrate. There was no course Mallinson could see that would keep him out of Ransley's black books, it was true. It was equally true that nothing Lady Clarissa did seemed to land her permanently in those same black books. Mallinson straightened up slowly.

She was begging Trenwick to rescue her from her guardian — and what could she possibly expect him to do, short of flying off with her to Gretna Green? She was much mistaken in Trenwick if she thought he'd marry her over the anvil… or at all. He'd certainly be willing to give her a tumble, but as his light o'love, not his wife. But she needn't know that.

Mallinson need only write back to her and tell her he was acting on Trenwick's behalf. Arrange to meet her someplace and pretend he'd come to deliver her to where her lover awaited her. She was so easily led, he could string her along for hours. And once she'd slept the night at an inn with him, she would be so utterly ruined that he was certain he could convince her she had no choice but to agree to marry him over the anvil.

There was a great deal to do and little time to do it. First, send a message back to Clarissa to arrange a meeting place, then hire a carriage…. Mallinson cursed, thinking of the lightness of his pockets. He went to his desk, dug out the money he kept hidden away from his prying valet, and weighed the bag of coin in his hand. It wouldn't be enough to get them to Gretna, but he rather thought he could get the little jobber he'd hired the carriage from last night to take a flyer on his prospects. He would, after all, be marrying an heiress in her own right. It would surely suit old Charlie to have a man in the position Mallinson would soon occupy beholden to him.

142

Mallinson might find himself supplanted by a child out of Ransley, but the duke positively doted on his ward. However much he despised Mallinson, Ransley would never cut Clarissa off. Once he married the chit, Mallinson could be assured of a roof over his head and a substantial income. He wouldn't have the title, it was true, but he'd have Lady Clarissa, and more to the point, Lady Clarissa's money. It was enough to settle for.

Chapter Eighteen

THEA realized she was staring across the room again and dragged her eyes back to her book. It was a Minerva Press novel, started largely because she knew she would not be able to focus on anything more demanding. Even so, she couldn't remember a thing she'd read that morning, couldn't keep her mind on anything for two minutes together before becoming distracted with thoughts of Ransley. She shuddered to think what a poor conversationalist she would make at the moment. It was as well, perhaps, that Mrs. Wellins was still keeping to her room, though Thea could wish it was for a less serious reason. She prayed Gabriel would be well.

With a sigh, she put the book down. She ought to be reading, or doing anything, in fact, other than thinking about Ransley. About whether he had yet left town, about his warmth, his strong arms, his kisses…

"Bother," Thea said aloud and picked the book up again. She struggled through three pages, forcing her mind back to the text every time it wandered and despite the fact that she was quite certain the heroine, Ophelia (and what lunatic would name their daughter that, knowing *Hamlet*?), was the most foolish, pigeon-brained female she'd ever had the misfortune of reading about.

She was relieved to be interrupted by a scratching at the door. One of the Neds stepped in when she called for him to enter. "Boy brought this for you, miss."

"Thank you, Ned." Her heart beat faster when she saw that it was a folded piece of Ransley's stationary. She opened it with trembling hands, and was quite irritated with herself when her heart fell at seeing a round, schoolgirl hand that could not possibly be Ransley's. Scolding herself for being full of foolish expectations, she began to read.

144

She finished only the first two lines before leaping to her feet and rushing to the door, calling out for Ned as she went.

"Miss?" he answered, startled by her urgency.

"Go out and find me a hackney as quick as you can."

"A *hackney*, Miss Ravenshaw?" he said, shocked.

"Yes, we haven't time to wait for a carriage to be brought round. I shall be down straightaway." With that, she caught up her skirts and dashed up the stairs in a manner entirely unladylike. She was in one of her older morning dresses, not planning on being "at home" for anyone today, but it would have to do. There wasn't time to change. There wasn't even time to ring for her maid. She rummaged through her wardrobe and took the first pelisse she found, only realizing she still had the letter in her hand when she did so. She snatched her reticule off the dressing table and stuffed the letter in it, grabbed her gloves, popped a bonnet on her head, and started back down the stairs, pulling on her gloves and tying the bonnet laces as she went.

She wasn't entirely certain if the Ned in the entryway was the same Ned she'd sent for a hackney, but it didn't signify, for he opened the door for her as soon as he saw her, and she exited to find the other Ned standing next to a hackney cab.

"Thank you," she said to him as he handed her into the carriage. "If Mrs. Wellins asks where I am, tell her there's been an emergency and I'll be back as soon as I can."

"Miss, are you sure you don't want to—"

"There isn't time. Thank you," she said again before turning to the driver. "The Duke of Ransley's townhouse, Grosvenor Square. As quickly as you can!"

"Yes, mum." He touched his hat, flicked his whip at the horse, and they were off.

Thea braced herself as best she could against the squabs and pulled the letter from her reticule (relieved to note as she did so that she had enough money to pay the hackney when she arrived — it would be too lowering to have to beg Ransley's butler to do so, no matter the mission she was on). She started again from the beginning, and had time to read it through twice before the hackney pulled up in front of Ransley's Town residence. Her heart in her throat, she pressed too much money into the driver's hand and took the stairs much faster than she ought, taking hold of the doorknocker and employing it vigorously. Finally, the door opened.

"Miss Ravenshaw?" The butler's expression shifted instantly from irritated to startled.

"I must see the duke immediately," she said, stepping smartly through the door so there was no chance he would close it on her. He retreated from her advance, looking shocked at her importunity. "Please tell me Lady Clarissa's still in the house!"

"She could hardly be anything else, being locked in her room." Thea looked up to see Ransley coming down the stairs in buckskins and a bottle-green coat. His expression stuck somewhere between grim and unwillingly amused, he added, "The only solution, I'm afraid, when she called me an unfeeling monster and said she'd do a flit rather than go home with me."

Relief tried to flood Thea, but could not seem to warm the coldness about her heart. "And you're certain she's still here?"

Hearing the urgency in her voice, his eyes sharpened upon her. He came to her and took her hands. "Whatever is amiss?"

Thea opened her mouth, then closed it as prudence stayed her. Old family retainer or no, it would not do to air the linen in front of the butler. In fact, now that Ransley's presence permitted her to draw a breath, she became aware that the entryway and staircase were full servants, all busily preparing to send their master and mistress off and close up the house.

Ransley instantly read her hesitation. "Hailston," he said, "check on Lady Clarissa, if you will." Then he drew her into the library with him, turning to her the moment the door was closed and possessing himself of her hands again. "What is the matter, Althea?"

Oh, her name was sweet on his lips! And oh, this was not at all the time. "It's Lady Clarissa… she's sent me a letter."

"A letter. About?"

Her nerve failed her. "Perhaps you ought to…" She retrieved the letter from her reticule and pressed it into his hand, then took herself off to the hearth to give him privacy to read it. The gray mask she'd worn at Vauxhall was still sitting on the mantelshelf, its shimmer in the indirect light of the sun seeming to say *here, it was here, remember how his lips felt against yours, how his body felt—*

Ransley ground out a curse.

"Just so," Thea said, trying again to swallow her heart, which just would not keep out of her throat.

She was talking to an empty room, for Ransley had dashed out and she could hear him running up the stairs. He must have met someone coming down, for there was a sudden babble of voices, punctuated by Ransley ordering, "Then *look* for her, damn you!" in quite the iciest tone she'd ever heard, and she'd found herself on the sharp side of his tongue on more than one occasion.

Not that she faulted him in this instance. Lady Clarissa's note — devoid of details but full of spurious reassurances that she was safe and knew what she was doing — did not say what, precisely, she intended, except for escape, but wherever she went, it would be without a guardian or chaperone. She would be lucky if it were only her reputation she lost.

Ransley came back in, going directly to the desk. In a moment, he had out a box that held a brace of pistols. One was in the box, the other still sitting on the corner of the desk where he'd left it last night. He busied himself in loading the second.

"Why you?" he said after a moment. "Why send you a letter and not..." Though his voice faltered, his hands never did.

"Because she feared being stopped if she left something for you. She likely thought that by the time I got her note..." She'd moved unconsciously back to him, but made herself stop before she reached the desk. She was standing near the chair where he'd draped his greatcoat the previous night. It said something about the upheaval of the house that none of the servants had collected it and hung it up where it belonged. The burgundy domino peeked out from beneath it and mocked her with its cheerfulness.

"Yes," Ransley said presently. "I had..." He cleared his throat. "I had wondered if I ought to have been more sympathetic. She was perfectly disagreeable this morning, and while I tried to be patient — doubtless she had quite a head from sampling arrack punch last night — when Hailston caught her sneaking out, I quite lost my temper. I've never actually locked her in before."

"Given how she's acted lately," Thea said tartly, feeling oddly as if a sympathetic voice might shatter him, "it's a wonder you haven't." And really, if she weren't shaken with worry for the girl, she'd be quite irritated. Lady Clarissa was far from muttonheaded, yet appeared prepared to scotch all her chances at once in what amounted to youthful pique. Thea sighed silently — the girl was, after all, scarcely eighteen and subject to the usual fits and starts of that age.

"Perhaps I ought to have kept her under lock and key," Ransley said without looking up from his task. "Perhaps, if I had..." His hands continued to work deftly, and Thea wished she could admire their certainty, but all she could think of was what those pistols would be used for and how much damage they could do. Clarissa was in danger and Ransley was going into danger and...

"This is my fault," she said.

He looked up at that. From somewhere, he found a smile. It looked ghastly, but she appreciated his instinct to reassure her. She doubted he'd feel it for much longer. "I don't see how. You've been the one bright spot in all this... for all I own I initially wished you to the devil," he added, a more genuine smile tugging at his lips.

In other circumstances, Thea would have smiled back, have said *Really, Your Grace? I never noticed,* but she couldn't. Every word he said only made the weight that bore down on her that much heavier.

"You've taken as much care for her as if she were your own kin," Ransley went on, and Thea devoutly wished that were true. His incipient smile vanished. "Better than I have."

She opened her mouth to damn herself, but nothing came out. She couldn't. She just couldn't. Instead, she said, "Nonsense."

"Hardly. My niece, who I've had the raising of for ten years, has turned into not only a hoyden but a ramshackle female who can think of no better reaction to brangling with me than to throw herself upon the mercy of strangers."

"Her note did not, to me, seem to indicate that she was dashing out into the wide world on her own. She sounded quite certain of her safety. Do you have any idea who she might go to?" Thea asked hopefully. Perhaps she'd read the situation wrong; perhaps Clarissa had merely taken herself off to some aunt.

He set the loaded pistol with its mate. "Had you not shown up here with her note, I should have expected to find her on your doorstep."

"Yes," Thea said heavily, her hopes dashed. She nerved herself to confess. "This *is* my fault. The people she's been thrown in with because of me—"

"Althea," Ransley said, getting up to come around the desk and once more take her hands in his. "Clary's hardly likely to have dashed off with *Wilford* of all people. A man less suited to rouse a girl's romantic pretensions doesn't exist."

"Not Wilford." Thea swallowed and forced out, "Lord Trenwick."

"Trenwick," Ransley said blankly. "How in the blazes could *Trenwick* be your fault?"

She could not, she simply could *not* look into his pale, piercing eyes while she said this. Thea dropped her gaze to his cravat and made herself start, her heart pounding nineteen to the dozen. "I… At Lady Ayleford's ball, Lord Trenwick…" There seemed to be heat roiling off Ransley's body; it beat upon her skin so that she could scarcely draw breath. *Oh heavens, Thea, just say it! You surely have at least that much backbone.* "Lord Trenwick bet me that Lady Clarissa would have to retire to the country before the end of the Season."

She heard Ransley take in a sharp breath, and for a moment, his fingers closed crushingly on hers. Then they sprang open and he stepped away, as if he could not bear to touch her, to even be in proximity with her. Thea forced her eyes up to his face with trepidation, but he was not looking at her, his eyes directed somewhere over her shoulder. His face was as cold and hard as she'd ever seen it. Quite without realizing she was going to, she started talking again, words spilling from her in a hurried jumble.

"I'd already decided that I wished to assist Clarissa, and I had no idea he'd take an actual hand in—"

Ransley cut her off in a voice like iron. "Enough, madam." Where a moment ago, she had been sweating in his heat, now she shivered at the ice coming off him. He smiled without looking at her, a smile without warmth or amusement. "The fault here is mine. I had the right of it at the start, but I allowed myself to be persuaded. By Clarissa, and by my own—" He bit back whatever he'd meant to say. "It was foolish of me to believe you ever had Clarissa's best interests at heart."

"Oh, but I—"

He cut her off with a look. "You have done quite enough, madam."

He'd said something similar the previous night. Then it had been an oblique thank you and a refusal of assistance. Today, it was an accusation. And a dismissal. But Thea felt frozen into place and could only gaze miserably at him.

Ransley swept up his greatcoat and the two pistols. He paused briefly at the door. "It would be well for you if you were not here when I returned. Neither in my house nor in Town."

Then he was gone, leaving the library door ajar. Thea heard him exchange a quick, sharp word with his butler, then the sound of the door closing behind him. For a moment, she couldn't move, so weak and sick she felt as if her legs would not hold her if she moved even an inch. Dazed, she looked around, scarcely seeing her surroundings. Last night, this room had seemed something out of a dream. Today, it was a nightmare. The gray mask on the mantelshelf grinned malevolently at her.

Eventually, she shifted a little. And though her knees felt weak, she did not fall. She took two steps, stopped, and wrapped her arms about herself. The room was warm, but she was not. She took in a careful breath, filling her lungs to their fullest. It did nothing to allay the pressure around her heart, which hardly seemed like it could keep beating under the weight it bore. Foolish, she chided herself. She'd held up fine through all her adult life without a man in it thus far; she would not crumble now. She'd had his regard for, really, only a short time, and she could surely go on in its absence, no matter how she felt now.

Besides, it was no more than she deserved.

She caught a glimpse of movement near the door, and her head came up fast. Ransley... No. No, of course not. Just the butler, hovering in the doorway wearing an uncertain expression that sat ill on his austere face. He looked gray and desperately worried, and fear had aged him unmercifully.

"My lady?"

He must truly be overset to make such a mistake in address. "I'm sorry, Hailston. I'm just going."

He shook himself slightly. "Miss Ravenshaw, it appears that Lady Clarissa's maid may know something of where she's gone. In His Grace's absence—"

Thea smiled, a pitiful thing as broken as her heart. "His Grace would not thank you for involving me."

"Perhaps not," Hailston admitted. Worry had unbent him enough to drop his formal façade. "But that does not matter so much as what Lady Clarissa needs. I've sent a boy after His Grace, but it seems to me there's not a moment to spare."

"Why?" Thea asked, his urgency forcing her to surface from her misery. "What did you find out?"

Hailston turned and jerked his head at someone in the hall. A moment later, Lady Clarissa's young maid was standing in the doorway, wringing her hands in her skirt. "Oh miss," she stammered. "Oh miss, it's horrible. My poor mistress, and the duke'll be that mad, and—"

"We can't worry about the duke just now," Thea said, as much to herself as the maid. She went to the girl and took her hands before she could do herself an injury, so tightly was she twisting her skirt. "Mariah, is it? If you know something about where Lady Clarissa has gone, you must tell me."

Mariah hesitated, peering doubtfully at Thea.

Hailston shifted impatiently. "Out with it, girl. Tell Miss Ravenshaw what you told me."

"Lady Clarissa was that excited, miss. She... she said she was... eloping." She dropped her voice on the last word so that it was barely audible. "Going to Gretna Green with Lord Trenwick."

Thea closed her eyes briefly. She would never have guessed he'd go so far. Trenwick was lost not only to propriety but all virtue or sense. To be willing to ruin a girl just to win a bet, and one on which not a penny was wagered... He must be mad for the wager itself, for the thrill of winning. And it was Thea who'd put Clarissa in his way.

"Oh miss," Mariah said, suddenly clasping Thea's hands tightly. "You must go after her."

"His Grace has already left on that very errand," Thea said. "And unless I miss my guess, he's on his way to Lord Trenwick's lodgings."

"But Lady Clarissa was to meet him down the road a pace. He said he'd have a carriage for her there and they'd go off straightaway."

"How long ago?" Thea asked, her heart pounding. If they were meeting nearby, there was still a chance Ransley might have spotted them when he left.

"Most half an hour now, miss."

Her heart sank. Ransley wouldn't have seen them, and was even now heading in the wrong direction, wasting time looking for Trenwick when the blasted man and Lady Clarissa were already on their way out of London. By the time the boy caught up with Ransley and the man returned to his house, they would have such a lead that it might not be possible to catch up. Not before Clarissa was ruined.

"Hailston, please get me a hackney." She didn't have the money with her to pay for it, having used all she had in getting there, but she would figure something out. There was no time to lose and no choice — she must go after Lady Clarissa upon the instant.

"His Grace's curricle is harnessed and ready for travel," Hailston said. "If you drive?"

"I do," Thea said, sounding more certain than she felt. It had been a while, as she hired carriages and coachmen to get her where she needed to go, her funds not running to driving purely for the sake of driving, but this was no time to be fainthearted.

"One minute," Hailston said. He went to Ransley's desk and took two items out of the drawers, bringing them to Thea.

When he handed her the fold of banknotes, she tried to refuse. "I can't take his money."

"You can. You're doing this for Lady Clarissa. Our Clary." And really, it oughtn't be so affecting to see the man unbend so. "You may need to change horses," he urged.

She hoped to heaven that Ransley had caught up by then. If he had not reached them by the time the horses flagged, it would be a sign of something seriously amiss. But Hailston was right — even driving the duke's carriage rather than having to hire her own, she could not afford to go out without any money in her reticule.

The second thing Hailston handed her was a little folding knife of the sort used to mend quill nibs, the blade less than two inches long and wickedly sharp.

Chapter Nineteen

RANSLEY was startled when Trenwick himself opened the door to his lodgings in response to Ransley's hammering, but surprise didn't slow him any. He leveled the pistol at Trenwick's chest and stepped into him, forcing the man to retreat back inside.

After ascertaining from Hailston where Trenwick kept lodgings — the only people who gossiped more than the *ton* were their servants — Ransley had determined he could get there quicker on foot than in any cab. It had left him mildly out of breath, but had the advantage of not giving him the opportunity to think too closely on either Clary's danger or Althea's... *Miss Ravenshaw's* betrayal.

He'd been a damn fool. His belly and chest filled with a cold, sick rage when he thought of how he'd fallen for her charms. He'd lain awake half the previous night, unable to banish the feel of her in his arms, of her lips under his — unable even to want to. Though he knew he had to get Clary away from Town, while he lay unsleeping, he'd spun plans for how and when he might see Althea again. It would not be easy — he could not invite her to Tynesfield and thought it unlikely they would both be invited to the same country house party. But he could get up to Town occasionally, surely, or find some excuse to visit whatever part of the country she returned to at the end of the Season. And there was next year. Once he got Clary married off and no longer need worry about her, he would have time for himself. Time to devote to Althea. But she'd turned out to be as perfidious as he'd first thought her — more so, for far from helping Clary, she seemed set on the girl's downfall. Well, not if he had anything to say in the matter.

He swung the door closed behind him and engaged the lock. He'd had to show his pistol to the attendant at the door of the building to convince the man to tell him which room Trenwick had taken, and if the man took it into his head to call on some of his fellows to evict Ransley, he did not wish to be interrupted before he had what he'd come for. In any case, this was not a conversation to be had where someone might overhear.

He looked about the modest-sized sitting room. There were two doors — the one back into the hall and a closed door that likely led to the bedroom. A small fire in the grate, a few pieces of furniture, some books and odds and ends. No Clary.

"Where is Lady Clarissa?"

"What?" Trenwick said stupidly. He'd thrown himself into a chair in front of the fire, where he lounged indolently, affecting not to notice Ransley's pistol. It made his finger itch to bear down upon the trigger.

"Lady Clarissa," he said slowly, as if to a simpleton. "I know she's here. Produce her."

"What the devil would make you think she was here?" Trenwick speared a hand through his tousled hair. "Do you think I regularly entertain *en dishabille*?"

Ransley had been too busy keeping an eye out for Trenwick's valet, who might prove a hazard to his plans, to notice before, but Trenwick's hair was mussed with sleep, his feet bare, and his dressing gown gaped over his bare chest. There was only one kind of entertaining he would do while dressed like that. A growl rose in Ransley's throat. Keeping the gun on Trenwick, he walked to the bedroom door and opened it cautiously, in case the valet waited on the other side. It was empty. The bed looked like a battle had been staged upon it, but there was no mark of any woman in the room. No sign of Clary. Relief vied with rage in his breast... and lost.

Accepting the calculated risk of taking his pistol off Trenwick, he stepped into the room and looked quickly under the bed and in the wardrobe. Just to make sure, though he could not believe Clary so desperate to escape him that she would hide from him. But then, he'd never have guessed she'd run away either. He was not entirely certain he believed she had. Oh, her note and the fact that she'd clearly climbed down the tree outside her bedroom window showed she left the house on her own, but that did not mean she *stayed* away of her own volition.

"I don't make a habit of hiding women in my wardrobe," Trenwick said.

Ransley wheeled to find him leaning negligently against the doorframe, his arms crossed over his chest. "Where is your valet?"

"Presumably out arranging some kind of breakfast for himself and me."

"You don't know?"

"I was asleep until you pounded on my door." Trenwick yawned too widely for it to be aught but show. "The devil take it! It's too early for this. If you aren't going to make any sense, then take yourself off. I'm going back to bed."

Before he got one step, Ransley put the pistol to his breastbone. The slight widening of Trenwick's eyes was all the reaction he showed. "Where is Lady Clarissa?"

Trenwick seemed to study him. When he responded, the blithe pretended irritation was gone and he was all seriousness. "The last I saw her was last night, when you took her from me while I was trying to get her out of Vauxhall."

"She was much taken with you," Ransley said coldly, sourness filling his belly at the thought of this dissipated wretch having more influence over Clary than he did; enough to spirit her from his house. "And you've never been one to let grass grow under your feet."

"I've never been one to seduce virgins either," Trenwick snapped, "and I certainly don't mean to start now." He took half a step back, just enough that the pistol no longer pressed against his skin. "It's too blasted early for you to be foxed, and I've never heard of the Duke of Ransley getting deep into his cups in any case. You must be cracked to think she'd come here—" He broke off, his eyes sharpening upon Ransley. "Why *did* you think she was here?"

Ransley lowered the pistol. There was little point in continuing to aim it at the fellow when he showed no sign of being influenced by it. He kept the gun at the ready, however. He might yet have need of it here. While it was clear Clary was not in Trenwick's lodgings, that did not mean he hadn't sent his servant to bestow her in some less-accessible place. "I know about the wager."

"Which one?" Trenwick asked with a jaded smile. "There are so many."

"Your wager with Miss Ravenshaw."

For a moment, Trenwick looked utterly blank. Then he said, "Never meant to follow up on that. It was the diversion of a moment, soon forgotten."

"Not by Miss Ravenshaw." Ransley's heart had leapt to hear that the wager had not been genuine, plummeted at the realization that Miss Ravenshaw had thought it was and so could not be excused on that account.

"I wish I'd known. I would have laid her mind to rest on the matter." He gave Ransley a very direct look and said again, "I do not seduce virgins."

"Just so." He put the pistol back in the pocket of his greatcoat. He was by no means convinced, but it was clear that if Trenwick was involved, he was playing a much deeper game than could be won by use of a gun. Ransley ran his hand through his hair and allowed some of his panic and confusion to show, not entirely, as it happened, by choice. "But if Lady Clarissa didn't come away with you...?"

"She was running from someone when she collided with me at Vauxhall," Trenwick said. "I don't suppose she told you who it was, or who took her to the masquerade? No," he answered himself, "if she had, you would hardly be here."

"I had thought you took her there," Ransley admitted.

"No, I just caught her when she ran blindly into me and got a mask on her before any more people saw her. How could I do anything else?" he asked impatiently when Ransley gave him a disbelieving look. "The girl's a complete innocent. Though I admit, at first I thought—" He stopped, his gaze turning inward.

Ransley waited a moment before realizing he was wasting time, lingering with Trenwick in the hopes he might, intentionally or otherwise, say something that would give his search some direction. He felt hopelessly adrift, with no clear idea where Clary might be if she hadn't made arrangements with Trenwick, which it appeared more and more likely she hadn't. But he would clearly not find his answers here, and looking for them in Trenwick only delayed him from finding them elsewhere.

He turned to the door, but had scarcely taken a step before Trenwick said slowly, "I think, for the author of this, you must look closer to home." When Ransley looked back at him, he added, "Your heir."

"What the devil has Josias Mallinson to do with this?" Ransley asked, startled.

"It was he who came to me at Lady Cathorn's ball and said he spoke on behalf of a young woman who wished to waltz with me. He implied she desired more," Trenwick said bluntly. "I had my doubts — a young miss of the *ton* so forward — but…" He shrugged expressively.

Ransley squeezed his eyes briefly shut. "When she stood up to dance with you…"

"Precisely. It wasn't until I found her, terrified and half-disguised with punch, at Vauxhall that I realized she was truly innocent."

"Why would—" Ransley started in a voice that felt shredded. He stopped himself. It was neither an appropriate subject, an appropriate audience, nor an appropriate time. *If* it was true and not merely an attempt to misdirect him. Ransley couldn't know for certain until he'd tracked Mallinson down and had it out with him. But the more he thought on it, the more he felt a sinking in his chest. "Thank you, Trenwick," he forced out, and headed for the door.

He heard Trenwick's voice behind him, but didn't know or care what he said. He was halfway through the sitting room when a sudden banging started up on the hall door.

"What the devil?" Trenwick strode past Ransley. He unlocked the door and pulled it open, yanked the author of the ruckus in by his collar, and shut the door behind him. "What is the meaning of this?"

" 'M just here for His Grace," the boy mumbled, shrinking back against the door. His skittering eyes landed on Ransley, and he instantly squared his shoulders and took a step away from the door. "Your Grace!"

"Yes…" It was that boy groom, the undercook's son Clary had hauled out to Hyde Park with her. What the devil was the boy's name? "…Jeremy. What is it?"

"Mr. Hailston sent me, sir; to find you, sir; Mariah says m'lady's up an' run off; left most half-hour ago without no baggage or nothing; Mariah said she's on her way to Gretna with some cove named Trenwick," he said on a single breath. "Sir."

Trenwick cursed. He turned to Ransley, his hands slightly raised as if Ransley still held the gun on him. "If I'd arranged to elope to Gretna, do you think you'd catch me still sitting about here in my dressing gown?"

Before Ransley could respond, the boy blurted, "But this weren't where she had me take the note." He quailed when both men turned to look at him.

"What note and where did you take it?" Ransley asked, forcing himself not to snap at the boy.

"The note Lady Clarissa had me run out this mornin' to some cove on Bond Street."

Trenwick said quietly, "Mallinson keeps lodgings on Bond Street."

* * *

Ransley made it back to his house in half the time it had taken to reach Trenwick's lodgings. He outstripped even Jeremy's young legs within a few minutes of starting off, but didn't bother himself over it — the boy certainly knew his way home.

Home, where all the information he needed to find Clary had been all along. If he hadn't dashed off after Trenwick... If it hadn't been for Althea's confession... He bit back that thought. There wasn't time now. There was only time to get after Clary as quickly as possible. Clary and *Mallinson*. If the boy'd taken the note to Mallinson, then clearly Mariah had the name of Clary's beau wrong. But Mallinson! It was enough to send one reeling. They'd spent not twenty minutes together in conversation and scarcely knew each other. Of course, she'd spent even less time with Trenwick, but he was at least a dashing figure of a man. Ransley couldn't imagine how Clary'd developed a *tendre* for his heir, of all people. It beggared understanding.

He dashed up the front steps and into the house. "Hailston." Thankfully the man was in the entryway when Ransley came in. He strode into the library, still talking. "Have my horse saddled immediately. Return the carriage to the stables; I won't be needing it." He pulled open the drawer in which he kept some banknotes easy to hand, only to find the money gone. "Where the devil is my blunt?"

"I gave it to Miss Ravenshaw, sir," Hailston said. "She's gone after Lady Clarissa in your carriage."

"She what?"

"She was still here when Mariah came to me with what she knew. We knew it would take the boy time to deliver the message to you, and Miss Ravenshaw felt it best to start after Lady Clarissa right away. She took Mariah with her," he added when Ransley found himself unable to do aught but gape at him.

"Am I to understand that Miss Ravenshaw has taken off in my carriage with my money and my niece's maid?"

"To rescue Lady Clarissa, yes sir." His mask of imperturbability was somewhat undercut by the worry graying his skin.

Ransley cursed.

"Indeed, sir." Hailston handed him a fold of banknotes. "I took the liberty of retrieving this from your bedroom, sir. The stablemaster is having a horse saddled for you even now."

"Make that two," Trenwick said from the doorway. Ransley hadn't heard the doorknocker, so the man must have simply walked in. He was dressed rather plainly, and though he was neat, it was clear his valet had not been involved in the process. His cravat was merely wrapped twice around his neck and tied in a loose knot, and his hair was uncombed.

"What the devil are *you* doing here?"

Trenwick gave Ransley a bland smile. "I'm coming with you. You'll have to provide me with a horse — I'll never get mine from the mews in time."

Ransley watched Hailston head out the door to order up another horse, and wondered quite when he'd lost control of his own servants. Dismissing the matter as unimportant at the moment, he turned back to Trenwick, who spoke before he could.

"I consider that I bear at least some responsibility for this state of affairs. Allow me to assist you," Trenwick said simply.

If Trenwick weren't somehow involved in this, Ransley might well need his help. He had no clear idea quite what had possessed Mallinson, nor whether he had any help in this outrage. And if Trenwick *were* somehow involved, it would be as well if Ransley kept him where he could find him. "You'd best be an accomplished rider."

"I am."

"Good. We shall have to ride hard to catch up with Mallinson, Lady Clarissa, and Miss Ravenshaw."

"Miss Ravenshaw! Whatever is she doing with them?"

"I'll explain on the way." Ransley ushered Trenwick out of the library.

Chapter Twenty

CLARISSA'S maid was a poor traveler, moaning with fear and clutching at the armrail every time the curricle swayed a bit too vigorously. Which it did frequently now that they had finally reached the outskirts of London and Thea was able to spring the horses. Even so, they weren't moving that fast, as Thea found it challenging enough to control the matched pair of bays at a moderate pace, as they were fresh and energetic.

One of the wheels dropped into a rut with a jolt, and Mariah shrieked. Thea calmly gave the reins a snap, the horses pulled a bit harder, and in a moment, they'd righted themselves again, with Thea's ears the only casualty. She was sincerely regretting having brought Mariah along. She would give anything to have one of the Neds with her. As that had been manifestly impossible, however, the little maid would have to do. It might, perhaps, have been better to bring one of the duke's grooms or footmen, but the carriage could only hold two comfortably, with a third in the groom's seat up behind. Not only did Thea not know Ransley's male servants sufficiently to feel comfortable driving alone out of Town with one of them, she felt it would be better for everyone's reputation if the third in their party was female. Once they caught up with Trenwick and Lady Clarissa and convinced her to return with them.

Thea worried it over in her mind — how was she going to convince Clarissa to abandon this foolhardy venture? The girl was as stubborn as the day was long, and if she'd agreed to run off with Trenwick, she'd surely convinced herself she was fathoms deep in love with the cad. It was not a combination to auger easy success. Especially if Trenwick was determined to keep her — he could be very convincing, as Thea knew to her sorrow. She could still make little sense of his carrying things this far — surely he would not do so much to win a very small bet. But then, Lady Clarissa was an heiress in her own right, and perhaps it was as simple as that. Though Thea hadn't heard so much as a whisper to suggest Trenwick was dangling out for a rich bride, one never knew. A man who gambled as frequently and as deeply as he did might well be halfway up the River Tick and no one the wiser.

Try as she might, Thea could not arrive at a satisfactory approach for either Clarissa's love-struck stubbornness or Trenwick's… whatever motivated him. Her attempts to do so were not helped by the fact that her mind — evil thing that it was — kept throwing up at her the expression on Ransley's face when she told him about the wager. Or rather, the lack of an expression. He had withdrawn from her as utterly as if he'd flown to the moon, and she shivered still at losing the warmth of his regard.

It was only what she deserved.

She slapped the reins, encouraging the horses to greater effort. She could not run them for long without causing them harm, but a little more speed would surely not come amiss. The increased speed required her to focus more upon her driving than the thorough disaster she'd made of everything, and she welcomed the respite even as she knew it left her woefully unprepared for what she must do when she eventually caught up.

It happened sooner than she'd expected. Trenwick's carriage had a half-hour's lead on her, and Thea saw little chance of catching up until he had to stop and change horses. But she would also need to change horses, and if he'd arranged this ahead of time, he would have new teams already waiting at each stage, while she would have to take whatever the coaching inns had available. She prayed that Lady Clarissa had not told him about the note she'd sent Thea or admitted to being free in what she told her maid — if Trenwick did not expect immediate pursuit, he might drive more moderately, for Clarissa's comfort, if for no other reason. If he knew, however… Well, he was rumored to be able to drive to an inch, and Thea doubted her ability to catch up with him.

They'd just passed a coaching inn — Thea having determined to drive on, though her horses were beginning to flag somewhat — when Mariah gave a cry that was not prompted by some heaving of the curricle.

"Oh miss, go back! Go back!" she exclaimed, clutching at Thea's arm.

"What is it?" Thea asked, shaking her off gently and correcting the horses, which had veered in response to the sudden pull at the reins.

"I saw her; I saw my lady back at that inn."

"You are certain?"

"Oh yes, miss!"

Praying Mariah wasn't mistaken, Thea drew up and tooled the curricle around to go back. There were several carriages in the yard — including one of the yellow-bounders hired by those who did not have their own equipage, which was listing at a dangerous angle — but none Thea could make herself certain was Trenwick's. Even were she intimately familiar with his carriage and cattle, however, it still might not answer. For all she knew, he had borrowed or hired a carriage for the trip. She pulled up and waited impatiently for one of the ostlers gathered about the yellow-bounder to cease arguing there and come hold the horses. It was only a moment or two before one did, but by that time, Mariah had slipped out of the carriage and darted into the building, and Thea felt quite as if she were going to jump out of her skin if she had to wait a moment more.

"See that they have water," she directed, climbing down from the carriage with his assistance, "but do not unharness them. We shall be off again directly." They'd either be after Clary again, if Mariah was mistaken, or if the fates were kind, back to London with the foolish chit.

She scarcely waited for his response, but headed into the building herself, wondering where Mariah had got off to and how she was going to find her. The inn was busy, with people bustling about in all directions and no one to take notice of her or ask what she needed. She peeped in at the taproom, then moved on past it — however little care he had for Lady Clarissa's reputation otherwise, Trenwick would surely arrange for a private parlor. It would not do to leave his wife-to-be rubbing elbows in the common room, and in any case, she might be seen by someone who would instantly report her whereabouts to Ransley. Trenwick must be very confident indeed that they would not be overtaken if he was breaking their journey so soon. Or perhaps something had gone amiss.

Hearing raised female voices coming from a room off to the right, Thea took a chance and opened the door in time to hear Lady Clarissa say, "You're too much above yourself, Mariah. I'll thank you to keep your nose out of my business."

"Someone must take an interest in it," Thea said, entering and closing the door firmly behind her. "For you're truly making a hash of your chances."

"Miss Ravenshaw!" Lady Clarissa looked taken aback — clearly she'd not thought a bit about how her maid came to be there — but only for a moment. Wrapping herself in a spurious dignity, she squared her shoulders, the light of battle shining in her eyes. "My chances are no business of yours. I love him and I'm going to marry him."

"For heaven's sake, child! You don't even know the man." Thea winced. That was, perhaps, a bit more blunt than she'd meant to be. But now that she'd found Clarissa, she was desperate to convince her to return home before Trenwick could re-enter the picture. Thea rather thought she'd find herself on the losing side if Trenwick took part in the conversation.

"I know all I need to know. He's handsome and charming and a hero and he rescued me. I love him, and that's all that matters."

Thea squeezed her eyes shut briefly. "Child—"

"I'm not a child," Clarissa said, undercutting her assertion by stamping her foot petulantly. "I'm perfectly capable of making my own decisions, despite what you and my uncle think."

"Your uncle is beside himself with worry." And hopefully not too far behind, though Thea wasn't fool enough to mention that.

"He's just angry that I'm not doing what he told me to. Well, he'll just have to content himself with ordering the servants about from now on. He doesn't listen to me and he doesn't care, and I'm going to attach myself to someone who does."

"And you think Trenwick's that person?"

"He loves me!"

"Clarissa…" Thea saw Lady Clarissa's eyes widen. She hadn't meant to sound so defeated. But there was clearly no way to convince Clarissa to come away except to tell her the truth. And Thea knew that would dash Clarissa's heart upon the rocks and destroy her trust. Bad enough that Thea had to tarnish Trenwick in Clarissa's eyes, dispelling her illusions so she could see he was the worst kind of gambling-mad fortune-hunter. But to at the same time admit that she'd taken Clarissa's friendship and confidences under false pretenses — for that was how the girl would inevitably see it — was beyond bearable. "You don't know him at all. This is all a lie. Trenwick doesn't mean to marry you for—"

"What have we here?" a man's voice intruded. Thea hadn't even noticed the door opening. She turned, thinking in passing that the oily voice was vaguely familiar, and found herself looking at Ransley's heir.

"Mr. Mallinson." Relief flooded her, for if Mallinson was here, he must have arrived with Ransley. Though she felt cold at the thought of facing the duke again, he was by far the best person to talk sense into his ward. Or bear her off home by main force if necessary.

"Miss Ravenshaw," he returned, giving her a mocking and insultingly shallow bow. "Come after the prodigal, are we? Shall I expect the duke to breathe fire down my neck any moment?" His tone was airy and unconcerned, but he moved quickly out of the doorway and closed the door behind him, and she noticed he locked it. What the devil was going on?

"I'm not quite certain what you mean, Mr. Mallinson," Thea said slowly. "Is he not with you?"

"With me?" He barked out a laugh. "I should hardly bring him along when dashing for Gretna Green with his ward!"

Lady Clarissa was looking back and forth between them, her brows drawn together with as much confusion as Thea felt. Though she did look unsurprised to see Mallinson, so was ahead of Thea in that, at least.

"*You're* eloping with Lady Clarissa? I thought Trenwick—"

"Cut line, madam," Mallinson said at the same moment Clarissa protested that she'd *never*. Ignoring Clarissa, Mallinson continued, "I know Wilford's opened his budget to you, and you'd hardly be here if you did not put two and two together and arrive at the correct answer. Now—"

"You said Lord Trenwick was meeting us," Clarissa exclaimed, her voice momentarily overriding his.

"I lied," Mallinson said without looking away from Thea. "Whatever you know, Ransley doubtless knows as well, so where is he?"

"I have no idea," Thea said honestly.

"You surely don't expect me to believe that."

"I don't care a fig what you believe," Thea said, exasperated by his unfathomable accusations and odd talk. She hadn't the faintest idea what Wilford had to do with this, nor what Mallinson thought she knew or had guessed. Though obviously it was enough to make him tip his hand, and equally obviously, he was up to something decidedly havey cavey. Lady Clarissa had clearly been brought there under false pretenses, though Thea could not get her head around the exact circumstances, nor whether Trenwick was actually involved or not. "It's the truth."

"Ransley would hardly allow his niece to be carried off without giving pursuit. If you're here, then he knows Clarissa is gone and which way she went. And if he's not with you, he'll be close behind." Mallinson appeared to be talking more for himself than her, and Thea saw no reason to dignify his ranting with a response. "The flash curricle outside with the two prime goers is either yours or Ransley's, I presume. As it happens, you arrived in good time. A wheel has broken on my hired carriage, and yours will do nicely to carry us to the border."

"Nonsense," Thea said stoutly, trying to project confidence in the face of his odd behavior. She walked over to join Lady Clarissa and took the girl's hand, which clung to hers as if to a lifeline. "We shall be going back to Town directly."

"We shall be going to Gretna. All of us. I can hardly leave you behind to direct Ransley." He smiled unpleasantly. "You can act as Clarissa's attendant and be the first to wish us happy."

Lady Clarissa gasped. "Never! I won't be marrying you."

"You will if you know what's good for you, girl. What kind of life do you think you'd have once it became known that you dashed off to Gretna with me, but then didn't exchange vows? Refuse to marry me, and I will ruin you, girl."

"You've got windmills in your head to think you can do such a thing," Thea told him with more certainty than she felt. The marriage laws in Scotland were different, with no requirement that bans be read or guardians consent, and while Mallinson couldn't marry Clarissa even there if she refused, if he could convince her she had no choice but to agree… "Come," she told Clarissa, "let us go. We will say that we took a drive together in the countryside with your maid, and no one will think anything of it."

"You will go where I tell you," Mallinson said, "and if you do not, I will have no hesitation about using this." He produced a pistol from inside his greatcoat. Thea stepped back, startled, and the little maid gave a shriek and fainted dead away. "Leave her," Mallinson ordered when Lady Clarissa stooped over Mariah with a low cry. "There isn't room for her in the carriage in any case." He flicked the muzzle of the gun toward the door. "Now, out to your carriage, and remember that I'm behind you and will shoot if you try to raise the alarm. And I'm not particular about which of you I shoot."

Thea tugged Clarissa gently away from her unconscious maid and took her hand again. "Come, my dear," she said, her voice low to hide the tremor in it. "We must do as he says."

They went to the door, where it took Thea two tries to disengage the lock, so badly were her hands shaking. Then down the hallway and out of the inn, Mallinson close behind. Thea dared a quick glance back, and the gun was not in sight, but Mallinson's right hand was in his greatcoat pocket, and there was an evil glint in his eye. She turned her face resolutely forward and guided Lady Clarissa to the curricle. The ostler had fed and watered the horses and was standing at the head of the near animal, rubbing the white blaze upon its face and cooing to it.

"Pay the man," Mallinson ordered and climbed up onto the groom's seat at the back of the curricle without offering to hand either of the ladies in.

Thea dug into her reticule and fumbled to extract some of Ransley's banknotes. She blindly gave the money — almost certainly too much — to the ostler, who helped first Thea, then Lady Clarissa into the carriage, bowed, and trotted off.

"Now drive," Mallinson said, "and don't forget I have a gun and will not hesitate to shoot if you make it necessary. I only need one of you to make the trip to Gretna... fruitful."

Thea reached for Clarissa's hand again and gave it a squeeze before gathering up the reins. She prayed to heaven Ransley had nearly caught them up, for Mallinson was clearly a madman to think he could get away with such a thing.

Chapter Twenty-One

"ENOUGH!" Trenwick shouted. "We'll lame the horses if we keep on."

Reluctantly, Ransley reined his mount in somewhat. He knew Trenwick was right and they could not continue to ride neck or nothing, but the pounding urgency inside him rankled at riding at a trot, or even a canter.

His mind whirled ceaselessly, trying without success to fit events into a coherent pattern. He couldn't imagine what Mallinson was thinking. If it *was* Mallinson, and Ransley was sharply aware that he only had Trenwick's word for that. Even assuming Trenwick was not playing some deeper game, his assertion that Mallinson was the author of this outrage was based entirely on supposition and guesswork. In truth, the only thing Ransley had to go on that was even moderately reliable was the second-hand report of the maid. If the girl had the right of it, Clary had expected to make a dash for the border with Trenwick. That she was most definitely *not* with Trenwick argued strongly for either Clary getting the wrong end of the stick or someone lying to her. While she'd proven herself a thorough ninnyhammer with the Vauxhall mess and this latest start, Clary was hardly goose-brained. Ransley couldn't imagine she'd get something this far wrong unless someone had deliberately misled her. Whether it was Mallinson or someone else, that did not auger well for either Clary or Althea, who had chased off after the girl believing she was putting a halt to an elopement. God only knew what kind of danger she would face, interfering with the plans of someone bent on something quite different from love. Mallinson, or whoever was behind this, must be desperate to even think of trying it, and Althea had no idea what she was walking into.

No matter how he argued with his heart, no matter how he reminded himself that Althea was as perfidious as they came and had worked her way into his and Clary's lives on the worst of false pretenses, Ransley could no more stop himself worrying than he could fly to the moon and back. His fear for Althea was quite as strong as for Clary, and he could not argue himself out of it. However much he hated what she'd done and how she'd lied, he could not stop loving her determination, her tart tongue, her selflessness in dashing off after Clary without a thought to her own safety or reputation. And wasn't that rich? Wonder of wonders, the Duke of Ransley had finally found himself in love! There must be snowballs in hell, he thought with a derisive snort that startled both his horse and, he saw out of the corner of his eye, Trenwick.

That gentleman refrained from comment, however, which was as well for him, and they rode in silence for several more miles. The road was not packed with travelers, but there were enough to keep Ransley occupied watching out for his carriage, his heir, his ward, and his… Althea.

"I suppose," Trenwick remarked after a time, "this explains Miss Ravenshaw's rather unsubtle hint the other night at Stanhope's ball that she was prepared to waltz with me." He appeared to be eyeing Ransley sidelong.

"What the devil has that to do with anything?" Damned if he knew what reaction the man was looking for and damned if he'd let show how the thought of Althea waltzing with Trenwick struck him to the heart.

"Didn't she say? That was the wager. That she would owe me a waltz if Lady Clarissa had to leave Town before the end of the Season." He paused, but Ransley said nothing, feeling as if Trenwick had just planted him a facer. He knew Trenwick's reputation for gambling deep, and had assumed there was a great deal of money on the line. "I'd quite forgotten the wager, but I suppose she must have been forfeiting. Don't know why she should, though."

"Because," Ransley said, several things coming suddenly clear, "she thought you were behind Lady Clarissa's mishaps."

"I?" Trenwick said with too much surprise for his shock to be counterfeited. "Why should I—"

"To win the bet, of course," Ransley snapped. "That was why she defended Wilford to me when I thought him responsible," he went on, largely to himself. "She believed she knew who the culprit was."

"I don't ruin innocent chits and I don't cheat," Trenwick said tightly. "Also, I wouldn't count Wilford out. He's easily led, and he's been very much in Mallinson's pocket lately."

Sick of silently and helplessly fulminating, Ransley attacked the only part of this mess that was near enough at hand. "Why the devil did you make such an infamous wager in the first place? And why did Miss Ravenshaw agree to it?" he added, unwillingly.

"I was bored and more than a little disguised," Trenwick said airily. Then he rubbed his ear with the hand not holding the reins and muttered, "And she was afraid someone would come out and find us on the terrace together. I said I'd leave if she took the wager." He had the good grace to look embarrassed. When Ransley only stared at him, disgusted that the man would put Althea and Clary in such a position for no reason other than ennui, Trenwick said, "I never claimed to be a good man."

"No," Ransley agreed.

"For god's sake! It's not like I was betting on who'd get killed in an affair of honor or which girl would be found to be increasing before being properly affianced. When I saw Miss Ravenshaw dash outside after Lady Clarissa, I became curious how far she'd go to protect the chit. I'd never have made the bet if I didn't expect to lose it, and I certainly didn't have any hand in Lady Clarissa's misfortunes."

"Except for waltzing with her."

Trenwick cursed. "Except the waltz, yes. Which I'd never have claimed if your own heir had not told me my advances would be welcomed. If you want to blame someone for this mess, blame Mallinson. I'd wager a monkey he's at fault here."

"There's more than enough fault to go around," Ransley said, for even if it was Mallinson's hand behind this, Trenwick and Clary and Althea and he himself had each played their part. All he could do now was make sure the women did not suffer for it.

His mount, sensing his urgency, shifted into a canter, and Ransley gave the bay his head. They passed several coaching inns, slowing up only enough to verify that neither Ransley's equipage nor any of the actors in this particular play were to be seen in the yard. Ransley only hoped he could catch up before it turned into a tragedy. They did not stop at any of the inns. His bay was flourishing under the pace and the gelding Trenwick was riding, which he'd recently purchased from Tattersall's, was doing well. They could move at a much faster pace than any carriage; surely they ought to come upon the others soon.

* * *

"What are we to do?" Clarissa whispered to Thea. The girl had a wild, wide-eyed look that Thea found nearly as unsettling as the madman sitting in the back of their carriage with a gun. She had no idea what he would do if Clarissa made some panicked start, but very much feared it would involve shooting the girl.

"Be calm," Thea murmured, keeping her eyes on the horses, who jogged along comfortably. They were, thankfully, too well-trained to be bothered by her uncertain touch on the reins — more high-strung horses would have run wild by now, driven to it by the shaking of her hands. She firmed up her grip, hoping to still the tremor before Clarissa noticed. She dropped her voice still further and said, "Your uncle will find us; he can't be far behind."

Oh god, please let him be nearly up with us. Please let him not have gotten waylaid or sidetracked. Thea had never so desperately wished to see anyone as she did Ransley.

"No talking," Mallinson said from the elevated groom's seat at the back of the carriage. He had a perfect vantage from there of everything the two women did, though at least he could not easily overhear so long as they spoke low. Thea's back crawled at the thought of the gun in his hand. He need not even *intend* to shoot. She'd risked one look back soon after they left the innyard, and saw him sitting there with the weapon resting on his knee, the muzzle pointed directly at her. Every time the carriage jolted over a rut in the road, her shoulders went up in anticipation of a misfire.

Thea risked taking one hand off the reins, reaching out to clasp Clarissa's hand. "It will be all right," she murmured. "He'll find us." Clarissa squeezed her hand in return and smiled tremulously at her. She was looking slightly less like a spooked horse now, thank heavens.

"I said no talking," Mallinson snapped. "And hurry up. I can walk faster than this." He was exaggerating, as they were going at a good clip. Though not, it was true, as fast as they might.

"The horses are growing tired," Thea lied. It might only be a mild stretching of the truth, given the distance they'd come since leaving London. However, their lagging was due more to the fact that she was reining them in as much as she dared. "I meant to hire fresh cattle at the last stop, but you insisted on leaving so quickly…."

Her shoulders hunched as she anticipated his displeasure, but he only said several things unsuitable for polite company, then barked, "Turn at the next crossroads."

Thea's heart stumbled, then raced ahead. If they left the main road, Ransley might make it all the way to Gretna before realizing he'd overshot them. And while Gretna was the closest village inside Scotland at which one could be married, any number of other locations would do. Mallinson could serve his purposes just as well by crossing the border elsewhere. "It is not the most direct route, Mr. Mallinson," she said carefully.

"Ransley will be looking on the main road," Mallinson said. "We can't outrun him, so we must out-think him."

Thea thought that was a tall order for the slimy bastard, but certainly had enough sense not to say so, instead remarking, "You have great faith in his perspicacity, Mr. Mallinson, to think he will guess your destination."

"I'm no slowtop, Miss Ravenshaw," he sneered, "to think you would be here in his carriage, and him none the wiser."

"The carriage was already prepared for a trip." Thea slowed still further as they neared the crossroads, desperately trying to think of some sign they could leave Ransley in the hopes he might realize they'd left the main road. Was there even any way to do it that Mallinson would not see? "When I received Lady Clarissa's letter of farewell, I was concerned and went to Ransley's house. He had gone off in search of her. I took the carriage and left before he returned."

"You expect me to believe that?"

"It is the truth," she said quietly, if not entirely accurately.

He snorted. "Turn at the crossroads."

As they made the turn, Clarissa suddenly lurched sideways with a moan, nearly toppling out of the carriage. Thea grabbed her arm and drew the girl against her side, where she listed weakly.

"Clarissa! Whatever is wrong?"

Clarissa moaned again, and said, "I'm sorry, Miss Ravenshaw. I suddenly feel most unwell. Please, may we stop?"

Mallinson laughed harshly. "You must think me an idiot. Pick up the pace, Miss Ravenshaw, or I shall become impatient."

Thea gave the reins a little slap, drawing greater speed from the horses. Soon, they were traveling at their previous pace, Clarissa still leaning against her side. However, though the girl moaned and shivered and made a good show of being half-collapsed against Thea, she was doing a remarkably good job of keeping her weight off Thea's arms, so as not to interfere with her driving. Thea ducked her head to peer quickly into the girl's face, and received a smile from the decidedly healthy chit.

She returned to looking at the horses and the road ahead of her, but not before noticing that Clarissa's lovely blue gown was now missing one of the bows that had adorned the skirt. She allowed herself a smile, knowing Mallinson could not see it. Nor was he likely to notice Clarissa had ripped her gown; he'd not, after all, been observant enough to notice her dropping the bow in the road. Very clever. Very clever indeed. She only hoped Ransley was not riding so hard as to miss the scrap of blue fabric.

It was a good start, but Thea hated to rely upon it. Too much could go amiss. For all she knew, the boy had been unable to find and alert Ransley, or Ransley too stubborn to listen. Or he could already have confronted Trenwick. She shivered in the midday warmth. What if he had refused to believe Trenwick's protestations of innocence and called him out? What if they were even now meeting on the field of honor? If Ransley killed Trenwick, Thea would be at fault — it was she who sent him off after the rake and she who would bear the guilt for the rest of her days. And if it were Ransley injured or killed...? Thea clenched her teeth to keep back the pain and fear that crawled up her throat — she didn't know what sound it would make if she allowed it to escape, but she knew she could not scare Clarissa so.

The horses slowed, responding to her suddenly lax grip on the reins, and Mallinson shouted at her. *Get ahold of yourself, Thea*, she thought, her mental scold falling into Mrs. Wellins' familiar intonation. She got the horses moving again. Then, forcing as rigorous a control on her mind as she did the horses, she began to think about how they were to get themselves out of this mess.

The first and most important thing was to get Clarissa away. Thea could look out for her own chances later, but she absolutely must see Clarissa safe. They were passing through a wooded area with trees coming in close on both sides of the road. Under other circumstances, Thea would have feared highwaymen. A curricle without groom or outriders, carrying two women and only one man would be a tempting target to anyone hiding in the trees. As it was, that was the least of her worries. But the thought gave her a lovely, terrifying idea.

Clarissa was still leaning against her, making it easy for Thea to speak quietly to her. "When I stop the carriage, run into the trees and hide. I'll distract Mallinson."

"What about you?" Clarissa asked, nearly inaudibly.

"Don't worry about me."

"I'm not going without you."

"You must. Get back to the main road and flag down any passing rider. They'll help you." They'd damn well better! She ignored the slight shake of Clarissa's head. The girl was stubborn, and Thea had to be more stubborn. "There's a knife in my reticule. Get it out and give it to me." She couldn't take her hands off the reins to get it herself.

"What the devil are you two jabbering about? I said quiet," Mallinson ordered from the back.

"Just telling Lady Clarissa to take courage," Thea said, making her voice clear and ringing to cover any noise Clarissa might make in digging for Thea's reticule where it had gotten shoved down between them. "I believe she's quite ill."

"I don't care if she's got the plague. She will be marrying me the moment we reach Scotland, even if I have to carry her before the altar."

What was there to say to that? Thea bit her tongue and kept her eyes forward. Clarissa's stealthy movements had stopped when Mallinson made his pronouncement. Thea hoped it was because she'd retrieved the knife, and not simply reaction to his harsh certainty. But no, she reached to take Thea's hand again, clutching at her as if she needed the clasp of a friendly hand to hold up under trying circumstances. The metal of the knife was hard between their gloved palms.

Thea curled her fingers around the knife and withdrew her hand from Clarissa's with a pat, keeping the knife hidden in her hand as she returned it to the reins. She would need both hands to manage the next bit. Slowly, she began gathering the reins more in her left hand than her right. As she took in the left-hand rein more and more, the horse on that side began to draw left and shake his head. Thea made a worried noise, pitching it so it was sure to reach Mallinson.

"What is it? I told you not to stop!" he shouted as she began to rein in the horses, her muscles quivering under the strain of handling them.

"The off-side horse looks like it's coming up lame. We'll need to check on it."

"No. Drive on."

"But I can't—"

"I said drive on."

"If the horses get out of step, the carriage may overturn," she said slowly, as if to a child. Which really, he was acting like not to realize that the horses were harnessed so close together when pulling a curricle that if they weren't on the same foot at all times, the vehicle might well overturn. Why did he think the demmed things were so challenging to drive? She was lucky the duke's horses were exquisitely trained or they'd have overturned the curricle long since. Thea continued to rein in, her hands sweating and shaking and her back crawling. It was the biggest gamble she'd ever taken, and Trenwick's prosing about gambling being something people did everyday, rather than just at the tables, popped inanely into her head. He wouldn't shoot. For all his threats, surely he wouldn't shoot. He needed them both — only one to marry, as he'd said, but the other to threaten so he could keep them both in line.

Mallinson was swearing a blue streak, the pitch of his voice rising as she continued to ignore him, but he had not fired by the time she brought the curricle to a stop. Though perhaps he was merely holding off out of fear of startling the horses at the same moment he left no one at the reins.

"I'll check the horses," Clarissa said, and slid quickly down from the carriage seat. It was a long drop to make without help, but she managed it easily, reminding Thea that she was dealing with a consummate horsewoman, and one, moreover, who didn't blanch at being unseated by her powerful horse.

"Get back here," Mallinson shouted, for all the world as if Clarissa could climb back into the high carriage seat without help. Clarissa ignored him, walking up to the horse's heads with a measured calm that Thea quite admired. Mallinson was still sputtering curses at her when she turned suddenly and darted into the trees. "Stupid girl!"

He stood, bringing the gun around like a striking snake, and like a snake, all instinct, his lofty plans forgotten in an instant as he drew a bead on the flash of blue that was Clarissa. Thea reacted just as instinctively, only later realizing how much had flown through her mind as she acted. She could flip the reins — the jolt as the horses started would likely throw him clean from the carriage. But she couldn't be certain he would be badly enough hurt that he couldn't go after Clarissa. She opened the folding knife and swung around, plunging the little blade into his calf.

Chapter Twenty-Two

THEY rode up on a coaching inn, which Ransley was startled to see was alive with frantic activity, men running about the yard like bees boiling out to protect a hive. He scanned the inn and yard, but could see nothing of note aside from a yellow-bounder with a broken wheel, which surely oughtn't cause such a furor. As they neared, a female voice rose above the rest, crying out something Ransley couldn't make out. A moment later, a woman dashed out into the road in front of them.

Cursing, Ransley forced his horse to veer to the side, unable to stop until he was several feet past the woman. The bay had shied violently, its eyes rolling at the woman's sudden appearance, but Ransley brought him easily under control. Trenwick was not so fortunate, as the woman had darted out nearly under his horse's hooves. The gelding reared, the woman cowered, and Trenwick shouted, throwing his weight forward and managing somehow to bring the beast down to one side, missing the foolish girl entirely. An accomplished rider indeed.

Reining his horse around, Ransley came back, arriving in time to hear Trenwick shout, "What the devil did you think you were doing?"

"Easy, Trenwick," he said, seeing Trenwick's still-agitated horse dancing in response to his rider's mood. Trenwick cursed under his breath and guided his horse away before jumping off and moving to hold its head, rubbing its neck and murmuring calming words.

The shock of the dangerous situation must be blamed for the fact that Ransley didn't recognize the girl until she stammered, "Oh, Your Grace, I'm so sorry, I didn't think, I just ran out to stop you!"

"Mariah? Miss Ravenshaw is here, then? What about Lady Clarissa?" He looked past the little maid into the innyard, but still didn't see his own carriage or either of the women.

"No, Your Grace." She stared up at him, her eyes brimming with tears and her voice trembling. Somehow, she managed to hold herself together enough to continue. "He took them both, sir."

"He?"

"Mr. Mallinson, sir." She was wringing her hands in her skirt, doing neither any good.

"How long ago?" Trenwick asked. He'd calmed the horse and himself, and walked the animal over to join them.

"I don't know," Mariah wailed. "I… I must have fainted, sir. When I saw the gun."

"Gun?" Ransley exclaimed. His horse snorted and tossed his head, and Ransley hastily let up on the reins.

"Yes, sir. Miss Ravenshaw was saying as how she and Lady Clarissa would not be going with Mr. Mallinson, and he said he'd shoot them if they didn't do as he said. Oh, sir, he said Lady Clarissa would marry him over the anvil or he'd ruin her! And then…" She looked down. "…and then I fainted, and when I woke up they were gone. I raised the alarm," she said with a disconsolate look back at the active yard, "but no one seems to know what to do and maybe they don't even believe me."

Ransley bit back a curse. "Did you tell them your mistress's name?"

"Oh, no, sir!" Mariah said, her eyes wide. Thank the heavens for that — Clary might yet survive this with something of her reputation left. It was an excellent thing he'd never been much inclined for putting his coat of arms on his carriage doors and that Mariah had sense enough not to go bruiting her mistress's name about an innyard.

"We'll catch them up and bring them back here," Ransley said, as calmly as he could manage. "We can't be far behind now. Mariah, engage a private parlor and remain here until we return."

"Oh, but—"

Trenwick was before him, pressing some coins into her hand. "Tell them you've just spoken with your master, and he sent you to arrange for the parlor and luncheon for four. Convey to the innkeeper your master's apologies that the game he and his friends were playing got out of hand and frightened you and them. Use no names. All right?"

Mariah looked to Ransley, who nodded, then back at Trenwick. "Yes, sir." She curtseyed, her eyes downcast, and trotted off toward the inn.

Trenwick swung into the saddle. "They won't think anything of it — just some hay-go-mad bucks raising a ruckus as usual."

"It's been a number of years since I was wet enough behind the ears to be called a buck, Trenwick," Ransley said forbiddingly.

"It will still answer," Trenwick said with a shrug. He touched his heels to his horse's sides and came up alongside Ransley, who fished out one of the pistols that were dragging down the pockets of his greatcoat and handed it to the other man. "Much obliged." Trenwick put the gun in his own pocket. "I can't feature how Mallinson expects to get away with this. He must be quite out of his mind."

"We had best hurry," Ransley said tightly. He nudged his horse into motion, Trenwick following suit, and they left the coaching inn at a hard gallop.

* * *

Mallinson howled and backhanded Thea with the hand holding the gun. The world exploded in red and black and white, pain ballooning across her left cheek and both eyes. Thea reeled, her head ringing like a giant bell. She thought dazedly that the clapper must have been a thunderbolt.

Dimly, she heard the horses' panicked neighing. The carriage jolted under her and she grabbed the armrail hard just before the curricle careened off, swaying wildly. She thought distantly that they'd overturn if she didn't get the reins, but could only cling blindly to the armrail and pray.

She only realized that Mallinson's shrieks were mixed in with the horses' when he landed clumsily on the seat beside her and snatched up the reins. The racketing carriage finally drew up, and Thea found she was able to breathe somewhat. She blinked, tears running down her face, her eyes burning so badly she couldn't keep them open long enough to see more than a too-bright blur. Her head felt overlarge, swollen with pain, and when she forced one of her hands off the armrail and gingerly touched her cheek, the pain made her suck in a sharp breath.

Thea had never been struck before, and the shock so addled her wits that it took several minutes for her to realize that the burning in her eyes and nose was sulfur. Black powder! The gun had gone off when Mallinson hit her with it — that explained the overwhelmingly loud crash that shivered even now through her chest and head. Her hand flew to her face again, wet with tears, or was it blood? She forced her eyes open against the glare, and saw enough to know that her tan gloves were not stained red, so probably tears. She released a shaky sigh.

Too soon. A moment later, her heart was kicking against her ribs, Mallinson's arm tight around her neck and his voice snarling in her ear. "I won't forget that little trick." His coat sleeve was rough on her skin as he squeezed her back against him, his arm tightening under her chin until she had to crane her neck back to avoid being choked. "Don't make the mistake of thinking I'm unarmed. You may have made me misfire, but you kindly gave me another weapon." Something pricked the tender skin just under her jaw, something sharp and bright that spun a trickle of warmth down her neck. "Now sit quiet," he growled, "and I might manage to forget that you're responsible for damaging my favorite pair of boots. Bloodstains are *not* fashionable."

He withdrew with a suddenness that left her reeling, but she only had a moment to realize she was free before his left hand clamped down on her right wrist. Not that there was much she could have done, even given more time, as she could hardly escape when she couldn't keep her eyes open. He yanked off her glove and pulled her hand across his thigh, but she only had a moment to be shocked at the indecency before the sharp little blade was pressed to her inner wrist.

"Don't move, and I won't cut you." His hands moved as he gathered the reins into his right hand, his left kept tight on her wrist, holding the blade solidly against her skin. He clucked to the horses and the curricle began to roll forward. "You've put the noose round your own neck, seeing to it the chit escaped and laming me so I can't follow. You must be positively *swooning* to marry me."

The knife bit sharply into Thea's skin, blood creeping out to meet it, his hard grip and the movement of the carriage cutting her no matter how still she stayed. It was needlessly cruel, for she couldn't escape him in any case, not with the carriage moving fast enough the wind whipped her wet face. Not when she couldn't see. Oh God, what if the blindness didn't pass? What if she never again looked onto a world clear and unblurred, a world that didn't stab at her eyes with its brightness? And how was she to escape Mallinson now? The knife bit deeper. She daren't complain, but caught her lower lip in a hard bite and kept her body as stiffly away from his as she could.

Oh please, she thought. *Please*. She couldn't have said whether she was praying for the merciful God to save her or for Ransley to do it. She was mildly surprised to realize that she had more faith in the Duke of Ransley.

* * *

"This way," Ransley shouted, crouching low to stay with his horse as it took the turning at speed. He heard Trenwick cursing behind him, likely at the lack of warning, but didn't slow up.

The flat crack of a gunshot had pierced through him several minutes ago, and he wasn't entirely certain he'd taken a breath since. It had sounded close, but gunshots could carry for remarkable distances. Rationally, he knew there were any number of reasons someone might be shooting in the vicinity. But there was something in him that was the furthest thing from rational. Something that could not stop thinking about the pistol Mariah said Mallinson threatened them with, about Clary or Althea hurt, bleeding...

When he saw the scrap of blue in the crossroads, he'd taken that turn without a thought. Now, as he galloped up the road with Trenwick close at his heels, he could only hope it was not the wrong decision. He could not remember whether Clary had a dress of that color. But surely she had. Surely.

"Uncle!"

Ransley was off his horse before the animal had come to a halt, taking several running steps to keep his balance. He didn't worry about his horse; the bay was too well trained to take off on him. "Clary." He swept her into an embrace, straining her to his chest with all the strength of his arms. She held him back just as tightly.

"I'm sorry. I'm sorry. I'm so sorry." She said it over and over, pressing her wet face against his neck and trembling in his arms.

"It's all right. It's all right," Ransley said, patting her back. He was vaguely aware of Trenwick riding up. "Are you hurt? Where's Thea?"

"I'm not hurt." Clary pulled herself away with a sniff, nearly falling when she stepped back. He grabbed her arm and she clung to him, grimacing. "Well, my ankle…" She shook herself. "Never mind me. You must save Miss Ravenshaw!"

"She's not with you?"

Clary shook her head. "She distracted him so I could escape. I think… Uncle, I think he shot her!"

A word he'd never said in front of Clary escaped Ransley. His eyes darted to his horse — sides heaving but not spent yet — then back to Clary, dress torn, hair all anyhow, and balancing gingerly on one foot. He couldn't just leave her.

"Go," Trenwick said. "I'll see her safe."

That… was not necessarily an improvement. Ransley hesitated unbearably. Every moment saw Mallinson and Thea getting farther away. He would not, could not, think about how precious those minutes were if Thea were injured, perhaps even dying. He had to get to her, but…

"Ransley. Go." Trenwick brought the gelding over close and bent from the saddle. "Give her to me. I'll take her back to the inn to join her maid."

"Mariah's there? I'll be fine," Clary said to him, her voice filled with all the certainty of her age, lips firmed up with a determination he knew well.

Decided, and already hoping he would not regret the decision, Ransley stroked Clary's hair and kissed her forehead, her arms clinging tightly around his neck for a moment.

"Be safe," she whispered.

"Stay out of trouble," he told her, finding a smile from somewhere to encourage her.

He scooped her up in his arms and lifted her onto the saddle in front of Trenwick, who put one arm around her and with the other handed Ransley his pistol. "Shoot that bastard for me."

"I won't be doing it for you." Ransley put the pistol in his coat pocket, where it would balance the weight of the other one, and strode to his horse, gathering up the reins and swinging into the saddle. He paused for one moment to look back, but Trenwick had already brought his horse about and begun to carry Clary back to the inn. For the sake of both the girl and the doubly burdened horse, he was taking it slow. Ransley resolutely turned his face back up the road and touched his heels to his horse's sides. The slight rest had given the bay his second wind, and he was off like a shot.

Chapter Twenty-Three

RANSLEY rode low over his horse's neck, the wind grabbing at his hair and coat, his heart thundering in time with the hooves. The gunshot was now proven to be Mallinson's. He'd fired. He'd fired at Thea. She could be badly injured, or even— He dragged his thoughts from that by main force and coolly began to calculate the chances that Mallinson had a second pistol.

He went a mile, two. Clary must have left the carriage some ways back — there was little chance of her getting far through the woods with a turned ankle. Though he didn't know if that had happened at the moment of her escape or only later. No matter. There was only the one road, with no crossroads since he started. He must come upon them sooner or later, and his horse, even growing fatigued as it was, could make much better time than a curricle.

There was no chance of coming upon Mallinson unawares — not when riding *ventre à terre*, his horse's hooves beating against the hard-packed road. If Mallinson had a second pistol, he might get off a shot before Ransley realized he was upon them. But to do that, he would have to stop — he was surely not foolish enough to think he could successfully aim at anything from the back of a moving carriage.

Ransley came around a bend in the road and saw them. The horses were running flat out, the curricle bouncing and swaying. The road was empty of traffic, as it had been since the crossroads, which was as well, as the carriage looked scarcely under control. Mallinson was not, as Ransley remembered, a member of the four-in-hand club or otherwise known for his handling of the ribbons. He was a damn fool to go so fast. Assuming he was even at the reins — Ransley couldn't see the occupants from this distance. For all he knew, he was chasing down an empty carriage.

He bent low over his horse's neck, encouraging him in a low voice. One ear swiveled back, and as if understanding his words, the bay put on a burst of speed. They were slowly gaining on the curricle. Soon, Ransley was close enough to see Mallinson driving, a woman huddled close to his side. Thea had lost her bonnet somewhere, and her inky tresses whipped wildly in the wind of their passage.

"Mallinson! Pull up!" Ransley shouted. "Damn you, man, pull up before you overturn!" He was near enough now to see that Thea's body was not, as he'd thought, lying limply against Mallinson. Her posture was stiff, and he saw her back stiffen still further at the sound of his voice.

Mallinson looked back. His eyes were wild, his teeth set in a snarl. For a moment, Ransley thought the man was going to hurl defiance at him, but he only turned back to the horses, slapping the reins in a mad attempt to draw even greater speed from them. It was clear to the veriest fool that they had no more to give, and moreover, that any more speed would be the death of them all. The curricle was swaying wildly now, and would surely end in a ditch or overturned if Mallinson kept on.

Ransley transferred the reins into his left hand and drew the pistol from his right-hand pocket. There was no chance of aiming at this pace, nor would it be safe to try. Even if he succeeded in hitting Mallinson and not the carriage, the horses, or Thea, that would only leave the panicked horses without any hand upon the reins. But Ransley had no intention of trying to hit anything. He aimed well over Mallinson's head and fired. The crack of the gun half-deafened him, and Mallinson's shoulders jerked as if he'd been shot.

Ransley's horse faltered. He dropped the gun and got both hands back on the reins. It was only a momentary misstep, however, and the bay quickly recovered. He was a game fellow and well trained, and though lathered in sweat, he kept running.

For a moment, it looked as if Mallinson might drive on, but Ransley soon saw that the curricle was slowing, its sway becoming less exaggerated. He felt relief bloom in his chest and tamped it down hard — it was too soon to celebrate any kind of victory. Ransley allowed the bay to drop down to a trot, then a walk. He fished the pistol out of his left-hand pocket and transferred it to his right hand, letting the reins fall loose over the bay's neck and controlling the horse with his knees. Neither Mallinson nor Thea turned as Ransley came even with the curricle. It was in sad condition, battered and splashed with mud, the poor horses blowing and shaking.

"Mallinson. This has gone quite far enough."

The other man's shoulders hunched. Then he threw them back and stood, dragging Thea up with him. "On the contrary. I haven't gotten near far enough yet. I mean to make it to Scotland." Mallinson turned, keeping Thea before him with one arm wrapped about her waist, the other hand tight across her neck, drawing her up cruelly. Ransley gasped to see her, her eyes rimmed with red and squeezed painfully shut, tears streaming down her face, half of which was a horrid dusky black, with blood smeared across her cheekbone and down her throat.

"Bloody bastard," he growled, his heart squeezing in his chest. His hand was perfectly steady as he aimed the pistol at the two of them. Mallinson was keeping Thea in front of him, forcing Ransley to aim the muzzle a bit wide of the mark so she was not in danger from it. "Let her go, you craven dog."

Mallinson showed his teeth. There was a feral look to him, as if the thin veneer of civilization had been stripped away to reveal the corruption underneath. Looking at him now, Ransley marveled that he had not seen it before. "It is you who will let us go. It's some distance yet to Scotland, and we have far to go before dark."

"The devil take you, you're not going anywhere."

"I beg to differ." He moved the hand at her neck, and Thea's lips parted in a soundless gasp as a trickle of blood spilled down her pale skin. Ransley went cold as he realized there was a small knife in Mallinson's hand. A knife he was pressing against Thea's tender throat. "Miss Ravenshaw and I will be going to Scotland."

"I shall certainly not be marrying *you*," Thea said, and though she did so with as little movement of her jaw as possible, the knife pricked out another runnel of blood. Ransley's bay took two steps forward, made restless by the tight squeeze of his legs. He forced himself to relax enough to stop unnerving the horse. *Stay still*, he prayed, wishing she could see him, could read the urgency in his eyes. Much as he admired her courage — she would hardly be Thea if she stayed a meek mouse even in the face of danger — it was far too chancy a thing to provoke Mallinson now.

"You will do as I say or you'll regret it," Mallinson snarled.

"Enough," Ransley ground out. "You're a candidate for Bedlam to think you can get away with this."

"Why not?" He laughed shrilly. "You can hardly disinherit me. And I shan't miss the monthly pittance you give me once I have her money. It'll hold me over until you drop short and I become the duke."

For a moment, Ransley couldn't speak, though he didn't know which he felt more strongly — rage or astonishment. "You really are a Bedlamite to think I'd ever let the dukedom come to you now. I shall hardly find it difficult to sire an heir."

"Without Miss Ravenshaw? The first woman you've shown an interest in these last fifteen years? Who will you marry with her... unavailable?"

"I will not—"

"Married or dead," Mallinson said, cutting Thea off with another jab of the knife. "It makes no difference to me. Either way, Ransley won't have you."

"Hurt her and I'll put you to bed with a shovel." Ransley's horse danced sideways. He controlled it with his knees and brought his pistol to bear. "Now let her go, or I *will* shoot you."

Mallinson sneered, for all the world as if his eyes weren't following the movement of the gun like a charmed snake. "Hardly a good show, shooting your own heir."

"You assume I care what people think."

Mallinson's tongue darted out to wet his lips. "Even you're not a good enough shot to shoot me without hitting her."

"I'm sure you think so." Ransley fired. At the same moment, Thea dropped like a stone, and for a heart-stopping moment, he feared he'd somehow hit her. But Mallinson had dropped the knife and clapped his hand to his shoulder, blood seeping through his fingers as he swore foully.

"Oh good," Thea said. She felt for the side of the carriage. "You got him. Someplace painful, I hope."

For a moment, relief made him incapable of speech. He ought to have known his Thea was clever enough to go limp in Mallinson's grip and let gravity take her out of the line of fire. He put the empty pistol back in his pocket and gathered up the reins, steering his horse in alongside the curricle. The bay had scarcely flinched at the shot, and the carriage horses, thankfully too tired to be skittish, had done little more than shift in the traces.

"Are you all right?" Ransley asked her gently.

"I will be." She turned blindly toward him and he reached for her.

"Here," he said, putting his hands on her slender waist and lifting her from the curricle onto the horse in front of him. He'd be damned if he'd leave her in the confines of the carriage with Mallinson for a moment longer than necessary. And he needed to have her in his arms, cradled close to his chest. For a moment, he did nothing more than that, letting the feel of her, solid in his arms, calm his racing heart. He rested his cheek against her hair and drank in her scent and the way she leaned against him, her arm going around his waist for balance.

Then he made himself straighten up and deal with his still-cursing heir. "Quiet, man. You're barely blooded."

"You shot me," Mallinson said. He sounded shocked. His hands shook as he tugged out a handkerchief and pressed it to his shoulder. It was difficult to tell with the excessive padding in his jacket, but from the location of the hole, Ransley doubted his bullet had done more than dig a furrow in the meat of Mallinson's shoulder. He was disappointed it hadn't done more damage.

"You will leave the country," he told Mallinson, his voice hard. "I don't care where you go so long as you go. You will continue up this road and take the first turning that will get you back to London. You will drive *slowly*, sparing the horses, and stop at the first inn you come to where they can be properly looked after." He hated to leave the horses with Mallinson, but he wanted the man gone as quickly as possible. And if he left him to walk back to London, Mallinson would doubtless take ages about it, especially as he appeared to have blood running down his boot. Ransley took vicious pleasure in the thought that Thea had wounded the man. Given the circumstances, it was either leave him the curricle or leave him the bay, and Ransley was too fond of his clever mount to do that. "When you get to London, you will stable the horses at a reputable mews and buy a ticket abroad on any boat you like, so long as it leaves within the week."

"That all takes money," Mallinson protested, "and I haven't any. And you can't make me leave in any case."

"I can and I will," Ransley swore. He fished the fold of banknotes out of his pocket and tossed it at the other man. He still had coin enough in his purse to pay their way home. "Present yourself and your ticket to my man of business within two days. He'll draw a thousand pounds for you—"

"A thous—"

"Which he will give you only upon the moment of embarkation," Ransley went on, overriding whatever Mallinson meant to say. It was difficult enough to keep the rage roiling in him from boiling over at the feel of Thea trembling against him in delayed reaction — if he had to listen to a single word out of Mallinson's mouth, he would not answer for his actions. "If the horses are harmed, you will get nothing. If you do not meet my man of business within two days *with* your ticket, you will get nothing. If you do not get on the boat, you will get nothing. And if even *one* rumor about either Miss Ravenshaw or Lady Clarissa reaches my ears, you will get nothing. Do you understand?"

"You can't treat your heir so," Mallinson protested with base bravado.

"You will not be my heir for any longer than it takes me to change that situation." Ransley's arm tightened involuntarily about Thea.

Mallinson's tongue darted out to wet his lips. "A thousand pounds?" he said finally, and there was something in his voice and on his weaselly features that made Ransley think of the demmed man's demmed "friends" and the amount of trouble he could cause, even from afar. A few letters, a few well-chosen words…

Ransley cursed silently. "A thousand pounds," he confirmed, though it rankled to give the man anything. "And so long as you do not return and I continue to hear no rumors about Miss Ravenshaw or Lady Clarissa, I will send you two hundred a year to live on."

"A mouse couldn't live on that!"

"Then you'd best make the thousand last. Two hundred is better than nothing and more than you deserve. If I did with you what I strongly desire to, you'd be eating grass before breakfast."

"Damn you," Mallinson hissed between his teeth. "And may you never get a living heir."

"If so, I'm certain my solicitor will have no trouble tracking you down."

Mallinson snarled again, but he was a toothless cur now, and he knew it. He sat down, gathered up the reins, and gave them a flip to get the horses started. Ransley watched the curricle depart, going appropriately slowly on account of the tired horses, and bid his heir good riddance. The man hadn't said he'd take the deal, but there was nothing else he could do. Not unless he wanted to work for a living.

Ransley and Thea sat in silence until even the creaking of the curricle had faded. Only then did he feel comfortable turning his back on Mallinson. If the man had had another pistol, he'd doubtless have used it instead of the knife, but

Ransley had no intention of being complacent. Complacency had gotten them into this mess and put Thea in grave danger.

He tightened his arm around her waist to secure her before he touched his heels to the bay's sides and turned its head back toward the coaching inn and, ultimately, London. The horse was tired, and now forced to carry double, so they went along at a walk, which was just as well for Thea's sake in any case. Though much of her warm weight was delightfully distributed across Ransley's thighs, she was sitting upon the pommel and that could become uncomfortable if they went much faster.

"Is Clarissa…?" Thea asked after a moment.

"She is fine but for a turned ankle. Trenwick is with her."

"Trenwick?!"

"After the boy found me, Trenwick said he considered himself partly at fault and insisted on coming along. Do you know, he said he was trying to get her out of Vauxhall when we found them last night?" Was it really only last night? It seemed an age. Ransley was mildly surprised to hear himself add, "He's a chancy fellow, but seems to be a regular brick for all that."

"And you trust him? No," she answered herself, "I needn't ask, need I? You'd hardly have left Clarissa with him otherwise."

"What choice did I have? I had to come after you," Ransley said simply. "Though you were doing amazingly well on your own." He could not keep the pride out of his voice, nor wish to.

"Not well enough," she said dismissively.

"You got after them when I was still far afield, and you got Clary away from him. I shudder to think what might have happened if he'd reached Gretna with her, or if he'd still had her as well as you when I caught up. It would have been very much harder to get you both away from him."

"Still, if you hadn't come up when you did…"

He tightened his left arm around her, wishing he could wrap the right one about her as well, but it would be best if he kept the reins. He relieved his feelings somewhat by pressing a kiss to her temple, though it left his lips tasting of copper and sulfur. A sound caught his ears, and he reined in the slowly ambling bay.

"What is it?"

"Water." Ransley steered his horse off the road into the trees. They were well-enough separated here that they could ride through them with ease, and once the horse caught scent of the water and realized his rider wanted him to head toward it, he went with a will. In a few minutes, they had come upon a stream — little more than a rill, really, but running deep and clear.

Ransley took Thea's hand and threaded the reins between her fingers, then slid regretfully out from under her warmth and dismounted. As soon as he was down, he reached up to wrap his hands about her waist and lift her down. She felt light as eiderdown in his arms, and he wished nothing more than to hold her there for a time, but the sight of her poor bloodied face kept him to his purpose.

"You can release the reins," he told her. He'd given them to her to help steady her while he dismounted. The moment his reins were released, the bay walked forward to stick his muzzle in the stream to drink. Ransley let him drink as much as was safe for him, then tied him to a nearby tree before going back to Thea. "Come," he said.

He guided Thea toward the stream, supporting and steadying her with an arm about her waist as she felt her way sightlessly over the uneven ground.

"I doubt I shall appear presentable whatever we do," Thea said, and if the forced lightheartedness in her voice failed to cover a faint tremor, Ransley loved her all the more for it. She'd been right as rain throughout, and deserved much more than he could do for her at present.

"You'll feel better if we get you somewhat cleaned up." He guided her to the water's edge and helped her kneel by the stream, kneeling beside her and stripping off his gloves. Thea appeared to have lost her right glove, and he took up the hand that still wore a glove to peel it off, baring her skin. How, he wondered, had she come to be wearing only the one? He had his answer when he lifted her other hand and saw the blood upon her inner wrist. "Your arm first. Just lean on me — I won't let you fall."

She did so trustingly, and he pushed her sleeve back and drew her hand gently into the water until he could rinse away the blood and see the extent of the damage. A dark, vicious thing took up residence in his chest, where it roiled and seethed at the sight of the cuts, two of them fairly deep, though not so much as to be a threat to Thea's life. But they might have been, so easily. Though it felt as if his heart vibrated in his chest, shaking him with rage, his hands were steady as he tied her one remaining glove about her injured wrist to stanch the blood that still welled slowly from the wounds.

His voice sounded remarkably calm when he said, "Just lean forward over the water, and we'll see if we can't get some of this off you." He marveled that the black anger growing in him did not come out in his voice.

Thea did as he asked without question. He steadied her with one hand upon her shoulder while he cupped up handful after handful of water to rinse blood and the residue of gunpowder off her face and neck. He shuddered to think how it was she came so close to Mallinson's pistol as to have burnt sulfur upon her skin. He very much feared he'd come within an ames ace of losing her, and that before he'd even told her he loved her. Though she should, he thought, have some idea how he felt after the kisses they'd shared.

He was very gentle, not knowing what injuries he might wake from under their mask of blood and powder. The water was cold and her skin delicate and soft under his fingers. When the water ran clear from her face, he said, "See if you can open your eyes in the water," and held his cupped hand over her eyes. Her lashes fanned his palm like the touch of butterfly wings. "Better?"

"I think so." She didn't move to sit up, perhaps not wishing to drip on her gown, though it could scarcely be saved after the rough handling it had taken.

Ransley drew out his handkerchief to finish cleaning her face, using the hand on her shoulder to tug her up so he might see what he was doing. He was relieved to find that he had been right that much of the blackening was gunpowder. But as he mopped her face tenderly with the handkerchief, he saw that there was one area that was neither blood nor gunpowder. A nasty bruise was coming up in black and red across her cheekbone, already beginning to tip the corner of her left eye with color. There was a half-inch cut over her cheekbone that thankfully seemed to have stopped bleeding. Ransley swore as he dabbed up the last of the water. "He's darkened your daylights, the bastard." The dark, seething thing in his chest boiled over and brought him to his feet.

"Wait!" Thea grabbed for his hand, the feel of her slender fingers on his bare skin freezing him in place. "What are you doing?" She rose and he steadied her when she wobbled slightly. There was just enough room in him for relief at seeing her looking at him out of clear, if reddened, eyes.

"I'm going to catch up with Mallinson and draw his damned cork," Ransley forced out through his teeth.

"Please don't."

"You're defending him?" The darkness flared.

"Not in the slightest. But you already did all that was needful. We're well rid of him, and that's sufficient." She stepped closer and rested her other hand over his heart. "I do not wish to see you kill anyone for me."

Ransley put his hand over hers, pressing it against his chest until the warmth of her skin penetrated his waistcoat and shirt. He took a cautious breath and tried to banish the tentacled thing that squeezed so hard about his heart. Though it would not go entirely, and certainly not when he looked at Thea's dear, wounded face, he was at last able to say with something approaching equanimity, "If that is what you wish."

"It is." She smiled with a hint of her usual impishness. "Besides, he strikes me as the kind of man who will not do well in straitened circumstances. Do, please, not keep him from 'enjoying' them for a very long time."

It startled a laugh from him. "A suitable punishment, then?"

"Eminently."

He reached to touch her face gently. "This will hurt," he warned her before gingerly feeling the extent of the bruising. Thea winced, but did not step away. Finally, he drew back with a relieved sigh. "Nothing broken, as near as I can tell. But you'll likely have to wear a veil at the wedding."

* * *

Thea took in a sharp breath. She looked up into the face she'd once thought cold and forbidding and saw only warmth and care. Her heart was pounding, and she felt lightheaded with relief, and something a great deal more. Her happiness at being able to see clearly was nearly overwhelming, which made it all the stranger to find the fact that *his* face had been the first thing she saw even more affecting.

She *was* a touch lightheaded, though, so perhaps she had misheard? "I own I was somewhat preoccupied, Your Grace," she said carefully. "But I don't remember talk of a wedding. Whose are we to attend?"

He smiled. A genuine and breathtakingly open smile, which touched both his lips and his eyes. "Why ours, of course."

Thea's heart tripped. She felt as if she'd stepped down in the dark onto a stair that wasn't there. Surely her poor, overworked heart couldn't go any faster. "I don't recall your asking me, Your Grace."

Ransley had the good grace to look abashed. He slid his fingertips the length of her arm to take her hand in his. Bringing both of her hands to his lips, he kissed her fingers, his lips soft and shockingly warm. "I seem to recall your telling me once that you wouldn't accept me if I asked. Consequently, knowing your stubbornness, I'd hoped to make you think it was your idea. Please say you'll not dismiss me out of hand."

"I... would not do that," Thea managed somewhat breathlessly.

He smiled again, as if she had accepted him, and carried both her hands to his breast to press them against his heart with one large hand. The other reached to brush delicately over the cheek that did not throb with every pulse of her heart. His hands were large and just a little rough, calloused from handling reins and pistols, and yet so very gentle when he'd soothed her face with cold water and his warm touch. "Is there anyone whose permission I should ask to marry you?" he asked.

Thea laughed. "Just my own."

"Well then," he said, looking as if he wished to be serious, but could not do so for smiling. "Do I have it?"

"Have what, Your Grace?" she asked innocently.

"Permission to marry you, you imp. And you might call me Victor."

"I might?" she teased, full of a strange exhilaration. Perhaps it was freedom — not the kind that had once run light and prickling across her scalp, but the freedom to love him, to accept his suit and know she would still be herself and still free. His arms would hold her, but not confine her.

"If you marry me, you might."

"Then I suppose I must marry you, Victor."

He made a crowing noise and picked her up, swinging her about. Before she could catch her breath from laughing, his lips were on hers, and she lost herself in his excellent tutoring, as he once again taught her the dance of lips and tongue. By the time he released her, she was breathless and trembling from a different cause than had set her quaking at any previous time that day. Though she was no featherlight waif, Ransley... *Victor* seemed not in the least disposed to put her down. Thea laid her head against his shoulder and lost herself in the feeling of his heart beating strongly against hers.

Eventually, with a regretful sigh, Victor allowed her to come lightly back down to the ground, but even then kept her close, cradling her head in his hands to tip it back and look down at her with eyes that seemed almost to sparkle, they were so full of joy. She blushed, perhaps, more under that gaze than she had at the feeling of his mouth upon hers. He combed his fingers through her hair, bringing a semblance of order to the tumbled mess it had become, and Thea shivered at the touch of his fingertips against her scalp, scarcely able to credit how intimate it felt.

"I shall find it difficult to wait long ere we wed," Victor said in a confiding tone. "I'm all afire to make you mine."

Thea's face heated unmercifully. "We can hardly go on to Gretna," she pointed out reasonably. "Your poor horse would scarcely like to carry two so far, and Clarissa is waiting for us. Not to mention what it might do to her reputation if her guardian went dashing off to get married over the anvil, and…" Victor was laughing at her.

"I'm sorry, my love," he said when she glared at him, though his apology was undercut by the fact that he was still chuckling. He slid his hands down to lace their fingers together. "Gretna was not in my thoughts," he admitted, but before she could blush still further at her error, he brushed his fingers lightly over her lips, kindling a heat in her belly that made her gasp. "Though I'm glad to hear you're anticipating so quick a union." She opened her mouth to protest, though she did not know what she meant to say, and he stopped her words with his mouth, drawing finally from the kiss to say, "I *am* a duke, after all. I shall have no trouble procuring a Special License."

And truly, if she continued to blush like that, she was liable to take fire. Not to mention that her bruised cheek burned and itched with the increase of blood. "We shall be married after my bruises fade," she decreed, though it was difficult to be stern with him smiling down at her. "I won't have it said I wouldn't show my face at my own wedding."

Victor sighed. "So be it," he said, his regret not entirely for show. "My duchess has spoken." He gave her hands a gentle squeeze, then released her and went to retrieve his gloves and his horse.

"Oh heavens," Thea breathed as she suddenly twigged onto what she ought to have realized from the start. "I'm going to be a duchess."

"That you are," Victor said comfortably, if not rather proudly. "And a more regal duchess, I have not seen. Though you shall have to refrain from dashing out into dark gardens after wayward chits."

"I shall have no difficulty in that, so long as the girl in question is not Clarissa."

"Heaven forfend." He walked the bay over next to her. The horse drooped a bit, but seemed game after its drink and brief respite. Victor put his hands around Thea's waist and stayed there a moment, as if measuring whether he could span her waist with them. His hands were large enough he could nearly accomplish it, and so warm upon her waist there might almost be nothing between them and her bare skin. Then he lifted her, stealing a kiss along the way, into the saddle, settling her crosswise over the pommel as before. Thea took hold of the bay's mane to keep her balance, and with the other hand rubbed his proud neck.

Victor swung easily into the saddle behind Thea, settling her once more against him as soon as he was up there. She went with a will, blushing at the feel of his hard thighs under hers.

He gathered up the reins and spoke to the horse, who began to amble back towards the road. "Now," Victor said, "let us return to that coaching inn for a much-delayed luncheon and to see what new tempest Clary's gotten herself into."

"Lord knows," Thea said, though in truth she was not over-concerned. Now that she knew Trenwick wasn't betting-mad and willing to do anything to win, she trusted in his clear aversion to parson's mousetrap to keep Clary safe, even if she *had* lost her head over the fellow.

She leaned against Victor with her head upon his shoulder, secure in the circle of his arm. And to think that, were it not for Mallinson's machinations, she would not be here. However terrifying the route to this place, she was quite content to be precisely where she was. It occurred to her that she owed Mallinson her thanks. And Clary. If the duke had not despaired over launching his niece, he should scarcely have accepted Thea's help. Nor would she have offered it, in truth. So both Victor's heir and his ward had a hand in bringing about this match. Not that it would be a good idea to let either of them know that.

Though… Thea smiled to herself. It would be amusing, at some future date, to send Mallinson a note thanking him for his assistance in making her a duchess. It would make him absolutely livid.

But later. Now, she wanted only one thing: Victor. She turned her face against his shoulder, rubbing her cheek lazily against his lapel. His arm tightened around her and his chin came down to rest on her head as the horse continued to carry them slowly back towards the coaching inn and home.

FINIS

Lady Clarissa's story will be continued in *The Hoyden's Heart*, out soon.

And to see where Clarissa's and Ransley's stories began, and read more about Lady Ashburne and the murder mystery that influenced Ransley's actions in this book, read *The Lady's Ghost*, available in ebook and print format.

Also available from this author:

The Lady's Ghost

Ashburne Hall is decaying, the tiny staff is hostile, the money is running out, and then there's the ghost. Portia has no choice but to try making the Hall livable; the last thing she needs is some so-called ghost trying to drive her out, even if seeing him does take her breath away, and not because she's frightened.

Ten years ago, Giles Ashburne fled after being accused of murdering his fiancée. Now he's come back to the Hall to find evidence to exonerate himself. He didn't expect to find it occupied, or for the chit to be so blasted stubborn. Or beautiful. If she keeps trying to catch him out, she's going to get him killed. Worse, if she doesn't stop trying to prove him innocent, she's likely to get herself killed. That, he's growing to realize, really would be more than he could bear.

About the Author

Colleen Ladd lives in the mountains of northern Colorado with her family, which includes two goofball dogs and two lunatic cats. When she's not writing, she is a volunteer firefighter and emergency medical responder. She'd never make it as a Regency lady at a fancy ball, but would certainly enjoy looking on from the sidelines.

You can reach Colleen through her website (www.colleenladd.com) where you can also sign up to receive notifications about new books.

www.ingramcontent.com/pod-product-compliance
Lightning Source LLC
Chambersburg PA
CBHW021041130626
46552CB00005B/1951